ALSO BY ALISON RAGSDALE

D0062223

PRAISE FOR DIGNITY AND GRACE

Dignity and Grace is the atmospheric, heartwarming story of a young woman retracing the steps of her mother's last journey, on which she uncovers long buried secrets and difficult truths about the people she loves. Ragsdale confronts the emotionally charged issues of a tragic death with sensitivity, courage, and forgiveness. - **Kerry Anne King**, bestselling author of *Everything You Are*.

Alison Ragsdale's pace and prose sparkle in this beautifully crafted tale of a young woman losing her mother and finding herself. In a surprising series of twists and turns, Iona Muir follows the trail of letters her mother left behind and discovers a father's love far greater than she ever imagined. A page turner from start to finish. - **Bette Lee Crosby**, USA *Today* Bestselling *Author of Emily, Gone*

Dignity and Grace circles around a young woman's journey to unravel the secrets about her mother, and the unexpected path her journey takes. This poignant story delivers all of the familial pathos, love and redemption that I've come to expect from an Alison Ragsdale story. I look forward to her encore! - **Peggy Lampman**, bestselling author of *The Ruby of the Sea*.

This is a tender, emotional story of how strongly the threads of family and love hold us together. One you won't want to miss. - **Judith Keim**, bestselling author of *Breakfast at the Beach House Hotel*.

Alison Ragsdale mines the depths of love and forgiveness in this poignant story that leads readers on a journey of reflection and the true meaning of family. The rugged beauty of Scotland provides a splendid backdrop. - *Patricia Sands*, author of the bestselling *Love in Provence* series.

DIGNITY AND GRACE

ALISON RAGSDALE

This book is a work of fiction. Names, characters, organizations, places, events, and incidents either are products of the author's imagination or are used fictitiously.

DIGNITY AND GRACE

For information: info@alisonragsdale.com

ISBN: 978-1-7330377-5-4

For mothers and daughters everywhere, and for the love of music.

Music was my refuge. I could crawl into the space between the notes and curl my back to loneliness. — Maya Angelou

DIGNITY AND GRACE

Alison Ragsdale

PROLOGUE

ORKNEY, MARCH 2010

I ona Muir pushed through the squeaky wrought-iron gate, ran up the flagstone path, and burst through the front door into the cottage. After her walk home from school, the welcome warmth of home made her chilled face tingle as she dropped her bag under the coat stand and shrugged off her heavy coat.

Excited to share the news of the A she'd been given for her English essay on Beethoven, the studious eleven-year-old smiled to herself as the rich smell of a hearty soup floated out from the kitchen.

Rubbing her hands together, she kicked off her shoes, walked into the beamed living room, and stopped short.

Her father, Craig, was sitting in the armchair next to the fire-place, his head in his hands.

A stab of fear made Iona bolt toward the staircase, but before she could begin climbing, he called her back.

"Wait, pet. Come here. I want to talk to you." He beckoned to her.

Hesitating for a moment, she walked over and stood in front

of him, the prickle of dread creeping across her skin. "What's wrong, Daddy? Is Mummy asleep?"

Her father's pale-blue eyes were crimson-rimmed. "No, but I need to explain something to you before you go up." He blinked and took both her hands in his. "Iona, you'll have to try to be brave. O.K., love?"

She nodded, a lump closing off her throat as she slid onto the rug and crossed her legs.

"You know how we've explained to you that Mummy isn't going to get better?" He paused. "You understand that, right?"

She sucked in her bottom lip and nodded.

"Well, the doctor came today, and we talked to him."

"Mummy talked to him?" Iona felt a lift of hope, as her mother's voice was a rare commodity now.

"Well, she and I knew what we wanted to say. We'd discussed it a while ago, when it was easier for her to speak." He stared out the window for a few seconds before turning back to her.

"So, what did you say to him?"

"That Mummy has decided to stop taking all her medicine."

Despite the warmth of the room, a trail of cold splintered up Iona's back.

"She wants to accept what her illness means, Iona." He swallowed. "She's tired and she's ready to go, pet." At this, her father's face dissolved, his chin dipping to his chest and his eyes clamping shut.

She'd never seen him cry before, and a weight landed on her chest as a single tear oozed through his pale eyelashes. She wanted to jump up and comfort her father, but at the same time, as the meaning of his words, *ready to go,* permeated her young mind, a tingling paralysis held her to the spot.

Silence blanketed the room until the fire popped behind him, making her jump, and her breathing gradually grew shallower until finally he gathered himself.

"What she's decided was very difficult. And whether we agree or not, we need to help her now." He smoothed the sand-colored hair over his ears, then reached down and took her hand again.

Afraid to move, his words echoing inside her head, Iona let her mind float away from the room, conjuring images of her mother in the little music room off the kitchen. She was surrounded by piles of sheet music, her long dark hair piled on top of her head with a pencil anchoring it in place, as she embraced her cello. Iona imagined she could hear the sweet whine of the bow gliding across the strings, all the while her father's voice was fading in and out as he explained that her mother would be leaving the house the following week, and that Iona would need to say her goodbyes then.

It wasn't until Iona heard the words *say goodbye* that she snapped back to the moment, fully absorbing his message. "Why do I have to say goodbye now?" She let the stinging tears that had been pushing up, come. "Where is she going?" She swiped her nose with her palm.

Craig pulled her up from the floor and onto his lap, wood-smoke from the fire lingering on his sweater. "She's going to a special clinic, in Switzerland. Somewhere she can rest, and they'll take good care of her until she goes to sleep, for the last time." His voice trailed away.

Panic snatched at Iona's throat. "Can we go with her?"

Craig shook his head. "No, pet. You can't go, I'm afraid."

The word *you* sounded like a discordant B sharp. Iona twisted away from her father's arms—overcome by the sense that there was even more pain on its way—more than she would be able to bear. "Why not? I make her feel better. I can play my cello for her and help take care of her."

Craig pulled her closer and whispered. "I think it's best to say goodbye here, love. While she's in her own bed. It's easier for her to think of you here, at home with Nana, where you're safe and it's familiar. Do you understand?"

Iona's heart was thumping under her shirt as she pushed away from him and stood up, anger seeping in where sadness had been. "But *you* get to go?" She glared at him.

He closed his eyes and nodded. "I'm going with her, yes." "That's not fair, Daddy." Her voice rose. "I'm going up to ask Mummy. She'll say I can come." She made for the stairs.

"No, Iona." He jumped up from the chair, and the intensity of his whisper held her to the spot. "I don't want you asking her, O.K.?" He frowned. "The decision is made."

"But…"

He held up a finger. "No, do you hear me?"

Seeing the line of his mouth, she knew that on this he would not budge, and a new wave of anger crept up her chest. "And she's never coming back, is she?" Her voice cracked.

"No, darling. She's not." Craig shook his head, his eyes dimming.

Unable to find the exact words she needed, new tears flooded her eyes. "I hate you." Her voice was barely audible, but the look on her father's face told her that she had hit her target.

1

I ona heard the metallic clatter of the letterbox, followed by the distinctive thump of mail hitting the doormat. She shoved her mane of dark hair from her face, turned over, and blinked at the clock on the bedside table. She had slept in late after a rather overindulgent night out with her flatmate, Roz. They'd been celebrating Iona's twenty-first birthday a day early after a long shift at the Bonnie Prince, the Edinburgh restaurant where they both worked.

Having cleared their tables and discarded their black aprons, they'd run down the Royal Mile in the rain, arms linked and jostling a shared umbrella. They'd eaten at a chic bistro, drunk a ruby-colored whisky cocktail each, then drained a bottle of wine. Now, as she took inventory of the odd, chilly sensations that were trailing up and down her limbs, Iona couldn't clearly remember getting a taxi home.

As she rolled onto her back, the contents of her stomach sloshing under her diaphragm, she groaned, just as the bedroom door flew open.

Roz stood in her pajamas, her face blotchy, with a pile of envelopes in her hand. The edgy, bright-red pixie haircut that

Iona coveted but was too scared to emulate, now looked like a badly fitting hat as Roz jammed a fist into her eye. "Getting up?" She squinted at Iona. "It's after eleven."

Iona shook her head and pulled the duvet over her face. "Bugger off. I'm not on until four-o-clock."

Iona's feet were squeezed down by the quilt as Roz flopped onto the end of the bed. "Charming."

"Sorry. I'm feeling a bit rough." Iona spoke into the feathers, her stomach roiling.

"These are for you." Roz set the mail on Iona's stomach.

Even the slight increase in pressure was bothersome, so she moved the duvet away from her face and sat up. The light in her basement bedroom was dull at best, but this morning it was positively muddy. Edinburgh had a way of doing that in February, but then it could surprise you with a spear of sunlight that would split the sky and tease you with what might be.

Iona's eyes were gritty as she looked around the room, taking in the peeling paint on the walls and the tar-colored stain on the wooden floor, near the door. Her cello was propped up in the corner, and her clothes from the night before were draped over the imposing black case. As always happened now, the sight of the instrument pulled her throat into a tight knot.

"O.K. I'm getting up." Pushing down the sadness seeing the cello engendered, she smiled at Roz and gathered the handful of envelopes onto her lap.

Roz heaved herself up from the bed. "I'll stick the kettle on." She yawned. "Oh, happy *actual* birthday, by the way." She shuffled out into the hall.

"Thanks."

Iona sifted through the pile. There were a couple of envelopes that looked like cards, along with a credit-card bill and a gaudy flyer from a local restaurant. At the bottom was a thick brown envelope with a dirty smudge on the back. Discarding the other items, she flipped the envelope over, the sight of her father's distinct handwriting making her stomach dip.

He seldom wrote anymore, and this reminder of his presence on the planet unsettled her. She could push thoughts of him away for long periods of time, then she'd hear a particular piece of music, smell bacon cooking, or catch a glimpse of a woolen-clad shoulder. Even a shock of fair hair, and he'd be back, burrowing into her brain-space and reminding her that recently, she'd become a less-than-ideal daughter.

She frowned at the envelope, the familiar stamp from Orkney poking at her weighted conscience. She hadn't been back to her family home in almost two years, since leaving to study the cello at Edinburgh University's Reid School of Music, the same school her mother, Grace, had attended.

For the first year, Iona's father had written regularly and called her every week, but as she continued to defer his requests for her to visit, his efforts had trailed away. Now, the only contact was the occasional awkward phone call or stilted message left on her voicemail and the consistent Christmas and birthday cards. Nothing had been the same between them since her mother had passed away, and as Iona's eyes closed and her mind drifted back in time to the last days of Grace's life, images of home began to crash into each other, making her breathless.

Tragically struck down by motor neuron disease at just thirty-one, Grace Muir had been completely bed-ridden for her last months. Iona had spent all her free time either up in her parents' room or standing next to the hospital bed they'd eventually installed in the living room. Her mother preferred spending part of her day in the heart of their home, rather than isolated upstairs.

Iona would sit on the end of either bed, afraid to jolt or wake her mother if she'd dozed off, but reluctant to detach herself for more than a few minutes at a time, instantly bereft at creating any unnecessary distance between them.

Her father would let her stay for long periods of time, then he'd slip into the room and whisper to her that she needed to eat, catch up on her homework, or have a bath. She would reluctantly rise and gently kiss her mother's forehead, feeling the now ever-present tremor within Grace's body rippling under her lips.

Months earlier, when her mother's illness had finally robbed her of the ability to play her beloved cello, Iona had begun singing to her, as best she could, over the constant knot in her throat, or playing her own smaller cello, choosing Grace's favorite pieces. Bach's Cello Suite No. 1 in particular would make her mother's head rock from side to side, her smile beatific. The familiar notes drifted around them like old friends, binding them closer together, not only as mother and daughter, but as musical allies. This passion they shared was a private world they'd get lost in, a land from which, albeit unconsciously, Iona's father was often excluded.

Startling her, Roz nudged the door wider and walked in, carrying two steaming mugs. She set one down on the bedside table and resumed her post at the end of the bed.

She nodded at Iona's hands. "Did you get a pressie?"

Iona shrugged. "Dunno. It's from Dad."

"Oh, right." Roz said. "Going to open it?"

"Suppose so." Iona flapped the envelope. "I'm surprised he bothered."

Roz frowned. "It's your birthday."

"Right." Iona turned the package over and tore it open. As she tipped the contents out, a wad of ivory-colored paper and a single sheet of green, her father's color of choice, slid onto her lap.

"What is it?" Roz leaned in.

"Looks like two letters." Iona lifted the single sheet and unfolded it.

Roz moved in closer. "What does it say?"

Iona scanned the page. There were only four lines of text, but the characters seemed to shift around as she tried to focus on them.

"Well?" Roz's face was now hovering over the page.

"Hang on. I'm trying to read it." Iona leaned back against her pillows. "It says, Dear Iona. It was your mother's wish that you receive this on your twenty-first birthday. Please take the time to read it and try to understand. This was her legacy to you. Happy birthday. Love, Dad." The last word caught in her throat as she dropped the paper onto her lap.

"What does he mean, *legacy?*" Roz frowned.

"Not sure." Iona leaned her head against the headboard. "She must've wanted me to have something..." Her voice trailed.

"Are you O.K.?" Roz asked.

"I think so."

Roz reached down and lifted the thicker letter. "Aren't you going to read it?"

Iona took the folded pages from Roz's hand and pressed them onto her thigh.

"Not now. Maybe later." She shoved the pages back inside the envelope, her heart picking up its pace. "So, whose turn is it to make breakfast?"

～

They sat in the tiny kitchen at the chipped Formica table that Iona had picked up at a local garage sale. She had pulled one of the faded director's chairs up close to the rusty radiator as Roz made scrambled eggs on the two-ring stove, and Iona's feet were freezing inside her toed socks. "This place is pathetic in winter." She moaned. "We need to find somewhere else."

Roz nodded. "Well good luck with that, with what we can afford." She swung around and spooned egg onto two plates.

Iona shunted her chair over to the table. "I can see my breath."

"Any chance you'd accept the help your dad keeps offering?" Roz spoke around her mouthful. "My oldies are tapped out."

Iona shook her head, her recent choices sitting heavy in her chest. "No way. I can't bring myself to take it. I feel bad enough about everything—dropping out of university etcetera." She scooped up more egg. "I made that decision, so I'm responsible for myself now."

Roz shrugged.

Catching a movement out of the corner of her eye, Iona watched as a pair of woolen-clad legs passed the kitchen window. The fact that their flat on Morningside Road was referred to as a garden unit—with no garden in sight—rather than a dank, below-ground dungeon seemed newly ironic. She snorted.

"What?" Roz was staring at her.

Iona made an O shape with her mouth. "Ever considered a touch of street-walking for extra income?"

Roz stood up and wiggled her hips. "Cheeky." She grinned at Iona.

"You'd make a fortune."

~

Iona finished her breakfast then washed the dishes while Roz took over the bathroom. When the two women had met at a party on the university campus eighteen months earlier, they'd instantly clicked. Iona, petite, with her Gaelic complexion, aqua-marine eyes and quiet island ways, was the perfect antithesis to the scarlet-haired, lanky Roz, with her dark eyes and Glaswegian edge. Their friendship had blossomed, and the two had soon become inseparable. It had been Roz who'd got Iona the job at the Bonnie Prince when she'd left university, and while Roz worked around her engineering lectures, Iona picked up as many shifts as possible to make ends meet.

A crash from behind her made Iona jump. "You O.K.?"

She heard laughter. "Yep. Just smacked my head on the shelf again." Roz's head popped out from behind the bathroom door, and she rubbed a palm over her wet crown. "At least you won't be able to see the blood."

Iona laughed. "Finished in there?"

Wrapped in a towel, Roz tiptoed into the narrow hallway. "It's all yours." She bowed. "I might've used a wee bit of your shampoo."

"You'd better have left me some." Iona poked Roz's damp shoulder as she passed her.

Minutes later, standing under the shower, Iona closed her eyes and let the warm water patter her face. The bathroom was the best part of the whole flat, with a cast-iron Victorian bathtub and a massive brass shower head mounted high on the tiled wall. The water pressure was epic, and as the patters began to feel more like prickles, she turned her back on the spray. As she massaged her head, thick suds slid between her fingers and the scent of coconut, which she usually enjoyed, made her feel slightly queasy.

She tipped her head back and rinsed the foam away, picturing the letter that was lying on her bedside table. Her father's words circled her mind. *Her legacy to you.* She frowned. Whatever was in that letter, it wasn't the legacy she wanted from a mother she'd adored but now occasionally struggled to remember clearly.

After her mother had passed away, Iona, only eleven at the time, had slid into a dark place for many months. She couldn't remember for exactly how long, but she knew that during that time she'd wanted to leave the planet and go with her mother. The fear of death had seemed more bearable than the searing light of a world without Grace.

Thinking about her parents inevitably drew Iona's mind back to her island home. Their stone cottage sat on the edge of Stromness, only minutes from Craig's work at the maritime energy plant. It was a picturesque town with narrow winding lanes, terraced houses, and a network of mysterious passageways that led down to the iconic harbor.

Iona loved the wildness and diversity of Orkney: the rough-hewn rocks towering above deserted sandy beaches, the sparse, scrubby moors that stretched purple in September and grey-green much of the rest of the year, and the flat, arable pastures of the East Mainland. She was particularly drawn to the Ring of Brodgar, a spectacular ancient standing-stone circle on the West Mainland, where they would often go for family picnics. Once, when Iona was eight, Grace had taken her older cello along, the one she'd called *the old banger*. Iona and her father had lain in the dampening grass listening to Grace, having kicked off her espadrilles, play Elgar's Cello Concerto in E Minor as the summer evening faded to darkness around them. Those were the times when Iona had still believed in magic.

Her father's face materialized before her, and she closed her eyes against the image. He had done his best to explain why he'd made the decision to leave her behind when they'd gone to Switzerland, Iona understood that now, but at the time he had been the only available target for the arrows of her fear and pain. The subsequent months of isolating herself from him had bled into years, and the wedge that had formed between them had only thickened over time. Now, the thought of facing him made her nervous, as he brought with him the flood of memories that she'd spent years trying to suppress—reliving them being too hard to bear.

As the ruthless illness had progressed, stripping Grace of her life-energy, Iona had watched her father juggling his work commitments and her mother's care. He'd wash her shrinking limbs with soft cloths and brush her thinning hair with such tenderness that Iona would sense that she should leave the room.

This had been the pattern of their days, Grace becoming

more and more silent and frail, Craig growing grayer in the face, the weight melting from his already lean body. Iona resented whatever time she spent away from the cottage, at school or her music lessons, as precious time with her mother that was being stolen from her.

Shaking with the agonizing force of these freshly unearthed memories, Iona stepped out onto the bathmat and began toweling her hair. For all the small details that she had forgotten about her mother, she vividly remembered her hair. Grace had had the same long, dark tresses that twisted into natural curls at the ends, and Iona would stand behind her mother and push her pinkies inside the glistening tubes while Grace played the cello. The same cello that now languished in Iona's bedroom.

Grabbing one long tress, Iona wound it around her finger. She focused on the tension of the cool strap as it hugged her knuckle, imagining it to be her mother's hair, slick and fresh against her skin. There was always a rush of loss that accompanied this kind of memory and, recognizing its course toward her heart, Iona released her finger, flipped her hair back, and wiped away the condensation from the mottled mirror.

She also shared Grace's eyes and distinct oval face, the resemblance having deepened as Iona matured, and as she took in her reflection, her mouth dipped at the corners. How hard must it be for her father to see her becoming more like the wife he'd lost as the years passed? Another wave of conscience surged into her chest at her recent, and increasing, absence from his life.

~

The letter was bulky in her hand as Iona thumped her pillows and leaned back. She lifted the folded pages to her nose and inhaled, but there was nothing distinct about the way they smelled. Disappointed, she set them on her lap and unfolded them, the sheets of paper giving a dry crackle as she pressed them open against her thighs. Her father's note slid onto the bedcover as she eyed the first ivory-colored page.

Grace's handwriting was, as her personality had been, precise and artistic, and the sight of the script-like D drew Iona's throat tight.

December 15th, 2008
  My darling girl,

Her heart pounding, Iona slid from the bed and closed her bedroom door. Then, gathering the letter against her chest, she resumed her position.

First of all, I love you more than you'll ever know, and that will never change. As I write this, I know that by the time you read it, it will have been many years since I left you. It's a devastating and yet oddly tender concept that when I leave you, you'll still be a child, but now with this letter in your hand, you are an adult.

If I try, I can picture your face at 21, with the same soft, compassionate eyes but your other features perhaps a little more prominent, and your expression assured. If I close my eyes, I can hear your gentle voice and singsong laugh that I know will have remained unchanged. I also know that your beautiful spirit will be soaring, as you are undoubtedly surrounded by glorious music, so many of the pieces you and I were gifted to be able to share, and for that I am eternally grateful.

This letter is my way of speaking to you, as the amazing and accomplished person you've become. I have no doubt that you're well on your way to reaching those goals we talked of, your career blossoming and your talent taking you from strength to strength.

There's so much that I wanted you to know, but when this thing happened to me, and our lives changed forever, I felt that you were too young to absorb it all. Before I go on, I want to ask that you forgive me. If I could have changed anything about these events that are ahead of me, and yet are thankfully well behind you now, I would have.

Iona pressed her eyes closed. The image of her mother, withered, weakened by the disease that ultimately tore her music from her, was cruel beyond words. As Iona willed her breathing to slow, she read on.

More importantly, these words will be here after I'm not, and I hope you'll find some comfort in them. My greatest wish for you is that you know, and believe me when I say, that simply by exist-ing, you made my life the best life it could ever have been.

I believe that we'll find our way to each other, on the other side. I know we'll be together again. It'll be the whole me, too, the one that smiles and speaks and walks and plays the cello. If I'm lucky, the music will have transcended the terrestrial and become truly celestial.

I have two things to ask of you. First, that you trust me. I know it's hard, after everything that's happened, but I ask it, nonetheless. Second, I want you to visit Professor Douglas in Edinburgh. He was such a formative figure in my life, and I know you will enjoy talking with him. Please ask about the time I studied with him and believe that there's a reason for you to go.

I love you, now, tomorrow, and forever.

Mum

xoxo

Iona refolded the letter and blinked her tears away, the sight of the musical notes in place of the Os, painfully poignant. December 15ᵗʰ, 2008 had been just a few months after their last picnic at the Ring of Brodgar. Grace had become noticeably thinner after Christmas that year, but other than that there had been no significant changes, at least to Iona's knowledge. Her mother had played daily for hours in the tiny studio that Craig had created for her, in an extension to the back of the kitchen, and the schedule of music lessons that Grace gave at the local community center had been as full as ever.

Now, as Iona considered that time, she regretted once again not having known what was going on. If they'd told her, she might've been able to help in ways that a nine-year-old knew to. She could have been better behaved, made less fuss about homework, helped around the house, practiced more consistently—made her mother's life, whatever had remained of it, more pleasant.

Iona shifted against the pillows and turned to look out of the window. The sky was still February-dull and when she checked the clock, she saw that she had half an hour until she'd have to leave for work. Riding her bike, the two miles to the Bonnie Prince on the Royal Mile, was usually a pleasure. Today, however, with her tender head, she wasn't relishing the idea.

She glanced over at the cello in the corner, still draped with her clothes from the night before. As happened each time she looked at it now, she'd tap her fingertips together, testing the firmness of the pads that were gradually softening with lack of use, and the newly pliable skin would send a ripple of regret through her.

After Grace's passing, Iona had continued to play on a daily basis. While painful, the music kept her connected to her life as she'd known it, and to her mother. Over the years, the pieces that her teacher assigned had grown progressively more challenging until, at just fifteen, her repertoire was closing in on the complexity of her mother's. But the more pieces she played that had been Grace's favorites, the more Iona struggled, the music being a raw reminder of everything she'd lost.

Her instructor, Mrs. Macleod, a gruff island woman who'd once studied in London, was initially the taskmaster that Iona needed, but it was soon evident that the student's capabilities were exceeding those of the teacher.

Craig had encouraged Iona to use Grace's studio, but Iona had rarely been able to bring herself to play in the sunlit room, with the large window overlooking the hillside behind the cottage. The space was too evocative, and when Iona did venture in there, the musical scores that filled her head were not the ones she was looking at on the stand, but the ones she remembered hearing her mother play.

A twinge of pain made Iona shift up against her pillows as she focused on the small watercolor print of Orkney's eastern mainland that her father had packed for her when she'd left. The view was of a sandy beach near East Kirkwall where they'd often walked to collect oysters.

"Just so you don't forget home completely." As he'd placed it in her suitcase, he'd smiled at her, but she'd heard the profound sadness in his voice and now, as she took in the softly curved, green pasture sloping down to the familiar shore, she allowed herself to miss him, and her island home.

When Iona had first arrived in Edinburgh to study, she'd found the transition difficult. The initial freedom she'd felt on being released from the confines of her routine on Orkney had been both heady and lonely. Her quiet island ways had also served to separate her somewhat from her fellow students, who consequently tended to treat her like a little sister rather than a peer. However, as her obvious talent had shown itself, their attitude toward her had changed, and within a few months she'd felt accepted as a legitimate member of the gifted group.

As the first year passed, her teachers had worked concertedly to build on her technical skills and increase her repertoire, but Iona's resistance to playing certain pieces—those that brought her mother back with such a force it could leave her breathless—had caused tension. She'd been unable to share her reasoning, using the excuse that her technique wasn't compatible with the demands of those scores, until one particular teacher had taken her to task.

"Iona, I'm not hearing any deficiencies in your technique." Mr. Halloran had frowned behind his glasses, the trademark Harris tweed jacket smelling mildly of camphor. "If there's something else going on here, you need to explain it to me."

Iona had attempted a joke. "It's that old bugger Shostakovich. We've just never seen eye to eye."

"That's not sufficient. I want facts." He'd pressed her. "No serious musician can be this selective—not if they want to make a career of it. Which I assume you do?"

She'd eventually confided in him, and as a result he'd become her closest ally. He'd still insist that she tackle certain pieces that he assigned but, if she struggled, he would allow her to shift focus, take a brief walk before resuming, or would distract her with his own attempt at humor, which was not his forte. The fact that he tried caused Iona to warm even more to the prickly little man.

Now, she leaned over, checked the clock and then pushed herself up from the bed. She dressed quickly, pulled a comb through her still-damp hair and twisted it into a bun, then crammed a woolen hat on, grabbed her coat and scarf from the wardrobe, and turned toward the door. Hesitating, she spun around and flicked the clothes off the cello case, letting them settle in a pile on the floor. Perhaps she'd play something when she got home.

2

The restaurant was busy, and Iona was feeling the effects of her night out more keenly as the evening progressed. She'd drunk several glasses of water and eaten a light meal in her break, avoiding the grins and hangover jibes of her fellow servers, but all she could focus on was getting home and collapsing into bed. As she scanned the room, spotting two tables in her section that needed to be cleared, the phone in her pocket buzzed.

Her boss, Scott, was in the back office, so Iona eased the phone out and, seeing her father's number pulsing on the screen, stepped in behind the bar. Her finger hovered over the *Decline* button and then she hit *Accept*.

"Hello?" Craig sounded surprised. "Iona?"

"Hi, Dad." She turned to face the wall of bottles behind her, speaking in a forced whisper as a coworker squeezed past her. "I'm at work."

"Right. Well, I just wanted to say happy birthday."

Iona nodded silently, picturing Craig's face, his thick, fair hair and the blue eyes filled with concern.

"Have you had a good day?"

"Yeah. Not bad." She swung around to check for any signs of Scott. "Roz and I hit the town last night, so I'm not feeling the best." She shrugged. "But it was fun."

Craig cleared his throat. "Did you get the package?"

Iona closed her eyes. "Yes, it came."

A tap on her shoulder made her eyes snap open. Scott was pulling a face as he jabbed a thumb at the tables behind him. She nodded and mouthed "sorry" as he turned away from her. "Dad, I've got to go."

"O.K., love. Give me a ring soon, will you? I'd like to talk a bit more, when you're free."

"O.K. Maybe tomorrow, when I'm off." She suddenly felt his absence acutely. "Love you, Dad."

She heard him take a breath. "Me too, pet."

The shift dragged on for another hour and a half before she could finish clearing down her tables, grab her coat, and walk out into the frigid night. The bike ride home, which she'd been dreading, helped her head clear, and when she walked into the flat, she felt better than she had the entire day.

"Roz?" she called into the hall. "You here?"

The silence was a relief as Iona dumped her coat on the sofa. Across the hall, in her bedroom, she glanced at the cello, feeling its glossy accusing stare searing into her back as she picked up the letter from the bedside table. She'd eat something, read it again, and then play.

In the kitchen, she shivered as she opened a can of soup, tipped it into one of their two battered pots, and then pulled a chair up to the radiator while she waited for her meal to warm.

Iona's hands were shaking as she balanced the letter on her knee, this time reading more slowly, willing there to be more— perhaps something crucial she'd missed. Reaching the end without seeing anything new, she slid the letter and the note from her father back inside the envelope, set it on the table, and stirred the bubbling pot.

Half an hour later, Iona set her empty soup mug on the floor. Pushing the chair back a few inches, she lifted her feet up onto the radiator, gripping the warm metal rods with her toes. She closed her eyes and tried to picture her mother as she'd been at the time she'd written the letter. As she pulled an image of Grace's face into focus, Iona wondered if she had begun to see the changes by then. Had she noticed the shake of Grace's hand or the twitch in her leg? When her mother had been on the phone with Freya, her best friend and Iona's godmother, had Grace's speech begun to slur? Iona couldn't recall.

What she did remember clearly was the hilarity that filled the small living room during that autumn of 2008. Each Sunday night, after they'd eaten dinner, when there was little of interest on TV, Iona would raid her parents' wardrobe. Then, draped in shawls, a couple of her father's sweaters, multiple knitted hats layered on top of each other, and a pair of holey woolen tights she'd dragged from the dresser drawer, she would perform the entire Snow White and the Seven Dwarves story, peeling off layers of clothing as she transformed herself from wicked step-mother to dwarf—dancing as she recited sections of Sleepy, Grumpy, Bashful, and Doc's dialogue. As her parents would eventually beg her to stop, tears rolling down their cheeks, she'd finally reveal the pale-blue Snow White dress that Nana Jean had made for her, by then far too small and gaping at the back. She'd sing what she'd called *the bird song*, and at that her parents would lean into each other on the sofa, letting her young voice settle on them.

Smiling at the memory, Iona cast her mind forward to the Christmas of 2008. Craig's mother had taken over the cooking, and Freya had been her usual, larger-than-life self, being over-generous with her gifts, taking up too much room on the sofa, not leaving enough roast potatoes for anyone else, and drinking too much wine. Christmas just wouldn't have been the same without her mother's best friend, though the fact that Freya had all but disappeared from their lives since Grace's passing sent a fresh shard of hurt through Iona's middle.

Iona had been unaware that her father had been dressing her mother by that Christmas. That was something they'd hidden from her for weeks, until it was too much a part of the morning routine to be a secret. What she did remember clearly from that time had been the increasing silence coming from her mother's studio.

Iona refolded the letter and wiped her eyes just as she heard Roz's key in the lock. Tucking the letter up under her sweater, she stood up.

"Hey." Roz tossed her coat over the back of a chair. "How was work?"

"Not bad. I felt a bit rough earlier, but I'm better now." Iona pointed at the stove. "There's some soup left, if you want it?"

"Oh, brilliant." Roz lifted a mug from the draining board and emptied the pan into it. "I'm starving."

~

Roz beckoned Iona into the living room. The faded tartan armchairs, one on each side of the three-bar electric fire, sagged in welcome, so the women settled themselves under the glow of the overhead light and tucked blankets around their legs.

"So, did you read the letter?" Roz leaned over the narrow coffee table and poured wine into two mismatched glasses.

Iona held her hand up. "Ugh, not for me. It's a liver-reprieve day."

Roz shrugged and poured the wine from one glass into the other, then lifted the full one to her stomach. "So, what's it about?"

Iona felt a prick of irritation at the intrusion but, if she was honest, there was no one else in the world that she could share this with. "It's from Mum, like I thought. She wrote it about eighteen months before she died."

Roz's face fell. "Oh, sorry. I didn't mean to be insensitive."

Iona shook her head. "No, it's fine. It's just really hard to read."

Roz nodded. "Do you want to talk about it?"

Iona took a moment to consider. "I think so. I mean, it's so weird reading her thoughts. It feels like spying, somehow."

Roz shrugged. "But she wanted you to have it."

"I know. But still."

Roz pulled the blanket tighter around her. "So, does she write about you?"

Iona pulled the letter out from under her sweater. "Yes, and about how much she hated leaving me." She felt the weight of the envelope in her palms, somehow heavier than the first time she'd lifted it. "I know how scared she was, but there's no trace of fear in the letter." She swallowed. "I just wish I'd known more at the time."

"You were a kid. Like nine or something?" Roz was frowning. "They probably couldn't involve you more than they did until they absolutely had to, right?"

Iona nodded.

"It was natural for them to protect you from the reality of it all."

"Yes, I know that. But seeing things written down, in her own words, makes me feel like I wasn't actually there. I can't explain it."

Roz sipped her wine, her scarlet hair shining under the cast of the bare lightbulb above them.

"I can read you some, if you want?" Iona glanced at her friend.

"If you're comfortable to." Roz leaned forward and thumped at the flattened cushion behind her back.

Having read the contents to Roz, who was surreptitiously

wiping her nose on her sweater sleeve, Iona tucked the letter away. As she watched her friend, Iona was caught by the flash of a vivid memory from soon after Christmas, in January 2009. She remembered asking her mother why she couldn't take her to school anymore, and Grace had deflected, citing some schedule clash with her first lesson of the day.

"What's up?" Roz was staring at her. "If this is too hard…"

"No. I was just remembering when she stopped driving." Iona shook her head. "Poor Mum." She blinked, sharing any more suddenly feeling like too much of an exposure. "I think I'll go to bed. Do you mind?"

Roz shook her head. "Nope. I get it." She smiled. "You can tell me or not tell me, just let me know if there's anything I can do."

Iona smiled back. "I will, thanks."

~

Under the heavy duvet, Iona rubbed her socked feet together. The room was dark, but the strip of yellow from the streetlight above was reflecting off the windowsill. The dark shape of the cello loomed against the far wall, and she could see its distinct outline, even when she closed her eyes.

Her decision to drop out of university had come at the beginning of her second year. She'd continued to cut pieces from her repertoire, each one generating a different, blinding memory of her mother; her narrow back bending over her instrument, the long hair swaying with the movement of her body as she lost herself in the music. As Iona limited what she would play more and more, her course instructors had become increasingly frustrated. Eventually, even her ally, Mr. Halloran, had pulled her aside one afternoon in the music room.

"Iona, this can't go on." He'd blown his nose loudly into a white hanky. "I can't protect you any longer."

"I don't need protecting." She'd shrugged, having a sense, deep within herself, of what was coming.

"They want you out." His face had been flushed as he'd pushed the hanky into his breast pocket. "They see you as being obstructive—hampering your own progress by what they're interpreting as arrogance." He'd said kindly. "They don't understand, and it's not my place to tell them what's really going on."

"I appreciate that." She'd nodded. "But it's none of their business."

At this, he'd looked annoyed. "This is a place of learning. If you, for all intents and purposes, are refusing to learn, they have every right to offer your place to someone who will."

Iona remembered feeling a lift of hope. Perhaps this was when it would happen—when the burden of the music she so loved, but now tortured her to play, would be lifted from her shoulders.

"So, are they kicking me out?" She'd watched him shuffle his feet.

"I think it's a distinct possibility."

She'd set her cello against the wall and sunk to the floor. "What should I do?"

Halloran had, to her surprise, sat next to her on the dusty wooden floor. "My suggestion is that you ask to take a sabbatical." He'd hesitated. "If you leave of your own accord, you might have a chance of coming back at a later date—perhaps when you're more ready."

Iona had leant her head back against the wall and wondered if that time would ever come.

Three weeks later, she had requested an interview with the head of the School of Music and told her that she would be leaving. A week after that, she'd packed up her locker and left the arts building behind, and now, close to a year later, had all but stopped playing completely.

She turned over onto her side and eyed the cello. Never in

her wildest dreams had she imagined that she'd give it up, especially after the promise she'd made to her mother. Overcome, she pressed her eyes closed and whispered into her pillow. "I'm so sorry, Mum."

~

In Iona's dream, her mother was wearing a long kaftan. She was barefoot, her hair loose, and the wind that whipped it around her face was warm. Iona could sense the joy in Grace as she danced in a circle around a cello that seemed to be floating above the lush grass underneath it. Iona tried to say her mother's name, but no sound came. She tried to wave, but her hand was invisible in front of her face. Then Grace stopped twirling and focused on Iona, her pale eyes questioning and watery.

Iona woke with a start and, flipping over onto her side, checked the clock and then turned her back on the lime-green display. She knew that had her mother been alive, she'd have been devastated by Iona's current path—leaving the university and her precious music behind to wait tables. Her mother had often talked about when Iona would have her first concert—how she, Grace, would die of pride.

Iona pulled her legs up to her chest and breathed into her lower back. If only her mother had had the chance to die from sheer happiness. The stark reality of the manner of Grace's death had been almost impossible for Iona to process. The idea that her mother would choose to travel to Switzerland to end her life, before it was taken from her, still presented so many questions that Iona had consistently put it out of her mind. But now, as she tried to blink the thoughts away, as she did when they squeezed in on her, the same words flashed behind her eyelids like a script: *How could she go before she had to? And how could Dad have chosen to leave me behind?*

As Iona stared into the darkness, she could sense the letter pulsing on her bedside table. Rolling over in the bed, she flicked the lamp on and read it again.

As she set it back down, her memories drew her back to February of 2009, when her father had fully explained what was happening to her mother. He'd taken them both outside and walked up the hill a little, as far as Grace could manage, so they could look over to Ward Hill, on Hoy. It had been freezing, so they'd bundled up in several layers. Her dad had brought a flask of tea, and as they huddled together, he'd explained what was going on. Iona had been puzzled at first, frowning the way she did when trying to figure out a difficult phrase or movement in a score. As her parents had gradually filled in the gaps of information and answered her questions, the gravity of the truth had sunk in, and then the tears had come. Iona remembered lying with her head on her mother's lap, sobbing while Grace stroked her hair and talked to her in a new, breathy voice. Her father had eventually gone for a walk and left them alone for a while.

Now, as she pressed her eyes closed, Iona could picture him as he walked away, the line of his back like a much older man's. She vividly remembered the feel of the bitter cold day, the wind whistling down the hillside, the itch of the tartan blanket that Craig had laid on the grass for them, and the scalding tea that she'd sipped from a faintly musty plastic mug. Looming larger than all of that, however, was the memory that it was the first time she'd heard the words *motor neuron disease*, the first time she'd realized that her parents weren't immortal, the first time she'd been aware of their vulnerability as a family, and the first time she'd questioned God's existence.

3

R oz was soaking in the bath; the TV was burbling in the empty living room, and Iona had wrapped a blanket around her shoulders while she waited for the kettle to boil. Two dirty plates and a greasy casserole were floating in a basin of tepid water, and she poked the pile of dishes with her finger. Instead of washing up, she made two mugs of chamomile tea, left one on the kitchen table, and tiptoed past the bathroom door, heading for her bedroom.

The room was frigid, as usual. The small radiator under the window needed bleeding of air, but neither she nor Roz could find the special key intended for the purpose. Iona had left the caretaker another message on his voicemail but knew that he likely wouldn't call back until the following morning.

She slid into bed, pulled the covers tighter around her shoulders, and eyed the letter that was once again sitting on her bedside table. All afternoon at work she'd been distracted, trying to dash back to her bag during her short breaks, but had only been able to glance at it a couple of times. Now, as she settled herself against her pillows, her heart was pattering.

Not long after the picnic on the bitterly cold hillside, Valentine's Day 2009—Iona's tenth birthday—had come around. Grace had asked Iona to help her make a nice dinner, and while cooking was far from Iona's favorite thing to do, she'd willingly agreed. Spending time with her mother under any circumstances had trumped Iona's dislike of all things domestic.

With her mother unable to drive to the shops, they'd used whatever they could find in the house, and had ended up with a very presentable shepherds' pie and an apricot crumble. They'd laughed as they'd cooked, and Iona had savored every simple task they shared—measuring, assembling, stirring—but most of all, the sound of her mother talking her through the various stages of the recipe, until suddenly it had started to feel as if Grace was handing down something rather than sharing an experience they might repeat.

Now, as another minute flashed by on her clock's display, Iona wrapped her arms around her middle, pressing down the surge of grief that was forcing her breath to quicken. The memory of herself, at just age ten, understanding the subtlety of that realization still made her pause.

As they'd finished making the dessert, Iona recalled that her mother had cupped her face between cool palms, her eyes glittering. "I don't have enough candles, sweetheart." She'd held Iona's gaze. "Just the ones left over from last year." At this, her mother's eyes had filled.

Iona had seen a way to help. "Let's just stick a couple in the crumble. It doesn't matter." She'd smiled for her mother as relief had flooded Grace's ashen face.

Once they'd laid the table, Grace had asked Iona to help her get into a nice dress to surprise her dad. Her mother had chosen the rose-colored one he loved, with the lace sleeves, the one she always wore on this date—but Iona hadn't realized how much weight her mother had lost until she'd zipped it up and Grace was swimming in the filmy fabric. When she'd caught Iona looking at her, Iona, knowing that her face was a portrait of the shock that was rocking her and with wisdom far exceeding her years, had consciously rallied herself. She'd found a smile and said, "You look beautiful, Mum."

They'd both tried to brush off the searingly painful moment as Iona pulled the waist of the dress in with a broad belt. Craig had seemed delighted with their efforts, and as they sat around the table, eating and talking and each sharing accounts of the day, Iona had felt happy, as if when she closed her eyes and froze this moment in time, she might be able to look back and believe that everything was, for just a little while, normal again.

Now, she leaned her head back, vividly remembering the pink dress and that it had been her father's favorite. When she'd left for Edinburgh, her father had asked if she wanted to take it, and Iona had nodded, folding it into her suitcase. Now, it hung in her wardrobe under a plastic cover, and since arriving in the city she had never taken it out or looked at it.

Shoving the duvet away, she walked to the wardrobe and opened the mirrored door. She pushed the collection of hangers to one side and reached into the far-left corner. Finding the tacky plastic with her fingertips, she dragged the dress out. It seemed minute as she slid the clear cover off and then laid the garment on her bed. It had a deep V-neck and an A-line skirt that had skimmed her mother's kneecaps. The intricate lace sleeves were the most beautiful thing Iona had ever seen when she was a child, and she remembered fingering the material as Grace had smiled, telling her to be careful not to snag it with her nails.

Behind her, the door squeaked open. "You O.K.?" Roz was in her robe and a pair of lurid toe-socks. "You left the TV on."

"Oh, sorry. I forgot. I was so cold I just got into bed."

Roz made her way over and perched on the edge of the mattress. "Is that yours?" She nodded at the dress. "Not seen it before."

"No. It's actually Mum's."

Roz's eyebrows jumped. "Oh, wow. She was tiny."

"Yeah. About five feet two I think." Iona nodded. "I passed her height when I was eleven."

"To reach a heady five-five." Roz twisted her face. "Supermodel material. That's you."

"Well, at least I don't look like a matchstick without a box." Iona stuck her tongue out at her friend. "She always wore this on Valentine's day." She gestured toward the dress.

Roz said nothing as, lifting the hanger, Iona held the dress up for a moment then spun around to slide it back into the wardrobe.

"So, I'm guessing you read the letter a zillion times today?" Roz pulled her robe tighter across her chest.

"A couple." Iona nodded. "It's brought back so many memories. Like a flood." Her throat threatened to knot, so she took a deep breath. "I remembered the day they first told me about the MND."

"When was that again?"

"I was ten."

Roz pulled her mouth down at the corners. "God, you were so young to take all that in."

"I know." Iona slid back under her covers, her toes nudging Roz's thigh.

"When did they test you?" Roz frowned.

"Soon after that. I remember Dad telling me that I wasn't going to get Mum's illness." She felt a pinch of pain under her diaphragm. "He cried."

"What was it like, knowing that your mum was…" Roz hesitated.

"It didn't seem real. I was scared and sad and angry all at the same time, but even with all the facts they gave me, all the explanations, I think a part of me believed they were wrong. The doctors were wrong."

Roz nodded.

"Mum was just so alive. I couldn't imagine her any other way." Iona sipped her tea.

"But she deteriorated pretty quickly, didn't she?" Roz frowned.

"Yes. I think even as far as MND goes, it was a fast decline." Iona stared up at the dark window. "To some extent, even after all the time that's passed, it doesn't seem real. Whenever I think of home, of the house, or Orkney, she still seems alive there. But here, she's fading. Not the memory of her, but the depth of the memory. Sometimes I sense her around me, but it's like she's behind smoke." She paused. "It's so weird that I'm aging but she's stuck in time. What if all the memories I *do* have, the few that are clear, at least, start to go?" She looked at Roz. "Does any of that make sense?"

Her mother's presence lingered most strongly in a series of remembered moments, like in those first few seconds of darkness when the light goes out but there's no fear, because safety is just downstairs if you need it.

"Actually, it makes total sense." Roz squeezed Iona's toes through the duvet. "That's exactly why you haven't gone back to Orkney. Because she's still intact there, in your memory."

Iona stared at her friend, her heartbeat halting for a split second. Such a simple statement, and yet it held so much weight. "God, you're right." She sucked in her bottom lip. "I just haven't said it out loud."

Roz laughed. "Well, that's what you've got me for."

～

Roz had gone to bed, and Iona, not having talked to her father since he'd called her two days earlier, lifted the phone from the bedside table. After a few moments, he picked up.

"Hello?"

"Dad. It's me. Is it too late to call?" She slid farther down in the bed and pulled the quilt up to her chin. "Sorry it took me a while." She grimaced.

"S'O.K." There was a pause. "Is everything all right?"

"Yes, fine. But we didn't get a chance to talk properly." She frowned. "So, what's up?"

"Nothing's up. I just haven't heard from you in a while and I..." his voice faltered.

"Yes, sorry. My work schedule is jammed at the moment, and by the time I get home, it's so late." She closed her eyes against the lie. "So, how're things on the home front?"

"Same old stuff. House is falling apart at the seams. Work is busy. I got a good walk in this weekend, around Dingieshowe. Orkney is Orkney."

She nodded silently.

"Have you thought any more about coming home for a visit?"

"I was thinking about it yesterday, actually. Maybe in a few weeks." She screwed her face up again and waited for him to try to persuade her.

"Right. O.K." He sounded distant. "Whenever you can, then."

Iona chewed her bottom lip. While it wasn't like her father to capitulate so easily, it was more his defeated tone that alarmed her. She pushed herself up in the bed. "What's wrong, Dad?"

Craig coughed. "Nothing, Iona."

"No, tell me. What's wrong?"

"What's wrong is that my only daughter hasn't set foot in her home in over a year and a half." His voice was brittle. "I was hoping that once you got the letter, you might..." He halted.

Iona looked down at the envelope, lying in a pool of yellow lamplight. "I've read it, several times." She leaned over and lifted it to her cheek.

"Oh, good." His voice was his own again. "I don't mean to

pressure you, but it's really important to me—and it was to her."
He stopped.

"I know." Iona set the envelope down again. "It's just hard,
that's all."

"Yes. I understand, love." He sounded wrung out. "Look, I
have to go, but I just wanted to say that if you have any questions…" He paused. "Just call me, O.K.?"

Grace's request that Iona go to see the old music professor
surfaced again, the twist of both dread and confusion making her
sit up straighter.

"Dad, did you know she asked me to go and visit Professor
Douglas?"

He hesitated. "I didn't, actually."

"Can you think why?" Iona frowned.

"She must've felt it was important. Perhaps a way to know
her better?" He hesitated. "You will go, won't you?"

There was obvious angst underlying the question, and her
wish to be kinder to him surged into her heart. "Yes, of course. If
she wanted me to, I will."

"Thanks, love." Craig exhaled the words. "It's an important
first step."

Iona frowned. "First step?" She smoothed the duvet across
her thighs.

"Yes, just trust me." He sounded distant, the request echoing
her mother's.

"Mum asked me to trust her, too." She pressed her head back
against the headboard.

"Yes, I know."

As she scanned the wall opposite the bed, as if some clue as
to what this meant might materialize against the faded floral
wallpaper, she heard her father clear his throat.

"Well, goodnight, love." His rough voice cracked the last
word and simultaneously, a tiny crack split her heart.

"Goodnight, Dad."

Iona lifted the letter and read the second-to-last paragraph again. The notion of being reunited with her mother after death was something she'd ruminated over herself. As she'd catch sight of a narrow wrist or a long, dark ponytail, her thoughts would go to Grace. She'd follow the image, wondering if her mother would eventually be waiting for her on some spiritual plane or other, a cello balanced against her torso and those small, nimble hands beckoning.

Iona smiled at the words *If I'm lucky, the music will have transcended the terrestrial and become truly celestial.* This sounded just like her mother. She'd always said she wanted to play as if angels were guiding her fingers. Iona would giggle and flap her arms up and down as her mother's soft laugh lapped around her. As far as Iona was concerned, Grace's playing was heavenly—it had an ethereal quality that Iona felt she had never achieved herself.

She glanced over at the cello and suddenly wanted to feel its weight against her thighs, the taut strings under her fingertips, and balance its elegant neck against her shoulder, so she got up and hefted the heavy case onto the bed. Opening it, she lifted the gleaming hourglass out, along with the cloth she used to clean the strings.

Perching on the faded tapestry chair that sat under the window, Iona pulled the cello into her embrace and swept the rosin block over the bow, the musky antique-shop smell making her stomach contract with longing.

Having wiped the strings, she tossed the cloth onto the bed and settled into position. Without thinking, she slowly pulled the bow across the G string, letting it sing like a low, pealing bell. The Prelude to Bach's Suite in G was a perfect piece for her to start with, its momentum challenging and yet centering. When she'd first learned it, it had hurt her hands. She'd battled the ache and mastered it, but now, after months of musical hiatus, she felt the old pull in her palms, the burn of the strings as she moved her softened fingertips over the fingerboard and the tug in her shoulder as her right arm traced arcs in the dark room. Closing her eyes, she tried to lose herself in the first suite.

When she'd played this piece in the past, it had flowed like a sentence, each word seamlessly connected to the next. Now, it sounded like an argument and, her breath catching, Iona lifted the bow from the strings and pushed the cello away from herself. She couldn't damage a perfect piece of music this way.

With the cello safely closed away, she climbed back into bed, switched off the light, and pulled the duvet over her head.

4

Sitting at either end of Iona's bed, the women shared a heavy blanket. The small electric fire that they'd dragged in from the living room glowed in the dimness of the room.

"So, how's your mum?" Iona asked. "Over the flu?"

Roz nodded. "Yes. Sounds like she's over the worst. Dad's doing his best not to burn the house down, but he's a rotten cook." She smiled. "He tries, though, bless him."

A flash of memory took Iona by surprise. She saw her father whistling at the stove, a tea towel slung over his shoulder as he stirred a steaming pot. Her mother had primarily done the cooking in their household, not because of any gender role predilections but because she enjoyed it. The irony was that Craig loved it too, and Iona remembered them bumping shoulders in the tiny kitchen, laughing softly between themselves as they prepared a Sunday roast or made stock for the vats of soup that became a staple during the cold winter months on Orkney. She'd love to sneak up, lean against the door frame, and watch them, a profound feeling of safety leaching from their backs straight into her belly.

She closed her eyes against a wave of nostalgia.

"You O.K.?" Roz asked.

"Yeah. Just remembering stuff." Iona gave a half smile. "My Dad's pretty amazing in the kitchen. He took over after Mum…" She halted. "I wonder if he still cooks?"

Roz sipped her wine. "Not much fun cooking for one." She pulled her mouth down at the corners. No sooner had Roz said it than Iona saw realization dawn on her friend's face. "Oh, God. I didn't mean to make you feel bad." She grimaced. "Foot firmly in mouth, over here." She held a hand out to Iona.

Iona patted the air. "It's O.K. I think about that all the time. He is alone. Very alone." Hearing it out loud make Iona wince. Irrespective of the past and her beliefs about what had happened back then, keeping him at a distance, both emotionally and physically, felt increasingly unfair.

Roz nodded. "I know."

Iona settled back against the lumpy pillows, sadness clogging her chest. "I'm such a let-down." She sniffed. "I couldn't bear to stay there with him, even though he needed me, and then when I finally left, I couldn't keep playing, not even for Mum." She buried her face in her palms. "What's wrong with me?"

Roz patted her foot. "Nothing. You're still angry with your dad, that's all." She shrugged. "As for the music, you're just afraid. It's like you're afraid to play and afraid to stop."

Iona nodded.

"But you know you have to shit or get off the pot. Right?" Roz kicked her calf. "So to speak."

Despite herself, Iona laughed. "God, Roz."

"Well, I just mean that if you really can't play anymore, then you have to leave it behind. Once and for all." She held Iona's gaze. "Because this is a weird, half-life you're living at the moment."

Iona took in her friend's expression. The scarlet hair spiking away from the high forehead, the kindness radiating from the dark eyes.

"I know." Iona nodded. "I've known that for over a year, but something is stopping me from really letting go." She blinked to clear her vision. "When I think I've put it behind me—losing Mum, Dad and me being weird and distant with each other, leaving Orkney, all the issues I've been having with playing, and crapping out at uni—when I really think about hanging up the cello and taking the time to decide what the hell I want to do with my life—I freeze."

Roz nodded. "Right. Like I said—a half-life." She shifted awkwardly. "Look, do you really want to be waiting tables for overprivileged arseholes and tourists when you could be the next Yo-Yo friggin Ma?"

"Roz, really."

"Well, I'm just saying. You're pissing it away." She gave Iona another gentle shove. "I know I'm not an expert, but even from the little I know, you are extraordinary. You're a shit-hot musical genius, and every day you don't play, the sun dims a little." Roz smiled at her sadly. "I don't want to push you, but someone has to."

Iona gulped. "You're totally right. Not about the Yo-Yo Ma thing, but about the half-life." She swiped her sleeve over her eyes.

"O.K., well what was that woman's name, something Plat?" Roz frowned. "The one who peed herself at a concert, in that film we watched."

"Jacqueline Du Pré." She rolled her eyes. "Trust you to remember that particular detail. It was a film. That probably never happened." She shook her head. "She was a legend though, Roz. One in a million."

Roz's shoulders bounced. "So could you be." She pointed a finger at Iona's chest. "But only if you actually play the damn thing." She jerked a thumb over her shoulder.

Iona glanced at the cello, once again draped with her yoga gear.

"You need to get a grip and separate that from your mum. Her memory is intact. You playing won't change that." Roz's expression softened. "Right?"

Iona shrugged. "I suppose not."

Roz leaned forward and grabbed her hand. "No supposing. Just know."

Iona pressed her lips together.

"What was your mum's favorite piece of music?"

Iona turned to stare at the blank window. "Probably Elgar's Concerto."

"Go on, then." Roz pointed at the cello. "Pick it up."

Iona frowned. "Not now."

"Then when?" Roz held her palms up. "It's just me here. What's stopping you?"

Iona felt the press of new tears. "I'm sorry, I just can't."

5

I ona pulled her scarf up over her nose. The bitter wind was cutting across North Bridge, and the sky was still an ominous color. There was a steady stream of people heading in both directions as she left the bridge and turned right onto the Royal Mile. This was one of her favorite parts of the city, the flinty streets and granite architecture that had stood for centuries, stretching from Castle Hill to Holyrood Palace. She particularly loved the layers of Old Town, the narrow alleyways and hidden staircases linking upper streets to lower ones—all begging to be photographed. There was a life force here, a pulse that emanated from the stones under her feet, like the thrum of the bagpipes that could often be heard throughout the city.

On her way to work, Iona walked past the Heart of Midlothian, the granite mosaic heart set into the pavement near St. Giles Cathedral, at the top of the Royal Mile. The heart marked the former administrative center of the town, and she'd read that in the fifteenth century there had been a toll booth on the spot, a prison, and even a place of public execution. Now, as she spotted the familiar outline on the pavement, for some reason her friend's words of the previous evening came back to her. Roz had, in one short, insightful statement, put the last eighteen months into perspective. Iona had been hiding not only from her father, but also from her music, her memories, and consequently, from the task of healing.

As she walked in, the restaurant was quiet, the early March rain keeping much of the usual lunch crowd inside their offices. Taking advantage of the lull, Iona slipped into the back room with a plate of pasta. She grabbed a bottle of water from the mini-fridge and the letter from her bag and settled herself at the small table kept for the staff. Just as she was about to eat, Scott clattered into the room behind her.

"Damn. I cut myself." He held a bloody thumb out to her.

"Can you...?"

She shoved the plate away and, grabbing a clean bar towel, wrapped it around the wound. "It looks deep." She frowned. "What did you cut it on?"

He reached across her and lifted some paper napkins from the table, then began swiping at a red stain on his sleeve. "Bloody corkscrew. I need to replace most of them." He tutted, pulling his hand back from Iona's grip. He was only a handful of years her senior, and his sand-colored hair was thick, layered back over his ears. His broad brow was now furrowed over his hazel eyes. "How's the carbonara today?" He nodded at the plate behind her.

"Dunno. I haven't had a chance to try it yet." She widened her eyes at him.

"Oh, in that case, excuse me for bleeding on your lunch." Scott grinned. "May I join you, m'lady?" He bowed.

Iona swept her hand across the table. "Why not."

He pulled the other chair back, sat opposite her, and gingerly unwrapped the towel.

"Em, do you mind? I'm trying to eat." She grimaced.

He shrugged and re-wrapped the offending digit. "S'O.K. It's stopping anyway."

"Do you want me to check it?"

"No. It's fine." He leaned back, his long frame dwarfing the small wooden chair. "So, what're you reading?"

Iona pulled the letter closer to her. "Nothing."

Scott frowned. "So, what's it about, this nothing?"

She sighed. Scott meant well, and his humor and easy manner were usually a welcome release from the stresses of the restaurant, but today she just wanted him to leave her to read in peace. "It's a letter. Just personal stuff." She forked some pasta into her mouth.

"Personal as in bugger off Scott, or personal to share, like Virginia Woolf to Vita Sackville-West kind of stuff?"

For a moment, she considered telling him about it, but then shook her head. "Definitely not Virginia Woolf." She spoke around her mouthful. "Much less scandalous."

"Boring, then." He shrugged and stood up, shoving the chair noisily back from the table. Just as he was about to turn away, he hesitated. "Can I ask you something?"

Surprised, Iona nodded. "Sure."

"Is everything all right?" His brow creased. "I mean, with you." He tipped his head to the right. "You've been a bit quiet these past few days. Not your usual, irritating self."

Touched by his concern, Iona wiped her mouth on a paper napkin. "I'm fine. I just have some family stuff to deal with, that's all." She said. "Nothing to worry about."

Scott moved back to the table, his long fingers wrapping around the back of a chair. "Well, if there's anything you need, I'm here. You know that, right?" He scanned her face. "Anytime."

Iona took in his kind eyes, the evening shadow of facial fuzz and the tiny scar that ran from below his right ear toward his chin. Despite his taunting, scathing wit, and usual deflection tactics whenever anything personal came up, his was a face to trust. "I know that." She nodded. "Thank you."

Scott straightened, rolling his shoulders back, and Iona caught the slight creep of color across his neck and the signs of discomfort tugging at his mouth.

"You better watch it," she quipped. "You're going soft on me."

"Yeah, that'll be right." He laughed, the sound splitting the momentary tension that had risen between them. "Candy floss and puppies this way, please." He swept his hand toward the door.

She rolled her eyes, glad that they were back to their customary manner of communicating.

"Get that down you and get back out there, Muir." He jabbed a finger at her plate. "You're not paid to loaf around and eat all day."

Iona grinned and flicked her middle finger at him.

"Charming." He shook his head. "Blatant insubordination." Returning the gesture, he turned and walked out the door.

Having got the room back to herself, she flipped back to Craig's note. Each time she returned to the letter, she'd read the note from her father as a preface to the pages that lay ahead. *This was her legacy to you.*

The food had begun to congeal, so she shoved the plate away and sipped some water. The simple act of drinking was something she did numerous times a day, and never considered. Now, as the cool liquid ran down her throat, she considered struggling with something so seemingly unconscious, and it was another startling snapshot of her mother's experience.

Twisting the top back onto the bottle, she pushed down a bubble of sadness. She and Grace had struggled sometimes, as any parent and child do, but they'd been fortunate that in addition to the mother-daughter bond, they'd been so tightly connected through their music. It was something they shared that, when tensions rose, drew them together—so the fact that she, Iona, had willingly let that go was a heavy burden to bear.

Music was also common ground that her father didn't share with them, and sometimes Iona had felt bad about that. He was so good. So loving. So supportive. Back then, she'd never wanted him to feel excluded.

Thinking of exclusion, Iona blinked several times, shoved the letter into her bag, and tucked it inside her locker. The image of her mother lying awake in the dark, overcome by all that was happening to her and the ravages of MND on her delicate body, and coming to the heartbreakingly courageous conclusion that she had, was almost too much to contemplate. Not for the first time, Iona wished that she'd been more aware of the struggles that had been going on behind closed doors.

While certain memories had faded around the edges, one thing that she remembered clearly was when her mother's voice had changed. Iona's shock at noticing that the lilting quality was gone, and, in its place, a raspier, harsh timbre had taken over, was still very much alive in her. She'd watch Grace eating or, more often, shoving food around her plate, and the odd sounds coming from her mother would make Iona want to clear her own throat, like one yawn spawning another.

~

As she gathered her belongings and headed for the door, Scott was behind her.

"Off then?"

She swung around to face him. "God. You made me jump."

"Creeping out without saying goodbye?" He mimed shock.

"Not creeping. Well, maybe." She grimaced. "Sorry."

"I dinny rate a cheerio, then?"

His exaggerated Glaswegian accent always made her smile, so, relieved, she grinned. "You're a bampot."

Scott laughed. "There she is."

Iona slipped her coat on as the two remaining customers walked out into the grey afternoon.

"What're you up to tonight?" His eyebrows danced. "Hot date?"

She pulled her hat down over her ears. "Yeah. Not likely. The only hot thing about tonight will be my cocoa." She rolled her eyes.

Scott was looking at her intently, the smile gone. "You know, you need to get out more." He frowned. "Now's the time to be enjoying."

"Oh, thanks, Granddad," she said, taking in the warm eyes that were assessing her. Before she could stop herself, she pointed a gloved finger. "How did you get that?"

Scott looked startled, his fingers going up to the scar. "Um, a bike accident."

"Sorry, I didn't mean…"

"No. It's fine." He shook his head. "No biggie. Off you go." He moved past her and opened the door. "M'lady."

She smiled warmly at him. The knowledge that the only difference between them was that *his* scar was visible made him more of an ally.

∽

The Royal Mile was teeming, despite the bitter cold. Iona rode slowly past the bagpiper who played, stalwart against the wintry weather, standing close to the wall near Boswell's Court. She waved at him, and he gave her a nod as the chorus of "Flower of Scotland" wafted into the late afternoon, propelling her down the hill toward the bridge.

Stopped at a traffic light, she pushed her glove back to check her watch. She had twenty minutes to get home before Roz would be back. They'd planned on driving to Glasgow to spend the night with Roz's parents, Gregor and June. It being her father's fiftieth birthday, Roz wanted to surprise him by turning up to the little gathering her mother had planned.

The cold was biting at her lips, so Iona yanked her scarf up over her mouth and waited for the lights to change. Just as she eased the bike forward, the car next to her lurched violently in her direction. Her heart in her mouth, she swerved as the car's tires squealed on the damp stone street. The vehicle jolted to a standstill, the glistening black body rocking as the driver obviously stomped on the brakes.

As the bike's wheels continued to skid underneath her, Iona twisted her body toward the curb and shouted, "What the hell's wrong with you?"

She battled to steady herself, a rush of heat moving up from her middle setting her heart clattering. The car slunk away, the dark eyes of the windows obliterating any glimpse she might have had of the occupants.

Still shaking, she pushed her bike off the road and lifted it onto the pavement and, propping it against a lamppost, she dragged her hat off, her face burning.

"Are you O.K.?" A young, raven-haired woman in a fluffy pink jacket touched her arm. "That was close."

Iona nodded, feeling her pulse steadying. "Yes. Just caught me by surprise. I'm fine, thanks."

The woman nodded, then turned and walked away.

The cold grabbing at her now clammy head, Iona tugged her hat back on and, looking behind her, rolled the bike onto the street.

As she made her way unsteadily down the hill and cycled over the bridge, her mind was reeling. A brush with a careless driver had just scared the life out of her, the force of the adrenaline surge still rushing through her. Now, an image of her mother's face flashed vividly. *How had Grace dealt with the certain knowledge that her life was running out and yet managed to go on as bravely as she had for as long as she had?* Since receiving the letter, the more Iona contemplated these questions, the more her mother's ultimate choice was clarifying itself for her.

Iona pressed her eyes closed briefly until she felt the bike jerk sideways, then her eyes shot open again and she squinted into the afternoon light, focusing on the traffic ahead.

~

"You're late." Roz was standing in the hall. She wore her dark-blue ski-jacket and her big floral bag was on the floor, bulging against the radiator. "C'mon, woman. I want to beat the traffic."

"Sorry, I had a slight disagreement with a Mercedes." Iona shrugged her coat off, feeling the crack of static across her shoulders.

"Oh, crap. Are you all right?" Roz frowned, scanning Iona from head to toe, then turning her attention to the bike.

"Fine. Just got a fright." Iona looped her coat over one of the wooden pegs behind the door. "Give me ten minutes?" She eased past Roz. "I'm desperate for a cuppa, and then I'll throw some stuff in a bag. Shove the kettle on, would you?"

"Sure you're O.K.?" Roz asked.

"Yep. Really."

As Roz headed for the kitchen, Iona approached her bedroom. The door seemed heavier to open than usual, and as she shoved it with her shoulder, she spotted what looked like a puddle on the floor. Puzzled, she stepped into the room. There was a dank smell and an odd hissing sound coming from the corner, and as she flipped the light on, she gasped. Water was trickling in a steady stream from the ceiling, the plaster having opened up into a strange, flaky mouth, shaped much like a fish's. The liquid trail was spattering steadily onto the top of her cello case, then cascading onto the floor around its base.

"Shit. Shit. Shit." Her heart racing, Iona dashed to grab the instrument out from under the stream. "Bastard dump of a flat."

She dragged the heavy case to the bed and propped it up, then returned to try to shift her chest of drawers, which was also getting soaked. "Roz. Can you help me?" She shouted over her shoulder.

Momentarily, Roz stood in the doorway, looking dumbstruck. "What the hell?"

"I know. Help me. This is too heavy. You pull and I'll push." Iona turned her back to the chest and jammed her hips against the dark wood, shoving with her legs until gradually it began to move.

"What the hell's going on?" Roz stared at the ceiling. "Is that coming from upstairs?"

"God knows." Iona shoved the damp hair from her face, giving the chest a final heave until it met the wall opposite the window. As she turned, Roz was staring at the cello. "Did that get wet?" Her eyes were wide.

"Oh, no." Iona rushed over to the tall case and hefted it onto her bed. The black vinyl glistened, large teardrops of water trickling onto her duvet as she reached for the steel clips. She lifted the heavy lid to see the cherry colored hourglass nestled in its red-lined coffin. She ran her hands down the face of the instrument, her fingers finding wetness near its base. "It's damp." She reached for her pillow and tore the case off, then began dabbing the wood.

Tears were pressing behind her eyes as Roz, having dashed to the kitchen, returned with a bucket which she set under the water that was now flowing more heavily from the ceiling. "I'll call the landlord. Or a plumber." She turned to Iona and grimaced. "Or both."

Two hours later, a local on-call plumber was working in Iona's bedroom. He has located and turned off the stopcock, halting the flow of water, which was apparently coming from the bathroom in the flat above theirs.

Iona paced across the small kitchen, chewing the skin around her thumb. Her clothes, that they'd yanked from the soaked chest of drawers, were now draped over all the available radiators. She had turned the oven on low and opened the door, and the cello case now stood open, its insides hugging the stove.

Roz, having just called her mother to tell them she'd be late, slapped her phone onto the table and sighed. "What a bloody disaster." She yanked the cork from an open bottle of wine. "At least this guy came quickly."

"Yeah. I'm just worried about the case." Iona stood behind the dark eight-shape and leaned over, trying to see inside. "The bottom was totally soaked." She tipped it backward, propping it against her chest.

"Hopefully it'll be all right once it's dried out." Roz set a glass on the table. "Here you go. Have a wee bevvy to settle your nerves."

Iona repositioned the case on its end, then sat at the table. As she pulled the glass toward her, she noticed a sliver of something white protruding from the case's lining, where it had separated from the hard shell, so she moved to the side of the case and crouched down. "What's this?" She gently peeled the crumpled lining farther away from the edge and gripped the corner of what looked like a piece of paper.

Roz was standing behind her. "Is it a maker's mark or something?"

Iona shrugged as the paper slid out from beneath the crimson lining. "Dunno." As she focused on it, the air rushed out of her lungs.

"What is it?" Roz was craning over her shoulder. "You're white as a sheet."

Iona smoothed the bent corner of the photograph she held. In it, her mother, at perhaps nineteen or twenty, stood next to a tall man with a mop of dark hair. Grace's hair was tied up in a bun, and her cheek was pressed against the man's chest. He looked significantly older than her, his bone structure sharp in contrast to Grace's youthful profile.

Iona blinked several times, then looked at Roz. "It's my mum."

Roz's eyes widened, and she leaned in to get a better look. "Wow. Is that your dad?"

Iona turned her gaze back to the photo. "No." Once again she took in the unfamiliar line of the man's jaw, the wide shoulders, and the long tapering fingers whose tips were visible, wrapped around her mother's waist. "I've no idea who he is."

"Maybe an old boyfriend?" Roz shrugged. "Good-looking."

Iona nodded silently, then turned the photograph over. On the back, in her mother's distinctive handwriting, were two sets of initials inside a heart. The GB and CM were artfully scripted, with ornate tails that had been shaded to give them a 3D appearance, and under the heart was written 1998. Iona forced herself to swallow. The GB, of course, stood for Grace Burns, her mother's maiden name, but the CM meant nothing to her.

Iona sat down and lay the photo on the table. Her mother looked happy, her eyes telling all one needed to know about her state of mind. Her palm was flat on the man's chest, and her foot was locked between his as if she were holding him in place. They were standing in a doorway, the heavy stone lintel above them engraved with something that was no longer visible.

"You should take it with you when you go to see your dad." Roz flashed a smile, then sipped her wine. "Ask him who the tall, dark stranger is."

Iona was suddenly certain of the immense error in doing that, as if she had been given a precious secret to keep. "No. Probably not the best idea." She let her fingertips settle on the edge of the picture. "Who knows who he is."

∾

"Are you sure you don't want to come?" Roz slung her bag over her shoulder. "They'll be gutted. You know they prefer you to me." She pursed her lips. "'Ohhh, sweet Iona. The daughter we never had.'" She rolled her eyes as she imitated her mother. Iona laughed. "No. Really. I'd better stay here and sort out the mess in my bedroom. Plus, I don't have any dry knickers."

"Go commando or borrow some of my mum's. They've got scaffolding built in." Roz grinned.

"God, what a visual." Iona shuddered comically. "You're terrible, Roz." She shook her head. "Your parents are so kind."

"I know. But if I didn't give them some shit, they wouldn't recognize me." She shrugged. "O.K. I'm off. Call me tonight."

Iona closed the door behind her friend and went back into her room. The plumber had finished his work, leaving an even larger hole in the ceiling, which he'd told them they'd need to get someone else to repair, but at least there was no more leakage from the fish-mouth.

The boards under her feet were damp, but most of the water had either been mopped up or had drained between the floorboards, seeping away to heaven knew where. Iona had dragged the soggy bed linen off and shoved it in the washing machine, so now the displaced bed sat perpendicular to the wall, the cello settled comfortably on top of the bare mattress.

As she tiptoed around the bed, she stopped short. The letter. Panicked, she shuffled through the accumulated books and curling magazines on top of her dresser, searching for the ivory envelope. Not finding it, she tugged open both top drawers of the sodden chest, knowing that they were already empty—as evidenced by her damp clothes still steaming on the radiators.

She turned around and wildly scanned the room, and as she consciously slowed her breathing she took herself back in time, retracing her movements since arriving home. She remembered having hung her bag on a hook behind the front door.

Out in the dim hall, the light from the glass panel in the door formed a watery oval on the floor. As she pushed her coat aside and saw her bag hanging there, relief flooded through her. She lifted the bag down and plunged her hand inside, her fingers finding the bulky envelope, but rather than pull it out, she let them settle there, feeling the rough edges of where she'd opened it. Leaning forward, she rested her forehead against the prickly wool of Roz's scarf.

∼

With her bed freshly made and her dry clothes stacked in neat piles on the chair, Iona pulled her robe on over her pajamas and shimmied down under the lemon-scented covers. She'd dragged the electric fire in from the living room to help dry out the floor, and consequently, her room, though still slightly dank, was warmer than usual.

She'd eaten a sandwich, and now, the combination of her weariness, the stress of the cleaning-up fiasco, and the unaccustomed warmth around her was dragging her eyelids closed.

As she switched off the light, an image of the photograph that now lay on her bedside table, materialized. GB and CM. She frowned in the darkness, but before she could delve into the myriad questions the photo had sparked in her, she let her taut muscles ease into the pulpy mattress, and sleep took over.

6

I ona sat in Arthur's, the coffee shop at the end of their street. The coffee and pastries were passable, but the atmosphere was what consistently drew her back. A handful of mismatched tables were scattered around an old wood-burning potbelly stove that occupied the far corner of the space. Several of the armchairs were so sunken that once in them, one could hardly get out without help, and the row of grubby, leaded-light windows on the opposite wall overlooked a small courtyard where bowls of water were regularly refilled for passing dogs. The chipped door stuck in the frame, the stone floor was uneven, and there was one enormous ship's timber beam splitting the pitted ceiling from front to back. Sitting in the cozy space, listening to Classic FM on the crackling sound system, felt like home, minus the memories.

The clientele was eclectic and familiar, and as Iona sipped her cappuccino, a young man she saw there regularly, with a gold stud embedded in his chin and black spacers in his earlobes, locked eyes with her and smiled. His long matted hair was shoved inside a woolen hat and, as usual, he was battering away at an ancient laptop. Iona had occasionally been tempted to venture over and ask if he was a writer but, reluctant to intrude, had hung back. She returned his smile, then turned her attention back to her book.

Having had the morning off, she'd checked in with Roz in Glasgow, who'd said that her parents sent their love and that Iona had missed a cracker of a party. Roz was heading back that evening, and Iona had promised to go to the supermarket and stock up the bare fridge. After a quick breakfast, she had paid some bills, thrown a load of washing in the machine, and then escaped the still-dank smell in her room.

Now, she leaned forward and thumped the lumpy cushion behind her. Her father's note, which she had been using as a bookmark, sat face down on the mosaic tabletop, and she laid her palm over it protectively as the image of her mother with the stranger flickered behind her eyes. *Who was this man who had let her mother wind herself around him like a tiny vine?*

As a new flutter of curiosity flooded through her, she refolded the note and drained the dregs of her coffee, the cold foam clogging the back of her throat, then stood up and went to the counter with her cup. "Carl. Can I have another one, please?" She pushed the empty cup toward the balding middle-aged man who owned the café. His face was florid, and his bulbous stomach pressed against the glass of the display cabinet as he reached for the cup.

"Not working th'day?" He winked. "Skiving, are we?"

Iona shook her head. "No. Just have a late shift."

"No cupcake?" He tapped the glass of the case. "Yesterday's are only fifty pence." He looked at her expectantly.

"Tempting, but no thanks." She patted her middle. "Watching the calories."

Carl shrugged and turned his broad back on her, filling the coffee dispenser of the huge espresso machine that was now hissing. "Bastard thing needs a couple of new valves," he muttered at his hands as Iona looked around the coffee shop.

Apart from the chin-stud guy, there were three other tables occupied: one by a couple with a curly-headed toddler, whom they were struggling to keep in her highchair, another by an elderly woman with pink-tinted hair whose face was buried in the *Times* crossword, and the third by a girl around Iona's age. She was skinny, and her peroxide-blonde hair was long and stringy. She wore a battered leather jacket and was eating a Danish pastry that, from her expression, was clearly a disappointment.

Iona turned back to Carl, who was pouring frothy milk into her cup.

"Still at the Bonnie Prince?" He grinned as he shoved the full cup toward her, sloshing some foam into the saucer. "Sure you don't want to come and work for me?" He bit down on the end of his exposed tongue, the gesture oddly incongruous and child-like coming from this gruff, bear of a man.

"You're too kind, but I have a job." She widened her eyes. "Unless, of course, you make me manager and double my meager salary. Oh, and give me weekends off." She held his gaze until they both broke into laughter.

"Aye, that'll be the day." Carl chuffed. "What does that Scott have that I don't? Eh?" He grinned at her.

"Well, when you put it like that." Iona smiled, an image of Scott—the long lean limbs, kind eyes, and the track of the thin scar on his cheek—bringing a bloom of heat to her face.

"Well, enjoy the brew. I think it's better than the first one." Carl jabbed a thumb at the cup as she lifted it and made her way back to her table.

Iona rummaged around inside her bag until she felt the edge of the photograph that she'd shoved in there as she left home. She stared down at the face of the dark-haired man, then scanned the coffee shop, as if someone around her might have the slightest idea—or at least more than she did—of his identity. Feeling the need to reconnect with her mother, she pulled out the now dog-eared letter and read it again. She blinked, realizing that she had no idea how to process the words of an adored parent who'd gone, leaving you before you were ready to let them go. She swallowed over a knot. What she'd give to have her mother back for a day, an hour.

As the coffee shop emptied around her, Iona cast her mind back. It had been January of 2009, when Grace had been performing at a local music festival, that Iona had seen her mother, for the first time ever, lose her place in the piece she was playing and then, catastrophically, drop her bow. Craig had trotted onto the platform, lifted the bow, and handed it to Grace, but the ending to Shostakovich's Concerto No. 2 had been choppy, arrhythmic, and not nearly up to her mother's standards. That memory in mind, Iona had not played the piece since Grace's death—each note a splintering reminder of the beginning of her mother's end.

In the car on the way home that evening, her parents had been silent—the usual banter missing from their customary, post-performance exchange. Iona had taken her cue from them, staying quiet in the back seat, wondering if perhaps they'd argued, or if her mother might be coming down with the flu.

There had been so much she hadn't known, but it didn't matter how much time she spent looking back, staggered at how quickly her mother seemed to fade from effervescent to absent. There could have been no other outcome than the current one. As Iona tried to reconcile it all, to some extent, she knew it was probably unjust to still resent her father for her exclusion from the trip her parents had taken to Zurich so that Grace could end her life, but resent him she still did.

She slipped the letter back into her bag, realizing that she was alone in the coffee shop. Carl was thumping around behind the counter as she glanced at her watch. She had only an hour to get home and then to work, so she pulled her coat on, set some money on the table, and slung her bag onto her shoulder. "Bye, Carl." She waved at him, then pushed her way out of the stubborn door and into the street.

7

While Scott calmed an irate customer, whose steak was too rare, Iona had slipped into the break room to call home. After initial greetings, she had filled her dad in on the burst pipe scenario, but he sounded uncharacteristically distracted. "Are you sure you're O.K.?" She glanced at the clock, calculating the remainder of her shift.

"Of course. I'm fine." He hesitated. "So, the leak's been fixed? Are you sure you let everything dry out properly? You don't want mold to set in."

"It's all dry now. Not to worry, worrywart." She used her mother's saying, and as soon as she'd said it, she heard him sigh. "Sorry, Dad. I didn't…"

"It's O.K., love. Some stuff will always get to me, I suppose." He laughed softly, but it was a hollow sound. "So, any more thoughts on coming home?"

"Not exact dates, but very soon." She pictured him sitting in the cottage, probably with his feet up on the coffee table by the fire.

"Well, let me know if you need any money. Those repairs sound expensive."

"I'm fine, honestly. Roz and I can cover it between us, and the landlord is taking care of the largest chunk, anyway."

"Right, right. Of course." Craig sniffed. "I could help you with your train fare, if that's a factor?"

Iona's conscience once again clogged her throat. "It's not the money, Dad. I'll make a plan, I promise."

Scott saw her slip back into the restaurant. He was wagging a finger at her, but underneath the theatrical frown, she could see his eyes twinkling. She held her hands out at her sides and grinned.

As she cleared the vacated tables, Iona mentally calculated how long she might be away if she were to go to Orkney. She had at least a week's holiday due, so could make it a decent visit.

When she got back to the flat, Roz was slouched on the sofa. Her toe-socked feet formed a stripy V-shape on the coffee table, and a blanket drooped from her thighs on to the floor. The TV was on, but as Iona approached, she saw that Roz was asleep. Her scarlet head was thrown back at an awkward angle, and her jaw was sagging open, a strange hissing noise coming from her slack lips.

Iona hesitated for only a moment before clamping her hands down on Roz's shoulders, and speaking close to her ear. "Dozing, are we, Grandma?"

Roz shot upright, flinging her arms over her head sending Iona jumping backward. "What the hell?" She whipped around and glared at Iona. "You daft cow. Are you trying to make me mess myself?"

"Sorry, I couldn't resist." She held her hands up as Roz gathered the blanket from the floor and slung it over the back of the sofa.

"My heart's still thumping." She laid her palm flat on her chest.

Still laughing, Iona tossed her bag on the chair and headed

for the kitchen. "Did you get any milk?" she called over her shoulder, not realizing that Roz had followed her. "No need to shout." Roz widened her eyes. "It's in the fridge." She flopped down in a chair. "Ugh, I'm still hung over." Iona put the kettle on, then hoisted herself up on the countertop. "How come?" She frowned. "You've been home a day and a half."

Roz shook her head. "Dunno." She screwed her face up as if she'd tasted something sour. "I need toast, or some mashed potato."

Iona slid to the ground and opened the fridge. "There's cheese, salad, and I got some pasta yesterday. Want mac and cheese?"

Roz mimed vomiting. "No." She shuddered. "Just shove a piece of toast in for me."

Iona pulled the loaf out, and dropped two slices into the dented toaster that Roz's parents had given them when they'd moved in.

"So, how was the shift? All quiet on the western front?" Roz shoved the seat back and let her chin drop onto her folded arms.

"Yeah. Not bad." Iona took the butter and a jar of jam out and put them on the table. "I managed to call Dad for a chat. He sounded a bit down. I really do need to go home."

Roz nodded against her forearm. "Any updates on the mysterious CM?" She closed her eyes.

"No. I can't ask him about that. I'm worried it might upset him." She paused. "And what if he knows nothing about the guy?"

Roz took the toast that Iona held out to her and spread it thickly with jam. She took a huge bite, then spoke around her mouthful. "Probably best to wait then. Maybe you could ask your great aunt?"

"I'm going to talk to Scott tomorrow about taking a few days off. I'll check out train fares and make a plan." She smiled at her friend.

"Good, it's about time. Your dad will be so chuffed. And Scott will be fine about it." Roz grinned. "He'd bottle your farts if he could."

"Oh, for God's sake. She grimaced.

"Come on. You know it's true."

~

Iona balanced her book on her rosy knees. The bathwater was soothing as it lapped around her, the cup of cocoa that she'd made was sitting next to the soap on the wire caddy that spanned the tub, and a rolled-up washcloth was wedged behind her head.

Roz had gone to bed, nursing her lingering headache, and Iona was luxuriating in the quiet of the steamy bathroom. As she reached behind her head to dry her fingertips on the washcloth, she imagined her father's face lighting up when she told him she was coming home. She tried to picture the cottage and wondered whether he was keeping it as spick and span as her mother used to.

He had been a willing helper but, aside from their shared cooking duties, her mother had taken care of most things domestic. Iona would often sit on the stairs and watch her tidying. Unaware that she was being watched, Grace would hum as she moved, usually a movement from Bach or Haydn, then she'd pause and tut to herself as she lifted a sweater of Craig's from the chair, or moved Iona's gym shoes back under the coat stand. Iona would sit still and wait for what she knew would come next and then, sure enough, her mother would go back and tuck the muddy laces inside the gym shoes or fold the sweater neatly and run a hand over the prickly Arran wool, all the while smiling indulgently, forgiving them their messy transgressions.

Those tables had finally turned in the May of 2009. After

Grace had received her diagnosis and her shockingly rapid decline had begun, there had been few things for them to laugh about, so the memory of the day that her mother had wet herself was deeply ingrained.

Iona had been doing one of her one-woman shows, being both Beauty and the Beast. She'd mastered all the voices and was slipping between the musical alto of Belle and the bass growl of the Beast, until she'd sneezed and farted at the same time. Craig had immediately disintegrated into peals of laughter, then of course Grace couldn't stop herself joining in. It was only when she started to cough, too, that things got out of hand—and then came the peeing. Her mother had said she was trying to control it, but once the flow had begun, it was a lost cause, and as she simultaneously laughed and coughed, her frail body had quaked with the effort. When she'd eventually caught her breath, she'd grabbed Craig's hand and said something Iona had never forgotten.

"This bloody disease has freed me from embarrassment over the many ways my body is letting me down." She had hiccupped then, leaning heavily on Craig's arm. "So, let there be pee."

After Craig had helped her get cleaned up, they'd all sat in front of the fire, until Grace's speech had seemed to take a sudden downturn, and she was slurring badly—likely from pure fatigue. Craig had carried her upstairs, and later, as Iona lay in her own bed, she had been aware of her parents whispering well into the night.

The bathroom door rattled in the frame, making her jump. When the wind picked up outside, it somehow found its way down the outer staircase and through the front door, snaking along the hallway into the inner rooms. She shivered and slumped farther down in the sudsy water. The page she'd been reading was curling at the corner as she searched for the spot where she'd left off. Scanning the words, Iona was suddenly flooded with a memory of another serial tidier, her great aunt Beth.

Iona adored Beth. She was a no-nonsense type who'd been married to Ted, a local police inspector, for four decades. They'd lived in South Queensferry, which was where Grace had grown up, and Iona had many happy memories of visiting the couple in their police house overlooking the Forth railway bridge. One summer, when Iona was six, they'd all taken a boat trip out to the small island in the Firth of Forth where Inchcolm Abbey stood. Her father and great uncle had built a rudimentary kite and taught her to fly it on the gentle hillside in front of the medieval ruins, and Iona had kept the battered kite for years.

After the premature deaths of Grace's father of a heart attack, then her mother of cancer, Beth had raised Grace as her own, and the profound love and respect that existed between the two women had endured to the end of Grace's life. As Iona thought about Beth, the kindest of women, with her ubiquitous cardigans and the smell of fresh baking in her hair, she took a deep breath and sent another silent thank-you out into the universe for the gift of her great aunt in all their lives.

Distracted, she shifted the cloth up higher behind her head and tossed the letter onto the floor. Beth and Iona's Nana Jean were cut from the same cloth, both hearty women who made those around them feel safe and precious, qualities that were rare and that Iona hoped she could emulate in some small way. Her thoughts shifting back to her nana, Iona recalled Jean coming to Orkney to take care of her when, in September of 2009, her parents had gone away for a few days.

Around this time, there had been a conversation with them that had left Iona hurt and confused, and as she pulled it to the forefront of her mind, she remembered that her mother had been struggling to enunciate, so her father had stepped in.

"I'm going to take Mum away for a couple of days, for a wee break and to visit some friends." He had seemed overly bright at the prospect. "We'll drive straight down south and then work our way home. We'll be back before you know it, and Nana Jean will be here to take care of you. O.K.?"

Iona had been crushed that there was no mention of her going too, but something deep in her young psyche had stopped her from complaining about it. As she'd sucked down her disappointment, overriding it had been her worry about her mother traveling.

"What if she gets ill on the way?" she'd asked.

Grace had shaken her head, forcing her broken voice out.

"I'll be fine, love. Dad'll be with me. Not to worry, worrywart." She'd patted the sofa, inviting Iona to sit with her.

"Who're you going to see?" Iona had leaned into her mother. With Grace's voice catching again, her father had explained.

"Mum's old teacher in Edinburgh, Professor Douglas, then on to your great aunt Beth in South Queensferry, up to Freya at the kennels in Inverness, and then home."

Iona had burrowed closer into her mother's bony side.

"Why doesn't Aunty Freya come here anymore?" At the time, she'd remembered hearing raised voices coming from her mother's studio the previous Christmas. Grace and Freya never argued, at least to Iona's knowledge, so the incident had stuck with her for some time afterward. Now, with everything she'd learned about that time, she'd surmised that that was when Freya had told Grace how opposed she was to the decision to end her life.

Back then, when Iona had asked them about it, her parents had remained silent, but the absence of her mother's closest friend in those last months had become a sore point. Iona had asked numerous times why Freya wasn't coming for the usual long weekend in February, around Iona's birthday, or for the week in May when Freya would sometimes bring a puppy from her kennel with her, as Iona looked forward to that visit all year. She'd been met with extended silences, catching her parents flashing concerned glances at each other, then her father would give some placatory excuse that Freya was too busy with the dogs, having a new litter to care for, or her car was in the garage and she didn't like to travel by train. Iona had surmised that all was not well between her mother and Freya, but due to her newly heightened sensibilities around her already failing mother, she had once again let it go.

Now, as she sat up and pulled the plug on the cooling water, listening to it gurgle away, Iona pictured the map of the east of Scotland, visualizing the journey that her parents had taken. As she imagined them both, stopping at the various locations, spending a precious day with each of these people when Grace's days were so numbered, the question that had haunted Iona for years was suddenly answered. What prompted her parents to leave her at home, subtracting an entire week from their truncated timeline together, had been her mother's intention to guard her from the truth of her goodbyes. Rather than being excluded, Iona was being sheltered in the most profound way, and the realization was both sad and intensely revealing.

As she stepped out of the bath and wrapped a towel tightly around her, an idea began to take root. *What if, by asking her to visit Professor Douglas, her mother was sending her on some kind of quest, perhaps having her retrace that last journey she had taken?* Iona shook her head, but despite her efforts to banish the notion, the seed had taken root. Even if Grace had not intended it, Iona retracing her mother's steps held a kind of nostalgic, mystery-solving quality that, the more she thought about it, became compelling.

If she started by seeing Professor Douglas, right here in town, perhaps he'd share with her what he'd talked about with Grace? If nothing else, it would be good to meet the man her mother had obviously admired and respected so greatly. Then she'd go to South Queensferry to see Beth, which was a visit that was overdue. The thought of being in her great aunt's cozy home, in the warmth of her accepting presence, brought a smile to Iona's face.

From there, she'd travel up to Inverness to visit Freya. If she saw Freya face-to-face, after almost two years, maybe she would share what had really happened between her and Grace during Freya's last visit. Iona understood that Freya had been against Grace's decision, but the fact that she'd stepped back from Grace's life with such finality at such a critical time was unfathomable to Iona.

From Inverness, she'd carry on up to Orkney and see her father and, as she dragged the brush through her hair, Iona felt a lift of excitement. Aside from possibly answering a few of her own questions, her overriding hope was that with each stop she might learn something about that priceless week she'd missed out on with her mother. Maybe by asking each person about their time with Grace, she'd regain something of those lost moments, the seemingly endless days that, as she'd waited on Orkney, she'd crossed off the calendar as one would track a life sentence on a prison wall.

~

The following morning, Roz was up before her and the clattering of pots in the kitchen indicated that she was making breakfast.

"God, what a racket." Iona rubbed her eyes. "Wake the dead, you would."

Roz spun around wielding a frying pan. "Want eggs, or a smack in the mouth?" She playfully shoved Iona out of the way and opened the fridge. "Where's the cheese?"

Iona stepped around her and pointed to the large block of cheddar. "Um, what's that then?"

Roz grabbed it and returned to the stove.

"So, have you booked your ticket yet?"

Iona perched her backside on the tepid radiator.

"Nope. But I'm going to ask Scott if I can take off from March second for a week." She yawned. "Should be O.K." Roz nodded as she stirred the pan. "I'm sure it will be." She added salt. "What's the plan then?"

Iona explained about her parents' last trip and her wish to retrace their steps while making her way back to Orkney.

"Sounds good." Roz flopped a plate of eggs in front of Iona, then sat opposite her. "But what do you hope to learn?"

Iona shrugged. "Anything would be good. What they said to her, what she wanted to say to them." She shoved the egg with her fork, her appetite suddenly waning. "I might not get anything out of it, but then again, I might." She lifted her gaze to her friend's. "You know, you remind me of Freya, a lot."

Roz's eyebrows danced. She swept a hand down her front, presenting herself like a prize. "Ah, so she's gorgeous, intelligent as all get out, and totally fun to be around?"

Iona giggled. "Yes, all of the above." She shoved the plate toward Roz. "She's also incredibly hardworking and resourceful. Insightful. Oh, and she makes better eggs than you do." Roz crossed her eyes.

"She totally adored my mum. They were thick as thieves since childhood. That's why I want to ask her about what happened between them."

Roz shoveled the egg from Iona's plate onto her own. "Well, it was obviously about your mum's choice to..." She met Iona's eyes.

"You can say it. To end her life." Iona held her friend's gaze. "It's O.K., Roz."

8

Scott had approved Iona's request for leave, and her tickets were booked. She'd called ahead to Beth, who'd sounded delighted to have her come. Freya had initially been guarded when Iona called her but had warmed to the idea when Iona assured her there was no agenda, other than to catch up after too long since they'd last met.

Her last call had been to her father, that morning, and his reaction had been predictably upbeat. "Oh, fabtastic," he'd said, using one of Iona's childhood word-melds. "I'd better muck this place out, it's a tip."

"Don't go to any bother, Dad. It's just me." She'd smiled at the thought of him noticing dust that had been there for months, thumping fusty carpets over the clothesline in the garden, and worrying about what food to buy in.

"When do you arrive?"

"The fifth. I'll stay four days, if that's all right?" She bit her lip, anticipating his disappointment at the short amount of time.

"Great. That's great." There was no sign of upset. "Anything special you want to do? It'll still be as cold as a whore's heart, mind you." He'd used his mother Jean's pet saying when it came to describing winter on Orkney.

Iona had laughed. "I want to get some walks in. Maybe we can go to the Ring of Brodgar, and to Westray to see the puffins?" This had been another of her favorite outings as a child. The three of them would take the ferry to the northern island and camp in the warmer weather. Iona would lie on her stomach in the long grass on the mounds above the beach and watch for hours as the stumpy little birds tended their young, then dived gracefully into the water in search of sand eels.

"That'll be a rough ferry ride in March, love. Perhaps we should stick to things closer to home?" Craig had sounded dubious, and Iona had felt bad at seeming less than tuned in to the seasonal twists and turns of home.

"Oh, right. Well let's drive up to North Gaulton Castle, then." She'd nodded to herself, reminded of the 170-foot stone sea-stack, referred to locally as a castle, that they'd often visited. One of the lesser-known stacks of Orkney, North Gaulton resembled a top-heavy wedge whose thin end disappeared into the churning sea, making it look vulnerable to being blown over by the fierce westerly winds that buffeted the coast.

"We can do that, right enough." Craig sounded wistful. "It'll be so good to have you home."

~

A few hours later, making her way to see Professor Douglas, Iona slid the letter into her pocket and turned her back to the wind. The address she'd noted down earlier was also in her pocket, and as she jumped on the bus, headed for the port of Leith, her nerves were tingling.

Professor Andrew Douglas had been her mother's first, serious music teacher. When Grace was fifteen and living in

South Queensferry with her aunt, Beth had driven her back and forth to Leith three times a week for her lessons. Douglas had made time in his packed tutoring schedule for Grace, and Iona remembered that whenever her mother had talked about him, a look of veneration had taken over her face. She'd hush her voice, as if the next appropriate step would be worship.

Aside from the fact that Douglas was the strictest teacher Grace had ever had, Iona knew little more about the man. Having done the calculation, she estimated him to be in his mid eighties by now, and when she'd called him the day before, he'd sounded confused.

"I'm Iona Muir. Grace's daughter." She'd waited for some sign of recognition. "You taught her before she went to the Reid School of Music."

"Ah, Grace. Yes, of course." His voice had been gravelly. "And your name again?"

He'd agreed to have her come to his home and now, as the bus bumped down Leith Walk toward the port, Iona began to doubt the wisdom of this meeting. Her mother's visit had been many years ago and, there was a distinct possibility that this old man would have little to no memory of it and nothing significant to share with Iona.

When they'd got home from their trip, her parents had told her that they'd broken their journey in Aviemore, staying in a bed and breakfast that they'd been to once before, when they'd gone for a long weekend to ski. Grace had been enchanted that the room was exactly the same, that the owner remembered them, and that even the family golden retriever seemed to know them when they'd arrived. Having spent a quiet night in their room, they'd set off for Edinburgh the following morning.

The memories filling her head, and unsure exactly where her stop was, Iona stared out the window, looking for a street sign. The sky was clear behind her but ominous over the water ahead, and she frowned as big, heavy raindrops began to slide down the outside of the glass to her right. Feeling observed, she caught the eye of an elderly woman sitting across from her.

"Lovely day." The woman smiled from under her plastic rain hat. It protected a cap of silver hair that was carefully curled, as if she'd just stepped out from under an old-fashioned hood dryer.

Iona nodded, the irony of the comment making her smile.

"Yes. It's not looking too good now, though."

The woman swatted the air. "Och, it'll be clear as a bell in five minutes."

"I hope so." Seeing her opportunity, she twisted around in her seat. "I wonder if you'd help me?"

The woman's face brightened. "Of course, dear."

"I'm going to Shore, but I'm not sure what stop to get off at?" She jabbed a thumb at the door of the bus.

"Oh, right. That'd be Bernard Street. It's the stop right after Constitution Street. You turn left, and Shore's about a five-minute walk." She tucked a stray strand of hair back under her snood.

"Thanks a million." Iona nodded at the kind face. The woman grinned, her face folding into a mass of powdery wrinkles as she turned back to look out the window.

Seeing the sign for Bernard Street ahead, Iona thanked the woman again, then wove to the front of the bus. Jumping off the platform, she oriented herself, turning left as she'd been instructed, and within a few moments, she spotted Shore.

She'd last been here with Roz, and they'd stopped at the Tardis Tea Co. housed in an iconic old police box that sat at the waterside edge of the cobblestone road, its back to a landmark floating restaurant.

Spotting the familiar Tardis, Iona checked the address she was carrying. If she was right, Andrew Douglas lived only a few feet away.

The row of tall sandstone buildings faced the water. Many had originally been dockside warehouses and still had the smooth archways set in the stone that gave access to courtyards at the back of the row. The stepped gables formed a jagged roofline that topped the now exclusive, water-view residences sitting above shops and a handful of gastropubs—all giving Shore its eclectic atmosphere. In the warmer weather, this street was hopping with activity.

She counted the doors, and by her calculation, Douglas lived on the ground floor of the building, right next to the arch in front of her. Just to the side of it was a red door with a brass letterbox set into the frontage. She bent over to check the number, hesitating for a second or two before ringing the bell. Her nerves were mounting as she saw a shadow approaching the door from inside.

"Yes?" The voice was rough and low-pitched.

"Um, hello. It's Iona Muir. Grace's daughter." She stepped back from the door. "Professor Douglas?"

The door opened, and the old man with a painful looking stoop beckoned her in. His hands were contorted with arthritis, and his remaining hair floated outward in wispy white feathers over each ear. He wore a dark-red waistcoat over a checked shirt, his trousers sagged around his rail-thin legs, and highly polished brogues peeped out from under the corduroy turn-ups. "Please, do come in." He bowed slightly, his head bobbing forward in a courtly manner, and she could hear the distinct high-pitched squeal of a hearing aid. "Excuse the mess." He turned and ambled up a narrow hallway, past a long table all but invisible under several messy stacks of sheet music.

Iona closed the door behind her and followed him through to the back of his home. She passed two closed doors in the dark hall and then stepped into a surprisingly bright kitchen with two large picture windows overlooking the courtyard behind.

Professor Douglas was lifting the kettle as he faced her. "Can I make you some tea, young lady?" He smiled, transforming the wizened face into a cheerful mask. "I have the good stuff from across the street."

"I'd love some, thank you." Iona stood by a small round table near the wall. On it, there was a tray set up with wafer-thin, china teacups and saucers, and a plate with a few chocolate biscuits in a neat row. The obvious effort the old man had made was endearing. "This looks lovely."

He smiled at her as he set the kettle back on the counter, then nodded at the tray. "My wife's." He shrugged. "She insisted we use the good cups. Trying to keep me from becoming a complete barbarian."

Startled, Iona looked back down the hallway. She'd not considered that he'd have a wife. How thoughtless of her. "I'm sorry. I didn't realize." She could feel her face coloring. "I should've brought you both something."

The old man frowned. "Oh, she's not here, dear. Been gone fifteen years, now." His face sagged. "Old habits, and all that."

Iona felt a surge of pity for his obvious loss, his situation drawing a sharp parallel with that of her own father.

She offered to carry the tray and followed him down the hall and through one of the doors they'd passed on the way in. The high-ceilinged room was warm, a welcoming fire crackling in the grate. Two wing-back chairs were angled toward the fireplace, and in the corner by the window was a beautiful grand piano. The lid was propped up, catching the light streaming through the glass.

On the opposite wall, two cello cases stood on stands, and on a set of deep shelves were numerous violin and viola cases. In between the instruments were more piles of sheet music, some tidily stacked, and others fanned out like decks of cards, drooping over the edges of the shelves.

She looked around for somewhere to set the tray. Catching her hesitation, Professor Douglas motioned toward a sagging leather pouf. "You can put it on there. It's quite safe."

She nodded, then balanced the tray on the soft leather. She poured and then, with tea in hand, they sat in the chairs and took each other in.

"So, you're Grace's girl. I can see that." He sipped his tea. "'Like mother like daughter' was never more apt."

"Thanks. I like to think I'm a little like her." She bit into a biscuit.

He watched her closely for a few seconds, then balanced his cup precariously on the arm of the chair. "Are you like her in other ways?" There was a slight twitch in his eyebrow as he motioned toward the piano. "Play?"

Iona shook her head. "No. Not piano, anyway."

He folded his tortured hands in his lap. "What then? Violin?"

Iona hesitated, knowing what could potentially follow her confession. A request to play might be what would send her packing, but his face was so genuine, his eyes holding hers, what could she do but tell the truth? "Cello. But not for a while." She licked a tiny flake of chocolate from her thumb.

His face opened up like a book, the watery eyes lightening and his mouth spreading into a smile. "Well, now. Who'd have thought."

Iona waited a second or two before realization struck. The old bugger knew she played cello and, in fact, had just played *her*. "Ah, I see you know that already." She feigned annoyance. "Sneaky trick."

He held his twisted hands, palms up. "Guilty as charged."

Iona set the cup back on the tray. "So, may I ask how you know?"

He nodded slowly. "Your mother told me. Said you were exceptionally gifted."

She straightened her back, letting his words sink in. The notion of Grace talking to him about her made Iona feel exposed, but it also signified a new level of connection between her and this man, the emergence of an un-severed cord that led back to her mother. "I didn't know you'd stayed in touch."

"By letter mostly. I was never a fan of the telephone, and Grace, well, she liked to write things down. I think it helped her focus." His gaze shifted to the window as if seeing her mother there, sitting on the low stool next to the piano, the neck of the cello resting on her shoulder and her eyes closed, as always happened when she lost herself in the music.

Iona's thoughts went to the letter, the mixture of both emotion-filled and stripped clean words that her mother had written, knowing that Iona would read them one day.

"She came to see you, in 2009." Iona watched as he smoothed the white feathers that flanked his bald crown. "And she wrote me a letter during her last months." She felt the weight of her bag against her foot, the envelope leaking its presence into the conversation.

"Ah, yes. She came with her husband. A charming fellow." He nodded. "Sad times indeed." His eyes once again clouded over as he searched Iona's face. "So sorry, m'dear. Can't have been easy for you, losing her so young."

Iona's throat tightened. "Thanks. No, it wasn't." She forced herself to swallow. "She was so…" Her voice faltered.

His forehead folded into deep lines. "Yes, she was incredibly special." He coughed, a racking sound that made Iona wince. With a handkerchief at his mouth, Douglas took several ragged breaths before continuing. "We played a little together, when she was here." He gestured toward the piano. "Brahms No. 1." He hesitated, as Iona tried to picture the scene in this cozy room. "But she was unhappy with the quality of her playing. Stiff fingers, etcetera." He held up his crooked index finger.

Unable to speak, Iona simply nodded.

"She was torturing herself over keeping you on Orkney, not sending you to a proper musical conservatory." He blinked, his eyes telling their own story. "She was worried about your teacher not being able to challenge you enough, but knowing what she knew…" He swept a hand across the gap between them. "She said she couldn't bring herself to do it. To give up the time with you." He shook his head, dipping his chin to his chest. "She wanted you with her for as long as she had left."

Iona felt the warning prickle of tears, so lifted her bag, searching for a tissue. There had never been any mention of her going away to school, as far as she was aware, so the idea that her mother had been so consumed with guilt over her decision to keep Iona at home was startling. As she considered whether she'd have wanted to leave Orkney, her parents making the ultimate sacrifice to send her somewhere she could've been immersed in music, and around others who felt the same way about it as she did, she dabbed her nose with a tissue and pushed down the re-emerging sense of loss that threatened to drown her, from the inside out.

Apparently seeing her struggling, Douglas heaved himself out of the chair and made his way to the wall of instruments. As Iona watched, he singled out a cello, reaching down toward the handle of the matte case. "This one's not up to the standard of your mother's, but it's a good, solid instrument."

Unsure what he wanted her to do, Iona stood up and hovered close behind him. "Can I help you?" She stepped to the side as he flicked open the clasps.

"Yes, please take this out." He opened the lid. "I'd like you to play something for me."

Iona's stomach folded in two. This was exactly why she'd doubted herself on this decision: calling him, coming here, afraid that this entire meeting was ill-advised. "Well, I don't really…"

"I beg your pardon?" He cut her off. "Once a musician, always a musician." His voice had taken on a tutorial edge, but then as he looked up and met her gaze, his face softened. "Do it for me." He held up his hands, which were now curled into

awkward fists. "If I could, I'd play from dawn to dusk, but..."
He lifted his paws higher. "It's not an option for me anymore."
Iona looked at his poor hands, and her heart sank. This
encounter was taking a tangential twist that was diverting her
from the questions she'd come to ask. His request was like a cold
clamp around her middle, and yet she was unable to deny this
kind, old man. "I'll be awful." She leaned down and lifted the
neck of the cello from the bed of the case. "It's been ages."
Professor Douglas had turned his back on her and was
walking back to his chair. "Then that's why you need to start
here." He pointed to the stool she'd been looking at earlier.
"Back to basics. Take the fear out of it."
She frowned. *How did he know?* She lifted the cello and bow
and made her way to the stool. Once seated, she positioned the
cello in front of her and ran her fingers over the strings. Her
fingertips felt instantly hot, skin against metal, the friction
making her suck in her lip. Plucking each string, she adjusted the
pegs, tuning the instrument by ear and instinct, and then, without
realizing it, as she drew the bow over the strings, she closed her
eyes, focusing on the pure cadences she was searching for. When
she opened them again, he was smiling at her.
"Yes. Like mother like daughter, indeed."
"What shall I play?" She balanced the neck on her shoulder
and wiped her hands down her thighs.
"Elgar. E minor."
Iona had known that would be his request, and as she raised
the neck from her shoulder, her eyes blurred. "I'm not sure I
can." She blinked to focus.
"I am."

∽

She set the cello back in the case and sat opposite the professor.
"I told you I'd be awful." She shrugged. "True to my word."

He shook his head. "Not as bad as you think. It's so much inside your soul that the music is safe with you, regardless."

She frowned. "But the slipped notes, the tempo was all over the place. I fluffed the second movement completely."

He stared at her. "But you played it, my dear. You played it all."

She willed herself not to contradict him. *What did it matter if she'd played less than perfectly?* It was just her and him. No one else would ever know.

Overcome by the desire to confide in him, and before she could stop herself, Iona blurted, "I left Reid, a year ago." She sucked in a breath, "I just couldn't play anymore."

His eyebrows drew together, but he remained silent.

"It's all her, the music is her." Her throat constricted.

He nodded. "Yes, I see." His hand twitched on his knee. "No one would condemn you for that."

Seeing him close his eyes, she checked her watch. She'd been here over an hour and a half but still hadn't learned everything she wanted about her mother's visit. "I'm sorry if I've tired you, Professor."

His eyes shot open and he shook his head. "Quite the contrary. I haven't heard that instrument played in many years. You couldn't have made me feel more alive." He grinned.

"Well, I'm glad." She eased forward on the stool. "Would you mind if I asked you something?"

Douglas crossed his arms. "Not at all. Ask away."

"When she came to see you that day, what did she... I mean, what was it like?" She sighed, disappointed with the way she'd posed the question.

"We talked about you, a great deal. How much she loved you, how immensely proud of you she was, and how hopeful for your musical future. She said that if only I could hear you play, she was sure I'd rank you with the greats."

Iona shook her head. "I doubt it."

Leaving her comment hanging, he went on. "We talked about her illness, of course. Hard to avoid that, as she was already so incapacitated." He frowned, shifting his gaze to his lap. "We talked about all the music, the years of it, the layers of it in both our lives." He looked up. "Then, about how it felt for her to accept letting it go."

Iona's pulse quickened and she focused on his mouth as he chewed on his lower lip.

"She was brave. I've never met anyone so brave." His voice cracked, so Iona carefully placed the cello back in its case, then walked to the side of his chair and squatted in front of him. "If it's too hard, we don't have to talk about it." She patted his arm.

At this, he refocused on her face. "No. It's important that you know." He pushed his shoulders back. "She asked your father to go for a walk, just to give us some time to talk. I felt for the young man, he was so obviously besotted with her."

Iona slid her legs out from under her and sat cross-legged on the faded rug.

"Once he'd gone, your mother told me what she was planning to do." He sought her eyes again. "About her choice, to go to Zurich, and the fact that your father was so against it."

Iona nodded silently, her heart faltering. Craig's position on that, having been unclear for all these years, was now a sharp-edged reality.

"I was taken aback. I hadn't seen her in years and, aside from our occasional letters, had little to do with her life anymore, and yet here she was asking me to weigh in on the most critical decision she'd ever have to make." He reached into his pocket, pulled out his handkerchief and dabbed his eyes.

Leaning forward, Iona dug her elbows into her knees. "She asked you what you thought about it?"

He nodded. "I was shocked initially, but then it struck me that this was her modus operandi. Whenever faced with a challenge, Grace always gathered as much information, considered as many opinions as she could, before setting her course." He paused, as if reliving his reaction at the time. "Aside from being afraid that I might give her appalling advice, I was deeply flattered."

Iona instantly liked him even more for his abject honesty, something Grace had often credited him with when she'd talked about him.

"We talked for a while and then she asked me what I would do if it were me." His head trembled slightly. "So, I told her." Iona's pulse quickened and she pressed her lips together, waiting for him to continue.

"I told her that if it were me, I'd undoubtedly make the same choice. That when your life is so linear, pre-destined and dedicated to an art that you have spent years mastering—to have that ebb away, while the ones you love watch you transform into someone they don't recognize, it's too much to contemplate." His chin trembled. "Such a tragedy." He wiped his eyes again. "She was a true delight to teach. So much enthusiasm. So much joy in her playing. In her very being." He coughed. "I'm sorry, dear girl. This can't be helpful."

His words were reverberating around her. Not that they were anything that she hadn't imagined, but to hear them out loud, in the very room where her mother had fallen in love with the cello, practiced for hours, and had ultimately confided her innermost fears to her beloved teacher, was overwhelming. The fact that Grace had trusted him that much, while polarizing, was not totally surprising. As she took in the timeworn face, the kind eyes, Iona was flooded with gratitude for Professor Douglas's ability to put himself in her mother's shoes when Grace had needed him to, with total empathy and no sign of judgment.

She reached up and gently took his hand in hers. "Actually, it is helpful. You've no idea how much."

"I pushed her to study, you know. When she first came to me, she'd not long lost her mother, and having lost her father a year before that, her whole life was in flux." He patted Iona's hand. "She was considering giving up, taking her mother's advice about studying medicine. It seemed she felt it would be a fitting tribute, as her parents had both wanted her to become a doctor." Iona leaned back from the new information, her brow creasing. It was the first she'd ever heard of this. There had been nothing but music for Grace for as long as Iona had any memories of her mother. "Medicine? Really?"

"Yes. Seems her father had been quite adamant about her not wasting her time on something as frivolous as music." Douglas smiled ruefully. "Needless to say, I wasn't the impartial advisor I might've been when she told me that."

Iona pushed herself up and resumed her position in the chair. She considered the man in front of her, and as she watched him smooth his hair again, his role in her mother's life began to solidify. At a terrifying juncture in her too-short life, Grace had needed a father figure, and Professor Douglas had, albeit subconsciously, taken up that mantle. The realization was both sweet and painful to absorb. "You helped her stick with music. It was her passion." Iona smiled at him. "No father could've done more or done better by his daughter."

Douglas's eyebrows jumped as he focused on her face. He appeared to be processing her statement, his mouth working on itself. "Well, if that's what I was to her, then it was an honor I'd gladly repeat." He said. "Mrs. Douglas and I were never fortunate enough..."

"I'm so sorry." Iona felt the pain of this obvious dearth in his life.

"Don't be. I'd not change a thing." He nodded to himself. "Not one thing."

Iona nodded, her eyes skipping to the framed photograph of a woman with an oval face, neatly waved hair held down by a scarf tied under her chin, and a broad, warm smile. "She was beautiful." She watched Douglas push his bony shoulders back.

"She was. Inside and out." He nodded. "Much like your mother." He turned his eyes to meet Iona's. "Grace gave me something for you." He pushed himself to the edge of the chair, wincing at some hidden pain.

"Something for me?" Her stomach knotting, she laid her palm on her chest.

"Yes. She asked me to keep it for you until you came to see me." He was once again pushing himself up from the chair. "I wasn't sure about it. I said, 'What if she doesn't come?' But she was adamant that you would."

He crossed the room as Iona stood up, unsure whether to follow him or not. Behind her, next to the overstuffed shelves of music, was an old secretary desk, the same kind Beth had in her living room. Professor Douglas gripped the brass key with a twisted fist and turned it, letting the front section fold down. Inside was a row of tiny drawers and letter slots stuffed with papers, more sheet music, and a few tattered envelopes. At the far-right side was a narrow door which the professor opened to reveal a single, ivory-colored envelope, much like the one nestled in Iona's bag. He pulled it out and turned to face her. "Here it is, my dear." He held it out to her, his tremor making the envelope flutter, as if tempting her to take it.

Iona could feel the blood coursing through her veins, each viscous surge in perfect time with her racing heart. She gently took the envelope from him, saw her name on the front in her mother's script-like writing, then instantly held it up to her nose. It smelled musty, no trace of the soft lilac of Grace's face cream, or her coconut shampoo. The room began to spin, so Iona carefully turned and sat back down as the professor shuffled over to the door.

"You'll want privacy to read it." He nodded at her hand. "I'll make some more tea."

Iona held the envelope on her lap, the paper seeming to burn through her jeans. Her hand shaking, she slid a finger under the flap and opened the letter, unfolding two new pages, each covered with words promising to bring her mother's presence back, if only for a few moments. As she heard cups clattering in the kitchen, Iona lifted the letter and read.

My darling girl,

I knew you would come. Thank you for doing this, for trusting me and for meeting the person who was responsible for igniting my passion for music. He really is the best of men, Iona, and has come to mean the world to me in more ways than I can ever tell you. I hope you find him well, still torturing young musicians and then plying them with chocolate biscuits.

When I last was there, in that room where I can picture you sitting now, it wasn't the easiest of visits, or conversations, but true to form, he gave me what I needed. No fuss or frills, just truth, laced with compassion. He's a rare human being.

We talked about hard things, the most momentous of which was my decision to control the way I left the world, and how that might impact the people I love. He heard me out and gave me the advice any caring parent would. I will forever be grateful to him for that, and that's why I wanted you to meet him, be there in my stead, shake his hand and let him know what that meant to me. Men like Professor Douglas, who are willing to take on more than is expected of them, and who do so with an open heart, come along rarely in life, Iona, and deserve to be honored for those qualities.

Now that you've done this, I'd like you to go and see Aunt Beth. I know you'll have been visiting her as much as you can, in between classes etc., but this visit is different and very important. Tell her that I love her and that she saved me, more than she'll ever know.

Stay brave, strong, funny, and kind. Those are the qualities I treasure in you the most.

I love you, now and for always.

Mum xxx

As she lowered the letter to her lap, Iona's insides were quaking, her suspicions now confirmed that her mother was leaving her a very specific trail to follow. As she pictured Grace planning this whole thing out, Iona's breaths were coming in short spurts, and just as she was considering grabbing her bag to make a quick exit, Professor Douglas peeked around the door, a fresh pot of tea held awkwardly in his hands. "Can I come in?" His eyes held hers as he hesitated in the doorway.

Iona's face began to color. "Of course, please." She gestured toward the empty chair, watching the old man make his way carefully across the room.

He set the pot on the tray and eased himself back into the chair. "Would you be Mother?" He pointed at the tea pot. "Pouring is a bit of a challenge." He held up the hand that was more of a fist.

Iona cleared her throat. "Sure." She shifted forward, slid the letter under her thigh, poured more tea, then handed a cup to him.

"So, I hope it wasn't too distressing?" He nodded at the letter protruding from under her leg.

She pulled it out and held it in her open palms, like an offering. "It's hard to see her writing, know she touched this." She drew her hands in to her middle. "When I read it, it's like I heard her voice again." At this her voice caught, and seeing her expression, Professor Douglas simply nodded. Grateful that he wasn't pressing her to talk, Iona sipped her tea, visualizing the hot liquid slipping over her palate and down her throat, cascading past her esophagus until it hit her center, warming away the gnawing knot of pain under her diaphragm.

Professor Douglas was staring at her now, his cup balanced

precariously on the arm of the chair. "I think that's the whole point." He lifted his chin, looking beyond her to the cello she'd played earlier. "That is her voice." He nodded. "That's how you keep her close."

Iona twisted in the chair and took in the shiny black hourglass, its long neck propped against the wall.

"She wanted to make sure you remembered her that way, through the music." His voice cracked as Iona turned back toward him. "I promised I'd make sure of it." His face was now a deep red, an intricate tapestry of tiny, broken capillaries scattered along each cheekbone, heightened by the rise of emotion.

Realization sucked at Iona's insides. It was as if her mother, by some cosmic telegraph, or telepathy, knew what she'd done, that she'd walked away from her music and by coming here, the old teacher would guide her back. Battling the press of tears and unwilling to have the old man read her eyes, Iona stared at her knees. "I know. I've let her down." She fumbled in her pocket for the tissue. "I've let myself down too."

Professor Douglas eased himself out of the chair and made his way to her side, then leaned over and put a twisted hand over hers. "Not at all, my dear. Quite the contrary." He patted her hand. "You have all the time in the world. You just need to see that."

9

B umped by a large man passing behind her, Roz thumped the glasses down, sloshing wine onto the already sticky tabletop. "Watch it, you pillock," she muttered over her shoulder.

The Castle pub was packed, and they'd been lucky to find a table on a Friday night. Roz had called in sick to work as soon as Iona had phoned her from the bus, her mind reeling from the meeting with Professor Douglas.

"You sure you won't get in trouble?" Iona leaned in, raising her voice above the raucous laughter coming from a group at the bar. "Scott might figure out that you're skiving, because I'm off too."

Roz swiped the air. "No, he's fine. I cited period pains, and no sane man's going to go there." She grinned, shrugging her coat off and onto the back of the rickety chair. "So, rewind and tell me everything."

Iona relayed as much of the day's interactions as she could recall, even the fact that she'd played for the old man.

"That's great." Roz smiled approvingly. "Perhaps you could take some lessons from him yourself?"

Iona shook her head. "He's retired. His poor hands are racked by arthritis." She shook her head. "Seems like the ultimate cruelty, for a musician."

Roz nodded. "Yeah. I suppose so."

"God, what am I saying. The ultimate cruelty is MND." Iona said sadly.

Roz took a draft of wine, her eyes locked on Iona's. "Are you glad you went to see him?"

"Yes. Definitely. I wanted to meet her teacher, but he turned out to be so much more than that. It felt right to shake his hand, tell him thank you."

"Good." Roz leaned forward on her elbows. "Did you ask him about the mysterious CM?"

Iona shook her head. "No. It didn't seem right."

"Right." Roz nodded. "So, how did you leave it with him?"

"I said I'd stay in touch. He asked me to drop round sometime, the only condition being that I must agree to play. Earn my supper, so to speak." She shoved her glass to the middle of the table just as a roar from the group behind made them both wince.

"What a racket." Roz rolled her eyes. "Want to go somewhere else?"

"It'll be just as bad elsewhere." Iona shouted. "Let's stick it out."

Unable to talk without shouting, they shifted around to the same side of the table.

"So, next is Great Aunt Beth, right?" Roz dug into the basket of chips she'd ordered. "Have some." She shoved them closer to Iona.

Iona helped herself. "Yes. I'm going tomorrow. I said I'd stay the night with her before heading up to Inverness." The thought of seeing her great aunt brought with it the customary sense of calm. "You sure you can't come with me?" Iona raised her eyebrows. "She's an amazing cook, and she'd be quite happy to have one more mouth to feed."

"I can't. I'd love to, but I've got an assignment I'm behind on, and if we want to pay the rent this month, I need to pick up a few extra shifts." She poked Iona's shoulder. "You'll just have to keep me updated by text."

Later, wrapped in their coats and scarves, and with their arms linked against the cold night, they walked back along Morningside Road. As midnight approached, there was just as much human traffic around them as they'd passed three hours earlier. Having dodged more than one group of well-oiled revelers enjoying the start of the weekend, they went down the stairs and let themselves into the dark apartment.

Neither of them had been home since that morning, so as Roz pushed the door open, the day's mail shuffled itself into a pile behind it. "Post's been," she chimed as Iona bent down to pick up the letters. "Anything for me?"

Iona sifted through the envelopes, handing two to Roz. "Just these."

Roz took them from her and tossed her coat in the vicinity of the rack, the dark wool landing in a pile on the floor. "Bugger. Missed." She laughed.

Feeling the effects of the wine, Iona stepped unsteadily over the coat. "Yeah. You're a real crack shot."

Roz blew a raspberry. "I'll get it tomorrow," she slurred. "Night." She waved the mail over her head as she wove toward her bedroom. "Turn off the lights, Wee Willie Winkie."

Iona locked the front door and hung Roz's coat up. She flipped the hall light off, went into her room, and closed the door. She had an early start and still hadn't packed, and as she yanked her hold-all from the cupboard, her phone buzzed in her pocket. Pulling it out, she saw a text from Scott.

Hey. How's it going?

Curious, she flopped onto the bed and replied. *OK. Thanks.* She waited only a few seconds before seeing the telltale dots indicating that he was typing. Then another message appeared.

Are you sure? I'm worried about you. Touched that he was thinking about her, she lay back, holding the phone above her head, and typed. *Why are you awake, ya big softie?*

The dots flickered again, then the next message made her pause.

I'm serious.

She frowned, staring at the letters, unsure how to respond. Scott was a friend, someone whose company she enjoyed. He was funny and kind, and as she pictured his face, the thick sandy hair and gentle eyes, the wide jaw and the tiny scar, she couldn't deny that she found him attractive. Roz was perpetually teasing Iona about how much he liked her, but despite their developing friendship and flirtatious banter, Iona had kept him at arm's length. Now, as she re-read his last message, on an impulse, she typed. *Don't worry. It's just more family stuff. I'm fine, really.*

As she waited for a reply, she pushed herself up against her pillows, a slight quickening in her chest making her eyebrows lift. Soon another message bloomed.

You know I'm here, right? Whatever you need. You can talk to me.

At this, she sucked in her bottom lip, the sudden pull to tell him everything making her lean forward as her thumbs began to fly across the screen. *How long have you got?*

Within a few seconds, he replied.

As long as you need...

She hesitated only a moment before typing. *I got a letter from my mum. It's a long story.*

She watched the dots then, seeing his reply, let herself exhale.

I'm listening.

∾

A clatter in the street above her window made Iona sit bolt upright. Her head was thumping as she fumbled, trying to turn the alarm clock to face her. It was 06:23 a.m., and as she blinked several times to clear her head, wondering why she felt so disoriented, she realized that she'd slept in her clothes. Mortified, she swung around and sat on the edge of the bed, feeling her insides lurch and regretting that third glass of wine.

Picking up her robe from the end of the bed, she opened the door slowly, trying to control the loud squeak that always accompanied the movement. The hall was dark as she tiptoed past Roz's door and let herself into the bathroom. She flipped on the light and opened the narrow glass cabinet above the sink, the first order of the day being aspirin.

As she popped the pills into her mouth, leaning down to drink from the tap, her texts with Scott came back to her. She'd told him about both letters, her mother's messages to her, the visit to Professor Douglas, and from there she'd gone back in time. She'd told him more about Grace than she'd ever shared with him—her mother's music, her illness, and her death—and as the conversation unfolded in her mind, a flash of regret made her press her eyes closed. By telling him all this, she had opened a door that she'd been keeping closed between them. Now it was ajar, and both her story and her carefully protected heart were visible.

~

Having showered and dressed, she began to feel the aspirin doing its work. Her headache was finally lifting, and the toast she'd stuffed down, along with the cup of strong coffee, were reviving her.

Her hold all was open on the bedroom floor, and inside it was over a dozen pairs of knickers, one black sock, her hairdryer, and the two letters. She assessed the contents and rolled her eyes at the drunken effort, emptied the bag on her bed and began again.

Packing for March in Inverness and Orkney was easy— layers, and lots of them.

She pulled out a heavy scarf and gloves, a hat, and some thick socks for inside the well-worn hiking boots that she knew were still standing inside the back door of the island cottage as if she'd never left. She selected two of her least scruffy sweaters and some pajamas, an extra pair of jeans, and two long-sleeved T-shirts, then crammed everything into the bag. With her cosmetics and the novel she was reading, it was full to bursting, the zip looking dangerously close to tearing open. She considered asking to borrow Roz's bigger bag, but then dismissed the idea, not wanting to disturb her friend whose snoring was now rumbling into the hall from under her closed door.

Iona made a mental note to call Roz from Beth's, just in case she overslept and missed her shift at the restaurant that evening.

The easiest way to get to South Queensferry was by bus. Iona had to make one change at George Street. Then, with easy traffic, she'd be at her great aunt's well before lunch.

As she settled herself at the back of the first bus, she revisited her conversation with Professor Douglas. What she'd learned about Grace's parents' wish for her to go into medicine had been playing on a loop at the back of her mind.

She closed her eyes and tried to imagine her mother in a white coat, a stethoscope slung around her neck, writing prescriptions or taking someone's pulse. The picture was ludicrous, quickly obliterated by others of Grace in her studio, polishing the lustrous wood of her cello, practicing scales, or sifting through sheet music. Most vivid of all was the image of her playing Elgar's Concerto in E minor at their last picnic at the Ring of Brodgar, the cello spearing the damp grass as the melody gathered momentum, from pathos-filled to passionate, the smell of night, the brightness of the stars, and the sense of contentment all that had engendered.

Iona kept her eyes closed, waiting for the wave of longing to pass. After a few moments, she lifted her bag to her lap, pulled out the second letter, and re-read it.

Thinking about seeing Beth again, Iona tried to summon an image of her great uncle Ted. She'd been seven when he'd passed away, and her overriding memory of him was his big boots and the tangy smell of his pipe tobacco. While Beth knitted at the fireside, he'd sit Iona on his knee and sing to her, occasionally tapping the pipe on his boot-heel as she fidgeted against the prickly wool of his uniform.

Iona put the letter away and glanced out the window, anxious not to pass her stop.

The remainder of the journey went without incident, and soon she was walking along Shore Road, taking in the picturesque winding street with its eclectic mixture of shops— the gourmet ice cream store and Italian restaurant—all comfortingly familiar. As she made her way toward her great aunt's house, she was suddenly acutely aware that Professor Douglas's address was almost identical to Beth's. Marveling at the odd coincidence, she spotted the Anchor Inn on her left, which sat directly across the cobbled street from her destination.

Beth's house was a whitewashed, semi-detached home with matching dormer windows in the dark slate roof, flanked by brick chimneys at each end. The sight of the blue front door, a throwback to the days when it had been a police house, transported Iona to her childhood visits. The neighboring dark-brown, pebble-dash home made the white of Beth's appear blinding in the morning light.

Her great aunt liked to hang decorative wreaths on the brass knocker, depending on the season, and as Iona waited to cross the road, she spotted the current embellishment—an intricate ivy twist dotted with pale lemon pansies and a single sunflower.

Beth was always counting the days until spring from as early as the previous October, and the optimistic wreath made Iona smile.

Rather than turn up empty-handed, she'd bought some tulips from a vendor on George Street, and as she reached the door, she let her bag slide from her shoulder to the ground. Before she could ring the bell, the door flew open.

"You're here." Beth threw her arms open, a tweed skirt skimming her sturdy knees and a caramel-colored cardigan buttoned tightly across her ample breasts. "Give me a big hug." She drew Iona in, kissing her. "I've missed you, pet. Och, are these for me?"

Iona handed her the flowers, then kissed Beth's powdery cheeks, aware that she seemed to have shrunk since the last time Iona had seen her. As she squeezed her great aunt close, Iona caught the sweet smell of fruit on Beth's breath. "Hello, Aunty B. How are you?" She stepped back, letting Beth scan her from head to toe.

"You're thin. Too thin. Are you not eating?" Beth frowned and screwed up her hazel eyes. "Och, sorry. Look at me keeping you on the doorstep." She moved backward into the house, still holding on to Iona's hand. "Come away in."

Iona grabbed her bag and allowed herself to be dragged inside the warm house, instantly smelling fresh-baked bread.

"I'll be back in a tick. Make yourself at home." Beth released her hand and, with the tulips cradled in her arm, walked toward the kitchen with the rolling gait of someone compensating for pain. Concerned—and with a flash of fear at the prospect of Beth not being hale and hearty—Iona hung her coat on the old-fashioned stand and dropped her bag next to the staircase.

The small living room was tidy, the floral sofa and armchair flanking the fire, as always, with the retro, glass-topped coffee table in between them. The old boxy TV sat on top of a packed bookcase, and the drop-leaf dining table in the corner near the door was laid with a checked cover. The ornate cage housing Henry, Beth's cockatoo, hung on its stand near the window. "Hello, Henry, you old sod. How are you?" Iona poked a finger through the bars as the bird shuffled closer on the perch, presenting its chest.

"Gimme a biscuit," Henry squawked. "Gimme a biscuit." Iona tutted. "Just a minute, greedy piglet."

She turned to see Beth coming in from the kitchen. Her face was flushed, and she was wafting a dishcloth.

"Jeepers, nearly burned the steak pie." She puffed her cheeks out theatrically. "What can I get you to drink? Did you have breakfast?"

"Nothing for now, thanks. I'm fine." Iona slipped her boots off, tucked them under the sofa and flopped down into the soft fabric.

Having fed Henry a cracker, Beth folded the dishcloth into a neat square and perched on the edge of the chair. Iona noticed that Beth's hands were shaking, and as she smiled at Iona again, the passage of time since their last meeting—albeit only eight weeks by Iona's calculation—seemed to have stripped her great aunt of something Iona couldn't quite define.

"Are you well?" She scanned the deeply etched lines on Beth's face, still unsure what had changed.

"Och, yes. I'm fine." Beth flapped a hand. "Still waiting for my new hip, and now I'm having some problems with my teeth." She rolled her eyes. "But other than that..."

Iona shifted her focus from the warm eyes and silver-streaked, curly hair to the wide mouth. While the trademark coral lipstick was in place, there was a sinking around the gum line which, now that Iona knew what to look for, had changed Beth's face quite distinctly. "What's going on with your teeth?"

"Oh, some gum issues. I've lost a few. Have a damn plate now, and it drives me spare." Beth massaged her face, her wrinkled hand moving in small circles around her mouth.

"I'm really sorry." Iona frowned. "Is there anything that can be done?"

"Apart from take them all out, not really." Beth grimaced. "Anyway, enough about my ailments. Tell me about you?"

"Oh, I'm fine. Just taking a few days off, you know. Time for a little break and, of course, to see you, and then go home." Beth's face twitched. "Your father will be chuffed."

Iona nodded. "Yep. I think he's pleased."

"How long's it been?" Beth frowned.

"A year or so." Iona shuffled her feet, shoving her toes under the edge of the heavy rug.

"Hmm, a bit more than that, no?" Beth dropped her chin and gave Iona a scolding look. "Closer to two, I'm thinking."

Iona sucked in her bottom lip. Beth had a way of seeing through her like no one had been able to, since her mother. The fact that she was so transparent to Beth was disquieting. "Yeah, I know." She shrugged. "But I'm going now."

Beth settled back in the chair, slipped her feet out of her shoes, and wiggled her crooked toes. Several of the joints cracked, reminding Iona of the way Grace would hyperextend her fingers, popping the joints before she started to play.

"Why did you leave it so long, love?" Beth was scrutinizing her.

"I think I just figured it out recently." She saw Beth's eyebrows jump. "I was talking to Roz about it."

Beth nodded, letting her continue.

"I think it's about being afraid of going home because when I left, Mum was still so present there." Saying it out loud seemed to detract from the sense of what she'd concluded just a few days before. "Like, if I go back and all the memories are gone, then she'll really be gone." She locked eyes with Beth. "Does that make any sense?"

Beth's lips were pursed, seeming to hold in what she wanted to say.

"Aunty B?"

Beth leaned forward, linking her hands across her lumpy knees. "It's not about avoiding your dad, then?"

Iona's stomach dipped. Beth had done it again. "Well, maybe, but I think it's mostly about Mum."

∼

They'd walked for a long time, following the wall that ran along the edge of the Firth of Forth until the magnificent red, crisscross construction of the railway bridge and the two stark-white suspension road bridges were all behind them. Despite the cold of the day, they'd stopped to get an ice cream cone from a café that overlooked the water.

"Seriously?" Iona teased.

"It's never too cold for ice cream," Beth quipped, licking a dribble of chocolate that was running down her wrist.

"If you say so." Iona shrugged.

The sun was breaking through the intermittent clouds, and as they walked back toward home, Iona felt the gentle warmth of it come and go across her shoulders. Sensing her moment, she moved in closer to her great aunt.

"So, Aunty B, I wanted to ask you something." She glanced sideways at Beth, who was concentrating on licking her ice cream into a peak.

"All right."

"Dad sent me a letter from Mum on my birthday." She watched as Beth's focus switched to the water beside them.

"Uh huh." Beth sounded less than surprised.

"She told Dad that she wanted me to have it when I turned twenty-one. She wrote about a few personal things, quite a bit about Professor Douglas, and asked that I go and see him." Iona paused as Beth moved up to the wall and leaned a hip against it. "Then, she left another letter with the professor, asking me to

come and see you, to thank you for everything you did for her."
Iona took a steadying breath. "She called you her savior."

Beth's eyes snapped to hers, and the color drained from her face. "Oh, for goodness' sake."

At Beth's reaction, Iona grabbed her arm. "I'm sorry, I didn't mean to upset you."

"Oh, it's fine. I'm just a wee bit sensitive about that time. That's all. It's not you, love." Beth patted Iona's hand. "Go on."

"Well, I was wondering if you'd tell me about the last time they came to see you. What you talked about." She pulled her collar closer to her throat, a sudden gust of wind seeming to cut through her coat.

Beth popped the last piece of wafer-thin cone into her mouth, then wiped her face with a tissue. "It was a long time ago, Iona. I'm not sure if…"

Beth was never one to hedge. She was honest to the point of causing pain, so this vague response took Iona by surprise.

"I don't mean to pry or anything. I'm just sort of following Mum's lead, to see if I can learn anything more about that trip, if she got what she needed from it." She halted, seeing Beth's frown deepen.

"I understand that." Beth nodded. "It's fair that you'd want to know as much as there is to know."

Iona released the breath she'd held. The last thing she wanted to do was make Beth uncomfortable or taint the easy dynamic that existed between them.

"Let's walk home and we can talk on the way." Beth beckoned to her.

Iona dropped the remainder of her ice cream into a bin and linked arms with her great aunt.

"First of all, they really struggled with whether to bring you with them on that trip. But they'd agreed that there were things that needed to be said that would be too hard if you were with them." She cleared her throat, her grip on Iona's arm tightening.

"She called me before they came, but I could barely hear her, so Craig came on the phone." At this, Beth's voice faltered, and Iona, her heart twinging, pulled her great aunt closer. "They wanted to protect you, at least from witnessing her goodbyes, because they couldn't protect you from the rest of what was to come."

"I understand that now." Iona nodded, her eyes stinging in the chilly breeze.

"When they got here, she was awfully thin and weak. Your dad was her crutch. Everywhere she went, he was there, holding her under her arms, lifting her from chairs, and even eating most of her food." Beth smiled sadly. "They thought I didn't notice but, I did." She dipped her chin.

"You don't have to tell me everything now." Iona saw the magnitude of what she was asking settling on Beth's shoulders.

"No, it's fine. I could understand her O.K. when they first arrived, but it wasn't long before her voice failed. I felt terrible because I kept asking her to repeat herself." Beth shook her head. "Heartbreaking to see her that way."

Iona squeezed Beth's arm. "I know."

"Well, the first evening, she had Craig help her get ready for bed, then she came and sat with me in the lounge. She looked like a little girl, all wet-haired and smelling of my lavender soap." Beth looked over at Iona, her eyes glittering. "Craig said he was going for a walk, so he left us together for a while. She sat next to me on the sofa and put her head here." Beth patted her collar bone. "I could barely hear her, but I heard enough to know what she was saying."

Iona nodded, afraid that if she spoke her voice would betray her.

"She said that she was sorry that I had to see her like that, having lost my sister, Margaret, so prematurely. I'll never forget what she said next." Beth forced a swallow. "She said it was both freakishly ironic and heartbreaking that you wouldn't have your mother close, just as she hadn't. Then she said she knew it was a lot to ask of me, but that she wanted me to be that for you." A soft sigh escaped Beth, so Iona released her grip on her great aunt's forearm, instead draping her arm around the narrow shoulder.

"She said that she knew in her heart that I'd be there when you graduated, and in the front row at your first concert. That I'd be there when you got your heart broken, then on your wedding day, and when you became a mother yourself."

Iona could no longer see clearly, and dipping her chin to her chest, she tried to focus on where she was stepping. Hearing her mother speak through Beth was eerie, the words so very Grace, and yet their being somewhat removed in this way making them all the more poignant.

As a few moments of silence allowed the two women to regain their composure, a young woman with a baby in a stroller came toward them. She was wearing a rainbow-striped sweater and ripped jeans, and her long hair was being whipped across her face as she flicked her head from side to side, trying to free herself from the blonde mask. Her round face was line-free and her cheeks a ruddy pink. As she spotted Iona and Beth she stopped, swiped the hair from her face and grinned.

"Hiya, Beth. How are you?" The child in the stroller opened its eyes and, taking one look at them, its face puckered, the tiny mouth opening into a curly circle as a tiny mewl brought Iona to a standstill.

"Hello, Ailene. How's the wee one?" Beth bent forward at the waist and extended a finger, which she gently slid under the baby's chin. "She's grown."

"Yeah. She's a mushroom." Ailene chuckled.

Beth turned to Iona. "This is my niece, well, my great niece." She gestured toward Iona.

"Nice to meet you, Ailene."

Ailene nodded. "You too."

"Ailene works in the wool shop. She takes great care of me when I'm in the market for more." Beth shifted her feet, pulling at the collar of her coat.

Ailene bent over the child and grabbed the pacifier that had fallen out onto the blanket bundled around the baby's middle. After popping it in her own mouth for a few seconds, she replaced it in the child's mouth. "It's nippy again." She shivered.

"You need a proper coat on a day like this." Beth tutted. "You young folk."

"Aye, you're right." She shrugged. "Well, I better be going."

Beth reached over and patted the young woman's shoulder. "See you soon, then."

Ailene maneuvered the stroller around them and raised a hand in goodbye.

As they moved on, turning back onto Beth's street, Beth linked her arm through Iona's again. "So, where were we?"

"You were saying how she said she knew you'd be there for me." Iona let her eyes close briefly, a shadow of an image of herself in a gauzy wedding dress sending her jaw into a knot.

"Yes. There was more, but I can't recall exactly." Beth sounded tired.

"Let's leave it for now. We're almost home."

Beth shook her head. "Might as well get it out. Now's as good as any other time."

They crossed the road and headed down Shore Road, the blue door now visible up ahead.

"She told me that Craig had intended on talking to you about what she'd decided to do, with the Zurich decision and every-thing, but she was so worried about not being able to answer your questions herself, she asked him to wait."

Iona caught her breath. Grace's words were echoing around her, but pulling her focus was Beth's referral to "the Zurich deci-sion." While Iona now knew the words' meaning, the way Beth branded the weighty choice Grace had made seemed unencumbered, almost too simplistic. Surely, choosing to end one's life deserved a more significant label or system of reference?

Seemingly unaware of Iona's momentary state of shock, Beth continued.

"She still wasn't sure at that point if they should tell you, it being so much for a little girl to take in, on top of everything else you were coping with." Beth steered her up to the front door and pulled her keys out of her coat pocket. "He reluctantly agreed to wait."

Iona felt herself sway, the anticipation of what came next messing with her equilibrium.

"She asked me if I'd be able to forgive her." Without looking at her, Beth inserted the key in the old brass lock.

Iona willed her throat to relax so that she could speak. "So, she didn't ask you what she should do?"

Opening the door, Beth shook her head. "No. She'd already made her mind up by then."

Taken aback, Iona followed Beth into the house.

Beth hung her coat on the rack, glanced in the hall mirror, and smoothed her windblown hair. There were new shadows under her eyes, and Iona felt a squeeze of guilt at putting this dear woman through this, making her relive her pain.

Back in the living room, Beth patted the sofa cushion next to her, and Iona sat down.

"I told her, 'Grace, my love, only you can know how hard it's been to make this decision. It's between you and your god, and if that is the manner in which you choose to leave this world, there's no man who'll judge you. At least, none that'll let me know about it.'"

At this, Iona smiled. Of course, Beth would defend Grace. To the death. Literally. "Was it very difficult?" Iona kept her voice low. "To support her like that?"

Beth considered her question for a few moments, then shook her head. "Her main concern was for you, and your father. She'd seen her own mother die a slow, painful death from cancer. She refused to let that be the legacy she left you, and I totally understood that. She just didn't want you to have to face that kind of lingering loss."

The word *legacy* struck Iona like a fist.

"You know, while it was the saddest conversation she and I ever had, there was also something freeing in it." She looked at Iona. "Do you know what I mean?"

Iona nodded, her eyes blurring.

"For her own part, she seemed peaceful with it all. She was resigned, but not scared." Beth sniffed and rifled in her pocket for a clean tissue. Iona lifted her bag, pulled one out, and handed it to her great aunt. "We talked for a while, well, as best as she could manage, then she asked me to stay close to you and your dad. So of course, I promised I would."

Iona nodded.

"I think that until they were leaving the next morning, I hadn't let myself believe that it would be the last time I'd see her." Beth placed her hand on Iona's forearm.

Iona blinked several times, the pain of Beth's memories leeching through her hand and onto Iona's skin.

"I tried to say that she still had time. That I'd come up to Orkney before she…" She swallowed. "But she refused. She was adamant about it. She wanted to say goodbye here, while she was, as she put it, mostly herself."

A tear broke loose and trickled over Iona's cheekbone.

"So, we said our goodbyes, and I cried like a baby for the rest of the day." Beth wiped both eyes. "I'd not wish it on anyone." She cleared her throat. "Life is cruel, Iona. But you know that better than most, my love." She grabbed Iona's hand as the clock on the mantle chimed four times. "Come on, now. Let's have a wee break, and I'll make us some dinner."

∾

With their evening meal cleared away, they sat on either side of the fire. Henry had chirruped and squeaked throughout dinner until Beth had slung a blanket over his cage. Now, in the peace of the room, as the flames licked up the sides of the logs in the grate, and with her stomach full, Iona felt her eyelids get heavy.

"Do you want to go to bed, love?" Beth whispered.

"No, I'm fine." Iona shifted up in the chair. "I'm just relaxed. It's so lovely to be here."

"It's wonderful to have you." Beth stared into the flames. "You should come more often."

As Iona flexed her back and flicked through their conversation earlier, her thoughts went to the photograph. "Aunty B. Do you mind if I ask you one more thing?"

"Not at all." Beth ran a hand through the feathery hair at her temple. "Ask away."

"I'll be back in a sec." Iona rose and made her way upstairs to the tiny guest bedroom. The single bed sat along the wall, and the chintz duvet cover was the same one she remembered from childhood visits. A miniature bedside table housed a lamp with fuzzy tassels hanging from the bottom of the shade. A small, white, kidney-shaped dressing table filled the remaining space in the room, and her bag was shoved under the low velvet stool that sat in the kneehole. She pulled it out and searched for the envelopes. Finding them, she opened the second letter, slipped the photograph of her mother and CM from between the pages, and went downstairs.

Beth was adjusting the blanket over Henry's cage, having probably given him his customary bedtime treat of a cuttlefish.

Her hands feeling clammy, Iona hovered near the sofa, waiting for Beth to resume her seat. Once her great aunt was settled, Iona perched on the arm of the chair and handed Beth the picture. "I found this old photo of Mum. Do you know who the man was?" She focused on Beth rather than the photo, anxious for her reaction, and possibly even some sign of recognition to register.

Beth screwed her face up, lifting the photo closer to her eyes. She frowned, flipped it over and read the back, then turned it face-up again. "I don't know him." She pushed the photo back toward Iona. "Where was it you found it?" There was something odd in her voice, almost defensive.

Iona explained about the burst pipe and how she'd discovered the photograph in the lining of the cello case. Beth listened, but seemed to be avoiding her eyes.

"I just thought you might recognize him. I think he and Mum were…" She hesitated. "Together, at one time."

Beth shook her head, almost violently. "No. I've never seen him before." At this, she stood up, causing Iona to have to jump off the arm of the chair. "Well, I think it's bedtime for me."

Iona slid the photograph into her pocket. "I'm sorry if I've been asking too many questions. Digging up memories." She reached for Beth's fingers.

"It's all right. You have a right to know as much as I have to tell. I'm just a wee bit tired now." Beth squeezed her fingers and smiled warmly. "You're her image, you know?"

Iona nodded. "So I'm told."

As Iona turned for the door, Beth held her hand tighter.

"Your father is the best of men, Iona. He was her rock, a pillar of strength, and he absolutely adores you. He'd move the heavens to make you safe and happy." Beth lifted Iona's hand and kissed the back of it. "Just keep that in mind when you're working through all your questions."

Curious as to what had prompted Beth's blatant redirection of the conversation, Iona still felt the gravity of the message. "I will, Aunty B. I promise."

As Beth headed for the door, something brought her to a standstill. She turned, an odd expression tugging at her mouth. "Iona, your mother left a letter with me too. The morning they were leaving." Her eyes flicked to the cabinet that ran along the wall opposite the window. "She asked me to keep it for you until now, until you'd received the others." Beth edged toward the long dark cabinet, her hands shaking slightly as she pulled open a deep drawer.

Iona pressed her lips together, her legs locking and her face tingling in anticipation. She watched as Beth moved several placemats to one side, then pulled out an ivory envelope, the exact same size and shape as the others. Turning to Iona, she held it out.

"I've no idea what it says, but here it is, love." She waggled the envelope, jolting Iona out of her paralysis. She stepped forward and took the envelope, her name in the familiar script drawing her eye like a magnet.

"Thank you." She pressed the envelope to her chest. "I think I'll read it in bed."

"Good idea." Beth nodded. "I'll be off to bed then, but you know where I am if you need me."

Iona moved in closer and kissed a powdery cheek. "I do, thanks. Sleep tight."

10

I ona snuggled down into the narrow bed. Beth's response to the photo had unnerved her and now, all she could think about was the image of her mother and the dark-haired man. The force of Beth's denial was intriguing, but rather than pursue it, Iona had let any remaining questions lie. She'd dragged the poor woman back into the past enough for one visit. Her stomach fluttering, she lifted the envelope from the bedside table and carefully opened it.

My darling girl,
So, you are with Beth. It makes me smile to picture the two of you sitting in her living room, feeding Henry crackers. That bird will live to be a hundred, I swear.
The thought of saying goodbye to Beth in a few minutes is devastating. I know it's the right thing to do, though, as she went through enough with my mum.
There was nothing Beth could've said to change my mind about this decision, not that she tried. The thing I love best about her is her total acceptance of me and my choices. Well, most of

*them, anyway. Barring some decisions I made at university, I
think she'd support me in anything I chose to do. She truly is
another rare human being whom I've been blessed to have in my
life.*

What choices had Grace made that Beth had disapproved of?
Iona frowned, shifted onto her side, and lifted the photo from the
bedside table. Holding it under the dim lamp, she scrutinized the
two faces. The curves of her mother's were familiar, although
more youthful than any memories Iona had of her. On closer
inspection, while handsome, the man's face was what she might
have called hard—his jawline sharp and his eyes deep set.

As she studied their stance, something unsettling began to
surface. Despite her mother's blissful expression, their body
language looked off, somehow. Grace was turned in fully toward
him, her leg trapping his, her cheek on his chest and her arm
around his middle. While his arm was around Grace's back, he
was leaning away from her, his shoulder tilted to the side, one
foot pointing toward the doorframe as if trying to escape the
manacle of her smaller one.

Iona leaned in, poring over the image more closely. Her
mother's eyes were alight. Although the picture was faded, Iona
could clearly see the glint of love, of infatuation, in the pale
irises. When she shifted focus to the man, his eyes were blank.
His smile was present, but he looked removed from the scene as
if humoring her mother rather than being immersed in the
moment as she was.

Disturbed, Iona set the photo down and lay on her back,
staring at the ceiling. Then, turning back to the letter, she
continued to read.

· · ·

Speaking of rare human beings, it's important to me that you know how incredibly happy I've been with your dad. When I first got to know him in Edinburgh, I thought he was the kindest man I'd ever met. And oh, those amazing eyes, and the wavy hair that just called for my fingers to run through it. Now, all these years later, my heart still skips when he comes into the room. His touch both stills and excites me (wasn't there a song about that)? Then, I remember those feelings, the very sensation of his touch, are impermanent, and I miss him already.

It's funny the things that you appreciate when time becomes more important, when the option of doing things again isn't a given. Each time I see you, my sweet girl, I want to hold on to the image of you. When I'm listening to the rain on the roof, seeing clouds move away from the sun, watching the water lick the shore, following a shooting star across the night sky, I'm wondering if it'll be the last time. Is this the last time I will hear my daughter's voice, taste wine, or feel a kiss with true passion behind it?

I'm getting a little morbid, but my point is that there is nothing as precious as knowing that you are truly loved and valued as a human being, and I have had that with your dad. More than anything else, I want that for you too. I don't know if by now there is someone special in your life, but what I will say is this: never settle for less than you deserve. Never let someone belittle your hopes or tarnish your dreams. Always believe that you are worthy of the best that life, and love, can offer.

I made my share of mistakes, but marrying your dad was the best decision I ever made. He has been my best friend, my protector, my refuge, my sounding board and sometimes my critic, but there has never been one day that I haven't felt loved. When you find that, Iona, and I know you will, hold on to it.

There's something else. I miss Freya so much. It's been brutal having my best friend in the world disappear from my life. I know she's angry with me, and afraid, but I'd hoped she'd be around for your dad and you, if not for me. All that aside, please go and see her next, Iona. Tell her that I understand and that I forgive her for everything, as I know she won't have forgiven herself.

> *I love you,*
> *Mum xxx*

Tears tracking down her cheeks, Iona refolded the letter. As she hiccupped, a picture of her godmother, Freya, monopolizing the sofa in the cottage on Orkney, her long legs draped over the arm and a glass of wine balanced on her stomach, snatched at Iona's breath.

Freya had been such a fixture in their home and their lives that the distance that had sprung up between her and Grace at the end had both perplexed and hurt Iona, but the thought of seeing her mother's best friend again now felt right. The fact that she'd been heading to see Freya next, even before knowing that her mother would ask it of her, felt like another tenuous string connecting them through the planes of existence that kept them apart.

Exhausted, Iona set the letter on the table and reached for the lamp switch, just as her phone buzzed. With a tiny lift in her chest, she picked it up and read the text from Scott.

How did it go with Beth?

She bit her bottom lip, lay back, and began to type.

~

Beth was cheerful when Iona came down to breakfast. She'd already lit the fire in the living room and had made a pile of potato scones. The teapot was on the table, covered by the faded Union Jack cozy that Iona used to put on her head as a child, and

Henry was out of his cage, perched on the back of the sofa. "Sleep well?" Beth set the scones on the table.

"Yes, thanks." Iona lied. "Bed's as comfy as ever."

Beth nodded. "Ted liked that bed. He'd scuttle in there, whenever I threw him out for snoring." She chuckled. "He was its most frequent guest."

"Well, lucky he liked it." Iona lifted the pot and poured the tea. "So, Henry's out and about this morning?" She nodded at the bird, whose beak was buried under its wing.

"Yes. He gets an hour or so of freedom while I have breakfast, and then clean the cage." She pulled out a chair and sat opposite Iona, "On pain of death, if he messes that sofa." She wagged a finger at the bird who, seeming to have picked up on her warning, tilted its head to the side, its beady eyes studying them both.

"Oh, shut up," He croaked, sending the two women into a fit of laughter.

An hour later, Iona slipped her coat on and turned to her great aunt.

"Thanks, Aunty B. Great being here." She hugged Beth close, feeling the warm breath on her cheek. "And when you get a date for your hip surgery, call me, and I'll take a few days off to come and take care of you."

"Bless you. That's so kind." She moved a tendril of hair away from Iona's eye. "Come back soon, m'love. You know you've a place here, anytime." Beth's eyes were watery. "Maybe bring that friend of yours next time."

Iona grimaced. "You'd need to stock up on food and wine if Roz comes along. Oh, and toilet paper." She winked as Beth pulled a face.

"Oh, too much information." She nudged Iona's arm. "Away you go now, and remember to phone me from Inverness."

"I will. I promise." Iona carved an X on her chest. "Love

you, Aunty B." She kissed Beth's cheek one more time before turning to the door.

The morning was breezy and crisp and, as she walked along Shore Road, Iona sucked in deep briny breaths as the wind flitted across the choppy water and buffeted her face. Before turning away, she stopped and squinted, as the firth shone like silver under the gentle March sunshine. All three bridges stretched into the distance, spanning the body of water, linking south to north, the direction she was now heading in.

The thought of seeing Freya was both exciting and making her nervous. Freya, the physical antithesis to Grace, was tall, fair, loud and, as Craig frequently commented, overly opinionated about most things. She was the brash to Grace's subtle, the tipsy to Grace's sober, and the shameless to Grace's reticent. As Iona considered the woman she was traveling to see, she was struck by the correlation between that friendship and her own with Roz. Thinking of her flatmate, she pulled out her phone to call her.

Roz picked up after a couple of rings.

"Hey. You O.K.? I meant to call last night." Iona checked for traffic and then crossed the road.

"Yeah, all good. I'm heading into work. Scott was desperate, as Katie called in sick today, so I said I'd go in early, help him set up for lunch, and do a back-to-back." Roz sniffed. "I need the money, anyway." She sounded breathless.

"Is everything O.K.?"

"Yeah. Just need to cut back on the wine, that's all." Roz laughed.

Iona edged past a flustered-looking woman pushing twins in an extra-wide stroller. She smiled at the red-cheeked babies, who were both gumming their fists.

"Listen, I've got to go. Can I call you tonight?" Roz sounded distracted. "I want to hear how it's all going."

"Sure, of course." Iona switched the phone to her opposite

ear as she took her place in the queue at the bus stop. "Sure you're all right?"

"Absolutely."

A few minutes later, Iona climbed onto the bus behind a young man in a utility kilt and black leather jacket. His Doc Martin boots were mud-caked, and his carrot-colored hair was twisted into a thick ponytail. As she settled in a seat across the aisle from him, he smiled shyly at her.

She smiled back, tucking her phone away. The trip to Dalmeny railway station wasn't long, then the train ride to Inverness would take around four hours, giving her plenty of time to relax and hopefully snooze before arriving.

Freya, having graduated from Edinburgh University as a veterinarian, had decided that a lifetime of treating overweight cats, sheep with foot-rot, and hamsters with anxiety was not for her after all. Much to her parents' chagrin, she had purchased a smallholding on the Black Isle, renovated the ramshackle stone house and outbuildings, and started breeding Border Collies. Her business had been running for over fifteen years, and in that time, Freya had built a reputation as the best source for top-notch sheepdogs in the region.

She had a way with the animals that impressed Iona. Even as puppies, they seemed to sense that Freya was alpha just by her decisive movements, the way she'd tap their little chests to get them to focus on her or click her fingers to have them sit, or stop barking.

Iona had been to the farm several times with her parents, but this would only be the second visit she'd made alone. When she'd called Freya to ask if she could stay for a couple of nights, the response she'd received had been initially tentative, then warm.

"I'd love it, kiddo." Freya had sighed. "It's been far too long."

"I know. I was trying to remember when I last saw you."

"It must be at least two years." Freya had sounded dubious. "Or maybe more."

Iona recalled that it had been on her way down to Edinburgh before she'd started at university. She'd arranged to stay at the farm for a night to break the journey.

"It was on my way down to uni. Remember?"

Freya had laughed, recalling how she'd let Iona have a little too much wine and had felt terrible sending her on her way with a hangover.

Iona enjoyed the sound of the familiar raucous laugh, letting it transport her back to the times when she'd hide on the stairs and listen to her mother and her best friend cackling well into the night, long after her father had given up and gone to bed. The symphony of their laughter had given Iona a deep-seated sense of safety, a warming in her belly that she now realized just how much she missed.

She glanced around her, the day beginning to lose its shine as purple clouds obscured the weakening springtime sun. The kilted man was waiting to get off the bus, and her stop was only a few minutes away, and as she kept an eye out for the sign for Dalmeny Station, she let another memory come. It was of another Christmas in Orkney, when Freya had brought a man with her. Grace had been taken aback when her friend had arrived with someone in tow, not having given them any warning. Iona recalled that her mother had been gracious, but that her dad had been less so. She'd overheard her parents talking in the kitchen, having shown Freya and her boyfriend up to the tiny guest room with the sagging single bed.

"What the hell was she thinking?" Craig's voice had been so low it had been more of a growl. "It's a bit much, Grace."

"Shhhh. She'll hear you." Grace had tried to placate him. "It's just a couple of nights, and if they're O.K. in that awful bed, what's the harm?"

"This is a family Christmas. Not a free-for-all, bring the

latest man you're shagging—or rather, emasculating—to dinner."

At this, Grace had giggled. "Craig. That's awful. She's not that bad."

Craig's voice had softened. "Oh, really? What was the last one like? A pathetic, hen-pecked chap from Aberdeen. I felt so sorry for him. He couldn't get a word in edgeways, and when he did, she corrected everything he said." They'd laughed together then, simultaneously shushing each other.

"Well at least this one looks like he can stand up for himself." Grace had laughed softly. "Here's hoping."

∽

The train was packed, and Iona was thankful she'd reserved a seat. As she wove through the carriage, looking for D34, her bag bumping against her hip, her phone rang. Spotting her seat, she thumped down into it and scrambled through her bag.

"Hello?"

"Hi. It's me."

"Oh, Dad. I'm just getting on the train to Inverness."

A tall, stocky man in overalls, with a heavy-looking rucksack on his shoulder, stood in the aisle. He was frowning and pointing to the seat beside hers, next to the window. Understanding she needed to move, she stood up and eased out of the way to let him in. As she took her seat again, she was aware that her father was speaking but was unable to hear him.

"Sorry, Dad. What did you say? It's pretty noisy in here."

"Never mind. Just have a good time with Freya and give her my best."

"Will do. I'll call you when I'm leaving there."

"All right, pet. See you soon."

"Bye, Dad."

An hour into the journey, with a hot drink she'd bought from the buffet car, Iona ate the packed lunch that Beth had given her. The noise level around her had settled somewhat as people plugged in earphones or opened laptops. A brother and sister, wedged in on either side of their frazzled-looking mother opposite Iona, were focused on a colorful book, and a baby was crying at the far end of the carriage. Rather than being a disturbance, the hum of activity gave Iona a sense of calm. She was able to let the hubbub sink away, to act as a buffer between her and the thrum of the train wheels, hard against the metal tracks beneath them.

To her relief, the man next to her quickly fell asleep, his big head leaning awkwardly against the cloudy window. Careful not to disturb him, she reached under the narrow table in front of her and lifted her bag to her lap. She pulled the last letter out and read it again, then folded it away. It was heartbreaking that these two women, who had been as close as sisters, had separated badly at such an intensely difficult time for her mother, when they should've been joining forces to face the inevitable, as they had all their lives.

She closed her eyes and Bach's Concerto No. 1 filtered into her mind. It was a piece that her mother had loved to play, so Iona exhaled and let it come. Her fingertips prickled, yearning for the smooth curve of the scroll, the feel of the strings, and the tension of the metal against the fingerboard as she'd trace it down to the bridge. As she followed the score in her head, she could see the notes on the stave, feel the pressure of the cello's body on the insides of her knees.

A sense of such longing overtook her that Iona pressed her head back against the grimy headrest, her heart pattering under her breastbone. She could see her cello, her mother's pride and joy, standing in the corner of her bedroom, neglected, draped with underwear, and then shame replaced the longing. *What was wrong with her?*

~

Not sure how long she'd slept, Iona opened her eyes just as the train pulled into a station. Panicked, she whipped around, looking for a sign on the platform. The man next to her was stirring. "Can I get past? This is my stop." He jabbed a thumb over his shoulder.

"Sure. Where are we?" She slipped out into the aisle.

"Inverkeithing." He spoke over his shoulder as he waited to pass a woman who was pulling a large bag down from the luggage rack.

"Oh, thanks. I change here." Iona yanked her coat on, grabbed her bag, and followed him to the door.

A little over two hours later, as she'd arranged with Freya, Iona stood outside the Royal Highland Hotel in Inverness. One of the last remaining classic Scottish railway hotels, the impressive sandstone structure loomed behind her. The sinking afternoon light gave the stone a pinkish hue as she stared up at the elegant sash windows of the top floor, the roof disappearing above an ornate architrave.

Being here made her miss her Nana Jean. Craig's mother had lived close to the station, and Iona had enjoyed visiting as a child. Jean had been another formative presence in Iona's young life and a tremendous support after her mother died. Craig had been devastated when his mother had been diagnosed with ovarian cancer just eight short months after he'd lost Grace, but true to her natural grit, Jean had battled for almost a year before succumbing to the disease. Iona remembered clearly the sadness of the funeral service, specifically the odd distance she'd picked up on between her father and Freya, who had come to pay her respects.

At the time, Iona had been only twelve, and not understanding what had happened between them, or previously between her mother and Freya, she'd tried to pull the two together at the hushed reception that had been held after the service. Freya had been unusually quiet and left early, citing a sick puppy that she needed to get back to, but Iona remembered being confused by her godmother leaving without hugging her dad goodbye.

A car horn sounding behind her made her jump, and she spun around to see Freya's Land Rover, the lights flashing from the far side of the parking area. Raising a hand, Iona eased between the taxis parked outside the hotel and made her way to the car.

Freya climbed out to greet her, her long legs encased in skinny jeans tucked into leather boots. Her green wax jacket flapped open, revealing a creamy Arran sweater, her long, fair hair was pulled into a tight ponytail, and her distinct turquoise eyes narrowed as she smiled. Iona noticed that a few more wrinkles had appeared on the attractive face but, rather than detracting from Freya's beauty, they somehow enhanced it.

"Look at you, kiddo. You're totally gorgeous." She hugged Iona tightly.

"Ha, thanks. You look fab yourself." Iona kissed Freya's cheek. "Not a day over sixty."

Freya flicked her backside. "Cheeky monkey." She laughed her trademark laugh. "Get in, it's nippy out here."

The fifteen-minute drive to the farm near Inchmore, flew by as they chatted. Iona enjoyed the easy repartee, filling Freya in about her journey, her visit with Beth, and how her job was going. Freya talked about the most recent litter of puppies she was dealing with and the improvements she'd been making to the house.

Their route along Clachnaharry Road was as stunning as Iona remembered, tracing the edge of the Beauly Firth, with spectacular views across the water to the Highlands beyond, the same vistas that Freya enjoyed from her home.

"It's as pretty as ever." She took in Freya's profile.

"Yes. I never tire of this landscape."

As the car began to climb a gentle hill, gradually becoming enclosed on either side by tall spruce and fir trees, Iona cracked her window open so the piney smell could filter into the car.

"Smells great."

Freya turned the car onto Newton Hill. "It does."

Iona soon recognized the long fence delineating the edge of Freya's land, and as they drove through the red farm gate, bumping over the rough driveway, the fieldstone house and a series of slate-roofed outbuildings stood before them, with Beauly Firth stretching away behind, a ribbon of startling blue.

"I forget how stunning this place is." She smiled at Freya, who yanked on the handbrake.

"Out you get. You must be in dire need of tea. Or perhaps something stronger?"

∿

Freya had gone out to the kennel to check on the dogs, having a litter of pups that was close to being weaned. She'd told Iona to settle into her room, then come out and join her.

Upstairs, Iona dumped her coat and bag on the floor. The guest bedroom had been decorated since the last time she'd been here, and the window overlooking the firth had elegant new sheer curtains that tipped the plush, creamy carpet. The walls were a soft beige, and the dark wood bedside cabinets, with brass handles glinting on the deep drawers, were a perfect contrast to the paleness of the room. The headboard was upholstered in an ivory-colored fabric, with brass nail heads outlining the arch, and the duvet cover was cream with an ivy design, soft green tendrils crawling from the base and thinning out toward the top of the bed.

It was a serene room, the view adding to the depth of the beauty and palpable calm of the space, and the knowledge that her parents had stood at this window, their shoulders inevitably touching as they looked out at this same view, was both comforting and heartbreaking.

Iona leant her knees against the warm radiator under the window as she scanned left and right, envying Freya this piece of the world. To the right was the long, slate-roofed building that Freya had converted into a kennel. The door was ajar, and as she watched, Freya came out with two black-and-white bundles of fur in her arms. She lifted one to her mouth and kissed the top of its head, then looked up at the window and, spotting Iona, raised one puppy up in the air, tempting her down. Iona waved, grabbed her coat, and headed down the stairs.

Inside the warm kennel building, the puppies' mother was lying on her side on top of a pile of soft blankets. She was in a small room with pine-paneled walls and a heat lamp mounted above her. Five tiny black-and-white puffballs were nosing her stomach, their little backsides and tails quivering as they pressed in, searching for a teat.

Freya leaned down and picked up a pup that had been edged out by its larger siblings. "Come on, little one. There's room for you too." She eased the pup's snout up to its mother, gently shifting a chubbier puppy to the side in order to let the smaller one in. "There's always one." She smiled over her shoulder.

Iona leaned in. "Can I pet her while they're feeding?"

Freya nodded. "It's fine. She's super mellow. This is Jessie."

Iona slipped inside the room and knelt at the dog's head. "Hello, Jessie. You're a beauty." She stroked the beautiful head, letting her fingertip trail along the distinct swath of white fur that ran from the forehead down to the end of the snout. The tip of Jessie's long tail ticked against the blanket. "What lovely babies you made," she crooned.

"They're seven weeks tomorrow." Freya was filling a long, shallow container with water at the deep farm sink on the opposite wall. "Soon time to go out into the world."

"They seem so small still." Iona leaned down and kissed Jessie's soft head. "Will she pine for them?" The dog raised its head and licked the back of Iona's hand. "Aww, thank you, Jessie."

"Sometimes they get a little depressed, but I'll keep her busy. Joe's here too. I keep him out while they're feeding. He's a great mate, even guards her while she sleeps. Adorable, really." There was a wistful quality to Freya's voice. "She's luckier than me in that respect."

To Iona's surprise, Freya had allowed herself to appear vulnerable. Her loneliness was tangible, for just a second, until she drew her shoulders back and turned to Iona. "Well, that was pathetic, wasn't it?"

"Not at all." Iona shook her head.

∽

The kitchen was warm, and Freya stood at the Aga, stirring a pot of something that smelled rich and meaty. She pinched some salt from a receptacle and added it to the pot. "Got everything you need in your room?"

"Yes. It's gorgeous up there. You've re-done both it and the bathroom since I was last here." Iona sat at the long farmhouse table.

Freya turned to face her. "Yes. My room too, so now all that's left is the kitchen." She traced an arc around herself.

"Not the Aga?" Iona frowned. "That's staying, surely?"

"Oh, yes. Not giving up my old pal." She patted the dark-green stove top.

The flagstone floor was chilling Iona's feet, so she lifted them up onto the chair, hugging her knees to her chest.

"So, it's officially wine-o-clock." Freya grinned. "Red or white?"

"Red, please." Iona ran her hands through her hair, twisting it into a knot at her neck. The warmth of the stove was permeating her chest, soothing away any residual anxiety at being here. Freya poured wine, set a dish of peanuts on the table, and sat opposite Iona. "Dinner will be about half an hour." She scooped up a handful of nuts in her fist, threw back her head, and funneled them into her mouth.

"Great." Iona lifted her glass and touched it to Freya's. "Thanks for letting me stay."

Freya eyed her over the rim of her glass. "Of course. I'm delighted to have you." She sipped some wine, and as she set her glass down, Iona caught a flash of sadness in the turquoise eyes.

"What?"

Freya shook her head. "You're so like her. It just makes me..." Her voice faltered.

Iona nodded. "I know. I get it."

Clearing her throat, Freya mimicked Iona by drawing her knees up to her middle. "So, tell me everything. What's going on with you? Work, music, men, I want all the gory details."

Iona snorted. "Well don't hold your breath on the man front." She grimaced. "Well, there's this guy at work—my boss, actually." She sipped some wine as Freya's eyes widened. "But we're more friends."

"Tell me." Iona shook her head.

"No, it's nothing really."

Freya frowned theatrically, picking up her glass. "And you're not playing much at the moment?"

Iona shook her head.

"How long's it been?" Freya scrutinized her face. "You haven't really said much about that."

Iona shrugged. "A few months. Well, honestly, almost a year. Since I left uni, really."

Freya's eyebrows shot up. "How come I didn't know this?"

"Well, we haven't really been in touch, and I don't exactly advertise it." Iona grimaced. "It makes me sad, but when I start to play, the music brings so much with it." She said. "The weight of the cello, the smell of the rosin, the feel of the strings." She tapped her fingertips together. "It's just Mum. All of it."

Freya's eyes were glittering.

"So, I just stop." Iona held her palm up.

Freya glanced out of the window. "I understand, love, but don't you think she'd be gutted if she knew?" She looked back at Iona. "She told me you had all of her talent in your one pinkie." She crooked her little finger. "She never doubted that you'd turn pro, and in a big way. Are you really O.K. just letting it all go? With all the work you've put in already." Iona shook her head. "No. But I can't seem to get past the memories." She felt her eyes burning. "Maybe one day I will, but at the moment they're stacked up like a bloody brick wall that I hit whenever I try to play."

Freya rubbed her eyes with her palms. "Perhaps if you keep trying, eventually you'll break through it." She sounded hopeful.

"Yes. Maybe." Iona assessed her mother's friend, a way out of the conversation beckoning to her. "You seeing anyone?"

Freya waved her glass back and forth. "Oh, no. We're not talking about me yet. We're still on you."

~

They passed the rest of the evening in easy conversation and cleaned their plates of the hearty stew that Freya had made. Having cleared the table, she'd poured them each a brandy, and they'd decamped into the living room and settled at either end of the sofa.

They talked more about Iona and her current, rather mundane existence, and when Freya asked her about her time with Beth, Iona opened up about her concern for her great aunt.

"She's frail." She swirled the amber fluid around in her

brandy glass. "I don't like to see the deterioration in her." She frowned. "I need to be better about visiting more often."

Freya nodded. "Yes. She's a sweetheart. Was always so good to me." Her eyes took on a distant look, and Iona wondered what memories were clouding them.

Talking about Beth reminded Iona of her great aunt's reaction to the photograph she'd shown her and, feeling confident in the ease of their conversation so far, she swung her legs around and stood up. "So, Mum asked Dad to send me a letter from her on my twenty-first birthday." She paced in front of the window, the view across the water having faded to various shades of black—the solitary twinkle of a boat light bobbing in the distance.

"Right." Freya's voice held steady.

Iona stood still, staring into the darkness. "It's not exactly light reading."

"I'd imagine not."

Iona turned to see Freya's smile fading. "She asked me to visit her old music teacher, Professor Douglas, and when I did, he had another letter for me, from her." Iona scanned the face she knew as well as her own, looking for signs of recognition. "Then, in that one, she asked me to visit Beth."

Freya sipped her brandy.

"When I got to Beth's, she had another letter." Iona held up three fingers. "Aside from some particular things Mum wanted me to know, each letter has directed me to someone else she visited during that last trip they took." She let her hand drop to her side.

Freya's eyes were now wide with what looked like alarm. "So, I suppose she asked you to come here next?"

Iona nodded. "The funny thing is, Freya, I'd already decided to come anyway."

"I suspect I didn't feature too positively, though. Right?" Freya pressed a palm to her chest.

Iona moved back to the sofa and reclaimed her spot, folding her legs under herself.

"Spare me the details. I can imagine." Freya pulled her lips together.

"She wrote about everything that happened, her illness, music, me, Dad, and you." Iona saw Freya's expression tighten, the lines that had grabbed her brow deepening. "I wondered if I could ask you something?" She scanned Freya's face. "If you don't mind?"

Freya nodded. "Um, O.K. Fire away."

"When they came here, that last time. I know it didn't exactly go well." She watched as Freya shifted awkwardly in the seat, as if suddenly uncomfortable in her skin. "Mum wrote about it."

Freya held a hand up. "I know I was an absolute arse to her. It was just something I couldn't get behind. The whole idea of her choosing that ending, that..." She closed her eyes. "I thought life was all about living as long as possible, but your mum just wanted to die on her own terms, and I should've supported her in that." She paused. "Then, with what happened that night." Freya shuddered. "I've had many years to think about how I behaved, Iona, and I'm not proud, let me tell you." Freya opened her eyes and the pain behind them was so obvious that Iona wanted to snatch back her question, but before she could speak again, Freya continued.

"I was so angry with her, so completely terrified of losing her, and how I'd cope without her—every moment with her seemed too precious to have her throw away even one of them." She swallowed. "I called her selfish." She locked eyes with Iona. "Can you believe that?" She shook her head. "Me, calling your mother selfish for wanting to end her own suffering, and by extension, yours and your dad's." She ran a hand over her hair, tucking a loose strand behind her ear. "I was drunk, and I completely blew it."

Trying to picture the heartrending scene, the heated argument that had served to split a lifelong friendship down the middle, Iona leaned forward and touched Freya's shin. "You followed your heart and did what you thought was best. I get that." She sat back and picked her brandy glass up from the floor, cradling the wafer-thin bowl against her stomach. "There was no right way to deal with it, I'm sure."

Freya was shaking her head. "No. Don't do that. Don't excuse me. I don't deserve it." A tear oozed over Freya's cheekbone and ran unchecked down the angular face. "I was a coward, self-centered and nasty, when she needed me the most. I have to live with that, Iona. It's mine to bear."

Iona's throat was thickening, the brandy doing nothing to ease the knot of sadness and growing unease that was gathering there. Beneath the obvious, something was taking root, a shaded question unasked and, as yet, unanswered. "I can't pretend to imagine what it would be like. If it were me and Roz, I'd be a wreck, and we haven't been friends for nearly as long as you and Mum were." She forced a smile as Freya swiped at her eyes. "So, you were a total arse. I'll give you that." She extended her leg and poked Freya's hip with her toe.

Freya let out a muffled laugh. "Thanks. I feel loads better now." She pulled her mouth down at the corner. "I wish I could've had the chance to take it all back." She gave a half smile. "But I didn't deserve that, after what I did."

Iona set her glass back down on the floor, Freya's still raw, and gut-twisting regret tugging at Iona's heart. "You have to let it go. She knew how much you loved her."

Freya's eyes locked on hers. "Did she, really?"

There was such a note of naked hope in her voice that Iona was flooded with compassion. "Yes. She wrote about it. Said she understood why you acted the way you did." Iona held her palm up. "She asked me to tell you that she forgave you, for everything."

At this, Freya's face disintegrated. The glass she held slipped sideways, the brandy cascading onto the carpet unnoticed as she let out a reedy whistle. "You have no idea how many years I've wanted to hear that. To know that she understood." Tears ran freely down her cheeks. "She always saw through my bullshit. She was the only one who ever did." She sniffed and wiped her nose with her palm.

With a growing sense that she was missing something, something critical to the whole truth she sought, Iona's pulse quickened, and she leaned forward. "Stop torturing yourself. She loved to you the very end. That never changed."

Freya was nodding now, the tip of her nose a rosy pink as she shoved the cushion away and stood up. "Thank you, sweetheart. Thanks for telling me that." She pulled her shoulders back. "I really needed to hear it, especially after what happened with your dad."

Iona pushed back against the cushions, the bubble of angst that had been forming in her middle now pressing up against her heart. *What was Freya talking about?* She eyed her godmother as the older woman raked her hair away from her face, her eyes darting around the room as if she were being hunted. An image of Freya and her father, their faces pressed close together, made Iona shake her head, trying to banish where it was taking her.

"What do you mean, what happened with Dad?" She sat up, planting her feet back on the carpet. "You mean how you two agreed that Mum was making the wrong decision, to go to Zurich?"

Freya's face paled, her brow creasing as she stared at Iona, then she moved carefully back to her seat.

"That's what you're talking about, right?" Now Iona was up, the fireplace warm at her back and her cheeks tingling. "Right?"

Freya's eyes were full, the firelight flecking the pale irises with glints of gold.

"Iona, listen to me." Freya gestured toward the sofa. "When you said she knew why I…that she forgave me everything, I…"

Freya's voice faltered, and her eyes closed. "I just assumed she'd told you about…that she must've known…" She opened her eyes and locked on Iona's.

Feeling as if the floor was shifting under her feet, Iona grabbed for the mantle behind her. This couldn't be happening. This new dark hole that was opening up around her threatened to consume her entirely. The face of the woman who had occupied such a position of trust, of love and friendship for her mother, was contorting, and all Iona knew was that she must keep gripping the warm wood with her numbing fingertips, feel the rug beneath her toes, both sensations anchoring her quivering body.

This was a moment she knew she'd look back on over and over, and in order to do her mother's memory justice, what she said next needed to count, make a dent in the thick atmosphere of the now over-warm room.

"You and Dad?" Iona whispered, the words tasting toxic.

Freya dropped her chin to her chest as Iona filled her lungs to bursting.

"You and my dad?" she shouted, the ripping sensation at the back of her throat, oddly satisfying. "When?"

Freya jumped up from the chair and moved toward her. "Iona, please…" She reached for Iona.

"Don't." Iona ducked away from the slender fingers and, circling the room, put the sofa between herself and her godmother.

Her heart clattering, and beads of sweat blooming on her forehead, Iona swayed, grabbing at the soft leather to steady herself. "Tell me what happened." Her mouth was so dry, her tongue stuck to her palate, distorting the words. "Freya?"

Freya nodded slowly and, after hesitating for a moment, resumed her seat at the fireside. "Can you sit down?" Her voice had a new, pleading quality that grated on Iona's nerves.

Shaking her head, she held Freya's gaze.

"O.K." Freya shakily set her empty glass on the table and

turned her focus to the flames that were licking at the edges of the remaining log in the grate. "It was that same night. The one your mum and I argued." She hesitated. "Your dad and I had drunk a lot of wine with dinner and then, after he helped your mum to bed, he came back down, and we had a couple of whiskies." She blinked several times, as if the memory was stinging her eyes.

"Go on." Iona whispered, her heart thumping wildly.

"It wasn't planned, Iona." Freya glanced up, her eyes filled with such remorse that Iona felt a tiny pinprick of sympathy bloom that she pushed down with a deep exhale.

Seeing that she could expect no response, Freya continued. "We cried together, talked about how afraid we were, what our lives would be like without her, and then somehow, we were kissing." She closed her eyes. "Next thing I knew, I woke up on the rug, and it was five a.m." She lifted her chin. "I shook him awake, and when we realized what had happened, what we'd done…" Her voice split the last word in two, and Freya doubled over at the waist, her messy ponytail dangling bizarrely between her knees, the gilded ends touching the carpet.

Iona heard a buzzing sound, as if a thousand bees were circling her head, looking for a way inside. She forced a swallow and shifted her weight to the opposite hip as Freya's sobs filtered through the buzzing, dragging Iona's focus back to the room. "Stop. Just stop crying." Her voice was cold, an empty, emotionless sound that didn't seem to belong to her. "Freya," she barked.

Freya sat upright, her face crimson and several strands of hair stuck to her damp cheeks. "I'm so sorry, Iona. You'll never know how…"

Unable to hear any more, as the buzzing reached a threatening crescendo, Iona swung around and bumped her way out of the door into the dark hallway. Taking a moment or two to orient herself, she headed for the stairs and began to climb.

"Iona." Freya, having run to the bottom of the staircase, called up after her. "Please, let's talk."

Iona turned at the top of the stairs and looked down at the ravaged face. "There's nothing to say that'll fix this, Freya. I can't even look at you now."

Freya's voice hitched. "Oh, Iona. Please…"

Iona held a hand up. "No. I just can't."

11

The taxi driver had dropped Iona outside the bed and breakfast, halfway down Douglas Row, a pretty street with terraced homes, all with friendly-looking dormer windows overlooking the River Ness.

She'd stumbled up the tiny front path and thanked the pleasant owner—Mrs. Ferguson, a plump woman, wearing a denim dress and sheepskin slippers—for taking her booking at such short notice. After a brief tour of the downstairs, she'd then climbed the narrow staircase to her room, thrown her bag on the floor, and flopped onto her stomach on the firm double bed.

The room was small, with the window overlooking the river now totally dark. The overhead light was dim, and the tartan carpet slightly worn, but the faded floral wallpaper had a homey quality that, despite her jangling nerves, made Iona feel safe.

As she breathed into the bedcovers, there was a faint scent of sandalwood, bringing with it an image of Scott's face, which she let linger for a few seconds. Then, rolling onto her back, she peered at the sliding door leading to the en-suite bathroom.

Suddenly, she longed for a hot bath, thinking about the huge cast-iron tub at her flat. Heaving herself up, she walked into the bathroom, trailing her fingers along the wall outside the door until she found the light switch. Flipping it on, she sighed with relief at the sight of a tidy white suite, complete with tub.

Tugging at her coat, she leaned over and began running the water. As the level slowly rose, she peeled off her clothes and heaped them on the floor next to the door, the need to get clean overwhelming.

She stepped into the water and slid down, letting it seep into her ears. The buzzing sound had faded, but now Freya's words, *somehow, we were kissing*, were playing on a nauseating loop, over and over, bringing her teeth together.

Unable to make it stop, she sat up and unwrapped the bar of soap that lay on the edge of the bath on top of a snowy-white washcloth, then began lathering her shoulders. With each circle she drew on her skin, the steady strokes served to ease the pain that had been mounting in her head since she'd darted from Freya's house an hour or so earlier.

Her insides were raw from crying, and recalling the kindness of the taxi driver asking her if she was all right, or if there was anyone he could call for her, threatened to reopen those floodgates.

Blinking rapidly, she continued soaping herself.

Under any other circumstances, the obvious choice would have been to call her father, but now that he had morphed into someone who had betrayed her mother in such a profound way, Iona couldn't bear to think about him.

Scrubbing the flannel across her face, she felt the sting of soap in her eyes, a fitting sensation, matching the sickening ache in her heart.

How could they? How could they do that to her mother when she was at her lowest ebb? The two people Grace trusted the most had stabbed her in the back, more devastatingly than if they'd used actual knives.

Taking a ragged breath, Iona pushed down another wave of

nausea as Freya's face came back to her, the expression rolling from fear to anxiety and then, finally, to crippling remorse. Shaking her head, Iona rinsed her face and body and lay back, letting the water lap around her shoulders. *Would there ever be enough remorse to make what they had done forgivable?*

~

Wrapped in her pajamas, her damp hair twisted up in one of the thin towels that hung on a rail in the bathroom, Iona hunkered down under the bedcovers. She'd turned up the radiator and drawn the heavy velvet curtains against the night, but there was a tremor inside her that refused to release its grip.

Checking her watch, she reached for her phone. She was desperate to talk to someone, spill the contents of her heart and seek comfort, support, but as she began to dial Roz's number, something stopped her.

Lying back against the lumpy pillows, she searched for another number and hit the call button.

"Hello, there." His voice was warm, and she could hear the smile in it.

"Hey." She swallowed, suddenly aware that if he was too kind to her, she was likely to lose control again. "How's tricks?" The absurdly flippant question made her grimace.

"Um, just working. It's bonkers here tonight." Scott covered the microphone and spoke to someone in a muffled tone, then his voice became clear again. "So, what's going on there? You must be bored stiff if you're calling me." He laughed softly, the sound bringing the prickle of new tears to her eyes.

When she didn't answer, he tried again. "You there, Muir?"

She nodded, pressing her tongue to the roof of her mouth, trying to dam the sob that was building at the back of her throat.

"Iona?" He sounded worried now. "Is everything O.K.?"

Unable to hold on any longer, she gasped. "No. Not really."

Her voice broke, an odd sound that brought with it a heaving in her middle like the force of an encroaching ocean.

"What's wrong?" Scott's voice grew intense. "Where are you?"

She took several deep breaths and tried again. "I'm in a B and B in Inverness. I left Freya's." She sniffed, tears trailing down her warm cheeks.

"Why? What happened?"

She closed her eyes and pictured his face, the intensity of his eyes, the shock of hair and the thin line of the scar, willing his presence closer. "How long have you got?" She pulled a tissue from her bag and wiped her nose.

"Just give me five minutes and I'll call you back, O.K.?"

"I'm sorry to bug you at work." She sucked in her lower lip.

"Don't be daft. And don't go anywhere. I'll call you right back." He hung up, and relief flooded her chilled insides.

A few minutes later, Scott called her from the small back office at the Bonnie Prince and now was speaking in hushed tones. "So, try to take a breath," he crooned. "I can only imagine how you're feeling about Freya, and your dad, but to just come back here, and not see this journey through..." He paused. "I think you'll regret it."

"I don't want to see her ever again, or him," she gasped. "How could they, Scott?"

"I know. I hear you." There was a sound in the background like breaking glass. "Shit," he growled.

"What was that?" Iona swiped her eyes and tugged the bedcovers up closer to her throat.

"Just someone's tips going down by a hundred percent," he sighed. "Sorry, I'm listening."

Iona glanced over at the window, the curtains bulging around the edges of the radiator. "I just want to come home. Perhaps this whole thing was a mistake. Sleeping dogs, and all that." She gulped. "I might check if there's an overnight train back tonight." The idea springing from nowhere, Iona played with it, seeing herself standing on cold, dark platforms waiting for dimly lit trains, filled with nighttime travelers, and the thought made her uneasy.

She could hear him breathing, imagining his brow creasing and his long fingers raking the hair from his forehead, something she'd seen him do whenever he was faced with a problem.

"It's far too late to be battling your way back tonight," he said. "See how you feel tomorrow, but I still think you need to see it through, Iona. If you're not going to go back to Freya's, then you should still go on to Orkney and at least talk to your dad about all this."

She tugged the damp towel from her hair and tossed it onto the floor.

"You both deserve to have that conversation." He sounded so centered, so sure of what she should do, that Iona was suddenly irritated. "I didn't call you for instructions," she snapped. "I just needed to talk to someone."

He stayed silent, sending a pulse of regret through her.

"God, I'm sorry, Scott." She closed her eyes. "I'm a mess."

"Listen, Muir. I get it. All I'm saying is sleep on it. I really think..." He stopped himself.

"No, go on. It's all right." She gathered her mane of damp hair onto one shoulder. "Please."

"I think you might feel differently when you let things settle down a bit and you've had some sleep."

Iona considered how bone-tired she was. Every muscle, tendon, and sinew ached, despite the hot bath she'd taken, and all she craved now was the oblivion of darkness, the comfort of no thought for a few hours. "You're probably right." She sighed. "I am absolutely shattered."

"Will you make me a promise?" His voice was low, warm.

"O.K."

"Sleep. Don't set your alarm, and have a long lie-in and a

good breakfast." There was a pause. "Don't rush into anything tomorrow. Take your time to decide what's next, O.K.?"

She nodded. "I will. I promise."

"I'll say goodnight then."

Iona closed her eyes, picturing his smile. "G'night, Scott, and thanks."

"Anytime, Muir."

~

The tap at the door pulled Iona from a deep sleep. Momentarily confused as to where she was, she blinked at the unfamiliar ceiling, then fumbled for her phone on the bedside table. Grabbing it up, she saw it was 9:40 a.m.

Surprised, she sat up, instantly feeling the muscles in her shoulders tighten as she shifted to the edge of the bed. As she took a steadying breath, her situation clarified itself, the events of the previous night all colliding with each other in her memory.

There was another tap at the door. "Miss Muir?" Mrs. Ferguson sounded concerned.

"Em, yes." Iona stood up, adjusting her pajamas that had twisted awkwardly around her thighs.

"Sorry to disturb you, but there's someone here to see you."

Iona frowned, picturing a contrite Freya, having bribed the taxi firm to find out where she'd gone, standing in the hallway, her face flushed and her eyes watery. Shrugging the unwanted image away, she approached the door. "Who is it?" She turned the handle and opened the door a few inches to see Mrs. Ferguson already halfway down the stairs.

"In the breakfast room." She spoke over her shoulder. "Oh, and I'm afraid you've missed breakfast. It finished at nine o'clock."

Iona pulled her pajama top closed at her throat. "What's their name?" she called into the empty hall, Mrs. Ferguson's hasty retreat having made it plain that she was no messenger.

Irritated, Iona shook her head and stepped back into the room, wondering who on earth could be waiting for her. *Had her father called Freya to speak to her, only to have Freya confess all, sending him on a frantic journey to intercept Iona before she returned to Edinburgh?* The idea of being confronted by him in this strange place, with everything that she might now say to him, made her stomach flip as she heaved her bag onto the bed and rummaged through the contents.

Having pulled on her jeans, a heavy sweater, and her suede boots, she combed out her bedraggled hair and secured it in a bun with a pair of chopsticks. She then brushed her teeth, checked herself in the mirror, and, tucking an errant twist of hair behind her ear, left the room.

She walked down the stairs and wandered into the little breakfast room Mrs. Ferguson had shown her the night before.

At the bay window, overlooking a narrow strip of lawn and a low stone wall, a broad back was facing her, the dark jacket one she didn't recognize. The shoulders were wide, wider than her father's, and the hair was wavy and sand colored. As she assimilated what she was seeing, Scott turned toward her and gave a half smile.

The sight of him made her catch her breath, a combination of shock, and surprising joy.

"So, are you going to hit me or hug me?" He grinned, holding his hands out at his sides.

Iona wove her way around the four empty tables that separated them, her feet soundless on the tightly woven carpet. Without speaking, she rose on tiptoe and put her arms around his neck, taking in the smell of sandalwood mixed with what could only be described as train dust.

His cheek was warm against hers, and the slight prickle of his morning-chin made her shiver.

He stepped back, obviously relieved. "Well, thank goodness. I wasn't sure, to be honest." He tipped his head to the side. "How are you?" His eyes were full of concern.

Her deep gratitude muzzling the emotion that was hovering so close to the surface she could taste it, Iona simply nodded. "Right. Good. Well, I'm starving." He grinned. "Fancy some breakfast?"

She looked around her, the tables empty of everything except thin white covers and a matching salt and pepper shaker set neatly at each center. She shrugged. "We've missed it."

"Not here." He shook his head, hefting a bulky rucksack up onto his shoulder. "Let me dump this in my room, and we'll explore Inverness. There must be a decent fried egg or a slice of toast somewhere in this town."

Iona blinked, his words making her frown. "Room?"

"Yeah. I'm not coming all this way to go straight back today." He said.

Suddenly panicked at the thought of staying another night at the B and B, with him in the next room, Iona stuttered. "But I wanted to go home today. I can't stay here." Her tongue felt thick and cumbersome.

"Why not stay, just tonight? We can head back tomorrow morning, if you really want to. Your boss is fine with it." He gave a lop-sided smile. "Besides, I've heard the food scene is pretty good on the Black Isle, so I thought I'd check it out." He winked. "Kill two birds."

Knowing that he was lying, purely for her benefit, Iona managed a smile. "You're a total bampot."

"So they tell me." He bounced his shoulders. "Now move, or I'm going to fade away to a shadow before your very eyes."

12

The scarlet-colored steel beams supporting the domed roof of the Victorian Market towered above them. A short walk from the B and B, the hundred-and-fifty-year-old covered market had been on Iona's list of things to do while she was staying with Freya. As they passed under a high stone archway and walked toward the café that Scott wanted to try, Iona breathed in the cocktail of coffee, fresh-baked bread, and warm spices floating in the light-filled space.

There was music playing. Something nondescript and elevator-like that neither made an impression nor particularly annoyed her, and it was pleasantly warm under the impressive canopy, a welcome contrast to the bite of the morning outside. As they strolled through the market, the shopfronts they passed were full of the character and old-world charm that Iona remembered from childhood visits.

Around them was a wide array of products—everything from hand-made chocolates and sleek leather purses to vats of rainbow-colored spices—so Iona slowed her pace, wanting to take it all in.

The feeling gradually seeping back into her numb face, she

slipped her gloves off. Scott had walked on ahead, and as she turned a corner, her attention was caught by a window display of glittering jewelry, row upon row of treasure, neatly set out in bulging glass cabinets.

The trays of sparkling gemstones and gilded bracelets pulled her to a standstill, transporting her back to a trip she'd taken to Edinburgh with her parents when she was eight, before the stuffing had begun to fall out of their lives.

Her father had been looking for an anniversary gift for her mother and, in a small jewelry shop on the iconic Rose Street, he'd bought them matching silver charms—two identical tiny cellos. Grace's had hung on a fine chain, the cello nestled safely between her collar bones, and Iona's had been attached to a delicate bracelet that she'd worn every day for years, until her wrist grew too wide for it.

Now, her fingers went to her empty wrist as she remembered tucking the bracelet away in her treasure box at the bottom of her wardrobe, forgotten and no doubt tarnishing as the years passed.

Allowing the poignant memory to smoke around her, she moved on to the window of a kilt maker, the rows of resplendent tartans an instant tonic to her troubled mood. The events of the previous day were still playing on a loop, only mildly displaced by her joy at the surprise arrival of her friend, and now, as she watched Scott up ahead of her, Iona frowned. *What was he doing here? Should she have called Roz instead? Had she given him the wrong idea by opening up to him about her life?* A slew of questions cascaded into her mind, one after the other, as she took a steadying breath. She couldn't think about that now, about him, or how she felt about him being here. She had to focus on what she'd learned about Freya and her father and figure out what she was going to do about that gut-churning reality.

Shaking her head, Iona turned, scanning the gentle course of people around her. A lift in her middle made her stop as she spotted Scott slightly off to her right. He was bending over an open cart full of colorful scarves when he caught her looking at him and smiled.

She raised a hand, and he beckoned to her, another waft of freshly ground coffee, and cinnamon, making her mouth moisten as she moved in next to him. "What've you got there?" She leaned over and fingered a pale-pink scarf, the butter-like fabric silky to the touch.

"What's your favorite color?" he asked, the scar shifting slightly at his jawline as he lifted the pink scarf from the pile.

"Oh, no." She held up a palm. "I mean, you don't..."

He widened his eyes. "What? I can't buy my pal a present?" He grinned at her, then, seeing her expression, a shadow dimmed his smile.

"No, I mean, yes..." She stepped backward. "Sorry, I..." She felt heat creeping across her cheeks.

He set the scarf down and straightened up to his full height. "O.K. O.K., don't panic." He patted the air. "I get the message."

Iona stepped forward and put her hand on his sleeve. "Sorry, Scott. I didn't mean to be..." She halted.

"Weird? Paranoid? Daft?" Behind his fading smile, she caught a flash of taut embarrassment that pulled at her conscience.

She shrugged. "Yes, all of the above." She met his gaze. "I'm just in a weird mind-space at the moment."

He assessed her, his kind eyes roving across her features as his expression eased back into a smile. "It's O.K. I can come on a bit strong, sometimes." He held his palms up. "Just another of my most endearing qualities."

At this, she laughed, the tension between them evaporating, and, as her gratitude toward him swelled, she took his hand. "You're the salt of the earth, you know." She squeezed his fingers. "You came all this way when I..."

He shook his head. "Hey. Don't get all mushy on me, Muir." He gently withdrew his hand. "Come on, I'm starving." He pointed over his shoulder. "The café's over there, and I smell bacon."

With a tiny dip of disappointment, Iona slowly followed him into the café and, spotting an empty table at the window overlooking the central walkway, she snaked between the occupied tables and pulled out an ornate wicker chair.

Scott shrugged his coat off, flopped down opposite her, and grabbed the menu. "So, what're you in the mood for?" He squinted at the card in his hand. "Eggs?"

~

The mid-afternoon light sparkled on the dark water of the River Ness and seemed to bounce off the line-up of waterfront houses that ran the length of Douglas Row.

Having spent two hours wandering around the city, then following the path of the river along Bank Street, they'd passed the Museum and Art Gallery. Neither of them wanting to spend too much time indoors, rather than go inside, Iona and Scott had walked on to Inverness Castle.

Seeing the impressive eighteenth-century sandstone structure and tower, perched on a cliff above the river, had brought Iona's mother back to her with staggering force. The image of Grace stroking her hair as she read Iona's favorite story of Rapunzel and murmuring, "Your hair is just as beautiful as hers," had caused Iona to take a moment to break away from Scott. She'd faced into the wind, and let the breeze dry her cheeks before eventually looping her arm through his and steering him inside.

After enjoying the stunning vistas along the river from the glass viewing room at the top of the tower, they had walked through the impressive grounds, companionably weaving around one another on the network of gravel paths.

Now, after crossing the river and confirming a dinner reservation at a popular fish restaurant, they walked back toward the

B and B, nothing but the sound of their breathing and the thrum of the occasional passing car surrounding them.

The decision having been taken to stay one more night, Iona had relaxed into the day and Scott's company, ignoring the frequent pings her phone was making in her pocket until eventually, Freya's pleading texts had ceased.

The fact that they hadn't talked again about what Iona had discovered had initially been a relief, but now, having spent a good part of a day together, that howling silence had created an unnatural vacuum between them.

Iona sidestepped to let a young woman walking a huge black dog get past, then trotted to catch up with Scott, who was focused on the dark ribbon of water on their left. "If we're going back tomorrow, we should probably book our train tickets." She skipped forward twice to stay in stride with him.

Scott glanced at her over his shoulder, frowning. "Can I be honest?"

A host of butterflies let loose in her chest as she took in his expression. "Aren't you always?"

"I try to be." He lifted her hand and looped it around his forearm, then moved them gently forward.

A gust of briny wind caught Iona square in the face, and she closed her eyes against its icy sting. Keeping them closed, she let him lead her, the sensation both unnerving and exhilarating. "Go on." She opened her eyes and felt them fill with protective tears.

"I really think you should still go and see your dad. In fact, you should consider going back to Freya's to sort things out, first."

At this, she yanked her hand away from his arm. "What?" She glared at him, her pulse quickening. "Why the hell would I do that? I can't face either of them, ever again." Her voice caught.

Scott pressed his lips together, no doubt to dam a hasty response.

She frowned, her assumption, or at least hopes, of him being firmly on her side slipping away.

"I think we should go." He nodded in the direction of the B and B.

"Wait. I want to know what you think." She paced after him. "Scott?"

His expression was dark as he shook his head, sending a shot of dread through her. "Come on, let's get back. We can talk more over dinner." He held a gloved hand out to her, and she tentatively slipped her fingers into his and then leaned in to the pressure of his shoulder as she fell into step beside him.

～

No sooner had she run up the stairs and closed the door to her room, than her phone buzzed in her pocket. Tugging it out, she expected to see Freya's number again, but instead, it was Roz calling. "Hey, Roz. Listen, I'm really sorry," she said breathlessly.

"Where the hell have you been?" Roz cut her off. "I've left you three voicemails. I was worried."

Iona squeezed her eyes shut. "I'm so sorry." She shrugged her coat off and dumped it on the bed. "I meant to call you, but I've been ignoring the phone." She scrolled down the missed calls list, seeing seven from Freya, but mercifully none from her father. At least Freya hadn't dragged him into things yet.

"Why are you screening calls? Is something wrong?" Roz's voice softened. "Are you still at Freya's?"

Iona flopped onto the bed. "Long story, actually." She looked over at the clock on the bedside table, calculating how long she had left to bathe, dress, and meet Scott downstairs.

"I'm listening." Roz sniffed.

Ten minutes later, with the phone still against her ear, Iona stood in the bathroom, staring in the mirror. Her hair was unruly, the dark coils twisting messily around her shoulders, and her mascara was smudged under her eyes, giving her a somewhat Halloween-like appearance. She licked her middle finger and swiped, making the smudge worse, then rolled her eyes at her reflection.

"I can't believe he's there, swooping in like some misguided bloody superhero." Roz huffed. "And why is he staying?"

Iona heard an unexpected trace of jealousy, and after everything she'd told Roz, her focus on Scott's presence was disconcerting. "He just thought I needed some moral support, I suppose." Iona shrugged, questioning her need to explain his presence. "He's a friend, Roz. There's no hidden agenda."

"Tell me that later, when you hear the tap at your door. He's a bloke, Iona." Roz said harshly.

At this, Iona frowned. "No. It's not like that. He's not like that."

"So, you're coming home tomorrow, without seeing your dad?" Roz sounded tired now.

Iona blinked, considering her options. "I think so." She sucked in her bottom lip, unsure why she was hesitating.

"Well, when you decide, let me know."

"Look, I didn't plan this. It was as much of a shock to me as it was to you." Iona checked her watch and began running water into the bath.

"Jesus, are you on the toilet?" Roz screeched.

"No, you daft cow." Iona laughed. "I'm running a bath."

"Well that's a relief." Roz chuckled. "I wouldn't put it past you, though."

Flooded with affection for her friend, Iona perched on the edge of the bath. "Roz, listen. There's no one I trust like you. You're my rock." She could hear Roz sigh. "My rock star."

"Just you remember that, please. Men come and go, but friends come and stay."

Laughing, Iona nodded. "Never a truer word."

"O.K. Go. But call me tomorrow with an update."

"I will. I love you, girl."

"Back at you. Just be careful, O.K.?"

"What do you mean?" Iona frowned, and turned off the tap.

"He's got it bad for you, you know." Roz sounded distant.

Shaking her head, Iona walked back to the mirror. "I don't think so." She tried again to wipe away the smudged makeup. "Especially if he could see me now."

Roz tutted. "You know it's true."

Iona blinked at her reflection, a face that was growing increasingly like her mother's. "He's barking up the wrong tree, then."

"Hmm. I'm not so sure."

"Night, Roz." She smiled at her reflection.

"Night, then."

Iona slid the phone onto the narrow shelf over the sink, slipped out of her clothes, and climbed into the bath, the water wrapping around her chilled limbs like warm silk. As an image of Scott's face materialized, she let her mind return to his motives for turning up, allowing that perhaps they were not as purely platonic as she'd thought. As she considered this, the chilling fear of letting someone in closed around her heart, so she shut her eyes and slipped under the water, blocking out all sound except the thumping of her pulse.

∿

The Riverbank Restaurant was low-ceilinged and warm, the wooden floor and porthole-shaped windows creating a fresh, maritime atmosphere. Each dark-wood table had a slim candle at its center next to a single red tulip in a vase, a splash of color against the starkness of the whitewashed brick walls. The gentle hum of conversation, underscored by a mellow soundtrack of classical guitar, welcomed them as they moved into the room.

Their table was at a window, adjacent to the long bar, that in the daylight would have had an impressive view of the river. As Iona settled in the seat, Scott scanned the menu, his lips moving slightly as his palm scrubbed the crown of his head, the same habit Iona had noticed numerous times and that now made her smile.

She cleared her throat. "So, what looks good?" Her face was flushed from having moved from the frigid evening into the cozy restaurant, and the smoky smell of garlic was stoking her appetite.

"Brill." His eyes caught the flicker of the candle. "It's supposed to be great here."

"Sounds good. I'll have the same."

"Sure you don't want to look?" He wafted the menu at her.

"Nope. I trust you." She saw his eyes narrow, warmth spreading up her chest under the light-blue cowl-necked sweater she'd chosen. "Seriously, I do."

"Hmm, O.K." He stuck his lower lip out. "This could be dangerous."

~

The meal was every bit as impressive as they'd hoped, the local fish and foraged vegetables melt-in-the-mouth delicious, and for almost two hours, Iona left everything behind and immersed herself in the present, in the ease of the conversation and the laughter that inevitably came about when she was with Scott. Now, as the waiter cleared their dessert plates, the abrupt ending to their conversation of earlier filtered back to her, and reluctantly, she raised the subject again. "I know I wasn't exactly receptive before, but I really do want to know what you think about what I told you." She paused. "I won't lie. I'm gutted that they could do that to Mum."

He seemed to take forever to consider his answer, his eyes

shifting from hers to the window and back again while he twisted the narrow vase back and forth, the top-heavy tulip rolling around in awkward circles.

Anxious about what was to come, she prepared to explain herself more when he tilted his head to the side. "If you want me to be honest, I will. But you might not like what I have to say."

Her throat began to narrow. She'd hoped he'd be an ally, her wingman in this giant mess, but if he couldn't support her thinking, while she'd be disappointed, she'd just have to go with her gut.

"Go on, please." She drained the remains of her wine, willing the ruby liquid to soothe her mounting nerves.

He pushed the vase back to the center of the table. "From what you've told me, while it was wrong, what happened was a one-off. A mistake they both recognized and immediately regretted." He searched her face. "Everyone makes mistakes, you know." He nodded to himself. "Iona, can you try to imagine how they felt?"

An arrow of pain slid into her heart at his so patently taking their side, seemingly not taking her position into account at all. Her pulse picking up, she watched the scar shifting as his brow rose toward his hairline, inviting a response.

Unable to keep the lid on her anger, she snapped. "Yes, I can, actually, because I was losing her too."

Scott dipped his chin. "Shit. I know that. I didn't mean to discount your own experience." He locked on her eyes. "That was thoughtless." His mouth dipped at the corners. "What I meant was, if you put yourself in their shoes, they were each the closest thing to your mum the other one had at that moment." His voice took on a hushed tone, as though he was observing something painful. "They were obviously terrified of losing her. Sort of trapped in a nightmare together, and the future was probably too hard to think about."

He blinked, a film-show of thoughts seeming to flicker behind his eyes. "I know it's a cliché, but perhaps that was the only bit of comfort they could find. So, they let go of the pain, for just a few minutes." His words swirled in the tense no-man's-land that had sprung up between them. "Obviously, neither of them could live with the guilt, so they removed themselves from each other's lives, and Freya did from yours, too."

Iona's mounting anger was making her thinking cloudy, but even as she formulated an acid comeback, she couldn't help but hear the message he was sending. *Was she being unreasonable?* As she watched, Scott seemed to slip away from her, his eyes becoming hooded and his expression closing her out. More than anything, she wanted to keep him here, with her, in the moment. "I hear you, Scott. I just think that some things are unforgivable, and this is one of them." She tried to keep her tone steady. "It was the worst kind of betrayal."

He lifted his chin, his eyes once again clear and focused. "I know it feels like it's unforgivable, but often, when we look back at things like this, we realize that's not necessarily true."

Her heart thumping now, she leaned forward on her elbows. "What do you mean?"

"Trust me. It's not always as straightforward as it seems." He lifted the wine bottle and emptied it into his glass.

Iona slammed back in her seat. "That's pretty cryptic, and annoyingly trite." She tapped her fingernails on the tabletop. "Can you elaborate?"

His surprise was evident as he leaned forward and placed a palm flat on the table. "Yes, I'll elaborate. You asked me once about how I got this." He traced his fingertip down the line of the scar on his cheek.

Iona nodded, intrigued. "Yes, you said it was a bike accident."

He shook his head. "I lied. I got it from my dad."

Taken aback, she felt the weight of the implication settle on her. "What happened?"

He sat back and pulled his glass toward him. "When I was sixteen, I came home the worse for wear one night. Not fall-down drunk, but I'd had too much." He pulled his lips together. "My dad was a nasty drunk himself, but it was one rule for him and another for everyone else."

His eyes took on a distant look, and Iona, her anger forgotten, leaned forward. "I'm sorry, Scott. I had no idea."

He shook his head. "Why would you? It's not something I talk about." He drained his glass. "Anyway, I was well out of order, shouting back at him and, for once, Mum tried to defend me, which of course set him off even worse." He turned to look out the window.

Iona swallowed, her sense of what was to come like a shadow hovering over them both.

"He was a bully, but he'd never actually hit me before." Scott turned back to her. "He swiped at me, narrowly missed Mum, and caught me with his ring." Once again, he tapped the scar. "I launched myself at him and, well, the rest you don't need to know, but it wasn't pretty."

Iona couldn't find words that adequately conveyed the spark of shock and sympathy she was feeling, so she simply nodded.

"I was sixteen, so I had brass balls, and was full of the resentment of a sullen kid who thought he'd been done wrong to, so I packed a bag and bolted. I stayed with a friend for a week or so, then gradually made my way from Glasgow over to Edinburgh, doing odd jobs and couch-surfing with anyone who'd put me up." He dropped his eyes to the tabletop. "I didn't go home for two years. Just occasionally kept in touch with Mum by phone." He shrugged. "I cut him out of my life and, by extension, her too."

Iona winced at the obvious pain in his voice. "So, then what happened?"

"I was working in a bar in Morningside when Mum called. She told me he was dying, and she begged me to come home." He closed his eyes. "It took me a month to make the decision to go back, and the day I arrived, Mum was in a terrible state. She'd been caring for him for over a year. Pancreatic cancer." He placed a palm over his side. "He looked like a ghost, and so did she." He shook his head. "Anyway, he and I talked, and it was gut-wrenching. He asked for my forgiveness, said he'd never forgiven himself for driving me away." Scott's eyes became filmy. "I was still angry, despite everything I was seeing. I wasn't gracious or accepting of his apology. Then I left to go and see a friend in the next street."

Iona's throat had narrowed to a thin pipe as she blinked her vision clear.

"I got home at two a.m. and Mum was sitting in the lounge, just staring at the empty fireplace." He stretched out his neck. "He'd passed away ten minutes before." His voice caught, and Iona let out an involuntary gasp. "I should've let it go. Let him off the hook. Accepted his apology. But I was a brat, and then, it was too late." He eyed her. "I made a stupid, immature decision and cut my nose off to spite my face." He dropped his gaze again. "I don't want that for you, Iona." He curled his hand into a fist. "I've regretted those years I stayed away every day since. I not only left him, but I left my mum, and she didn't deserve that."

"No." Iona found her voice. "She didn't."

"So please, think this through." His words were thick with emotion. "Because this is it. This one life is all we get. You've both lost so much already, and if you can't forgive your dad, and you end up alienating him over this one stupid thing he did, you might never have another chance to reconnect with him. You'll be condemning both of you to a lifetime of separation and heartache."

Iona's eyes blurred again as she tried to catch her breath.

This was so far from what she'd expected that she was rocked, unable to form a word. His confession had touched her so profoundly, hitting its target square on, that even through her own pain and sense of betrayal, she could see her father's face, the face of the man who'd raised her, loved her unconditionally —and try as she might, the idea of cutting him out of her life was inconceivable.

As her heart rate gradually slowed, she reached across the table again and covered Scott's fingers with hers. "Thanks for telling me that. I know it wasn't easy to relive."

He shook his head. "It's O.K. I just don't want you to make the same mistake. Whatever he and Freya did in a moment of weakness, he's still your dad, and she's your godmother. They both love you, Iona, and that's worth holding on to."

She nodded, withdrawing her hand. "I hear you. I do."

"So you'll reconsider?" He looked at her hopefully.

"I'll give it a go." She nodded. "I promise."

13

Scott had just left her outside the Bed and Breakfast, his hasty goodbye involving a rib-crushing hug and some awkward back-patting before he turned and paced away toward the station.

As she watched him leave, juggling a mixture of relief and disappointment, Iona let herself imagine that he was hers, her corresponding bookend, and how it might feel to know that while she'd said goodbye to him for now, he'd still be connected to her, possibly even miss her a little. Then, embarrassed at herself, she shook the sentimental notion off. His unexpectedly showing up had proved that he truly cared about her, which was deeply touching, but she couldn't afford to indulge in fantasies. Instead, she must continue to lock her heart away and focus on the next few days, on navigating her way through the emotional quagmire ahead.

Her Uber was due to arrive in moments, and as she paced at the end of the path, the river opposite the house roiled, stirred up by the high wind that plucked viciously at her coat.

The decision to go back to Freya's had come at 4:00 a.m. while Iona circled her room, wrapped in a blanket. Freya had

texted her again. The words, *Please. I just want to explain* were
simple, heartfelt, and, with Scott's story still spinning in the back
of her mind, had crumbled the remnants of Iona's anger. She'd
replied, *Can I come back tomorrow?* and Freya had responded,
You never have to ask.

Now, as she pictured the upcoming scene, a confrontation
that she could do without, Iona shivered and pulled her coat
closer around her, the smell of hot grease floating out from the B
and B behind her making her stomach churn.

The drive back to Freya's farmhouse seemed to melt away
time and now, as the car bumped between the open iron gates,
Iona was overcome with the urge to shout, "Stop." By coming
back, she was reopening the door to information that was barbed
with hurt, and having spent the last decade protecting herself as
best she could, the thought of walking directly into pain, freely
and willingly, sucked the moisture from her mouth.

Freya was standing on the doorstep, Joe sitting calmly on her
left, the whip of the wind separating his thick fur in a clean line
across his side. Freya looked haggard, as if she'd shed ten
pounds in the day that Iona had been absent, and seeing it,
sympathy swelled inside Iona.

Avoiding her godmother's eyes, she took her bag from the
driver, thanked him, and watched the car slink away—her last
chance at escape moving across the gravel toward the road.

"Come in." Freya stepped back, a tentative smile pulling at
her mouth. "Thank you for coming back."

Iona nodded, hefted her bag onto her shoulder, and followed
Freya inside. Joe padded after them, his nose nudging Iona's leg
as she dumped the bag at the foot of the stairs.

"Hello, you." She bent down and stroked his silky neck,
feeling the warm pink tongue find her wrist. "Good boy, Joe."

Freya hovered in the kitchen door, her fingers twisted in a
knot as she eyed Iona. Freya's sweater was hanging on her, her
denim-covered legs stick-like as they tapered away into her

brown-suede boots. There was a rich smell wafting out from the brightly lit kitchen, and as the thought of eating breakfast that morning had been nauseating, Iona now realized how hungry she was.

"I made soup. Thought you might want something warm." Freya jabbed a thumb over her shoulder. "Or perhaps some tea?"

Iona shrugged off her coat and hung it on one of the hooks by the front door. "Tea would be good." She denied herself the soup she craved.

"Maybe later, on the soup?" Freya's shoulders bounced.

"Yes, maybe." Iona followed Freya into the kitchen, pulled out a chair, and sat at the table, her back to the wall.

As she watched her godmother make tea, she nervously raked her hair into a ponytail, then let it drop down her back again. Her shoulders were taut, and so she stretched her neck to either side, feeling the muscles pulling like knotted ropes. As Freya set a steaming mug on the table, Iona smiled thankfully at her, drawing the hot drink closer.

"So, what made you decide to come back?" Freya slipped into the chair opposite her as Joe padded over to the Aga, circled twice, and flopped onto the knotted rug that lay in front of the great iron stove.

Iona sipped some tea, the warm liquid easing her tight throat. "It was a couple of things, actually." She cradled the mug between her palms. "But mostly, it was something Scott said." She leaned back in her chair, feeling the wooden bars bite into her back.

"Scott?" Freya frowned. "Your boss, right?"

"Yes, my friend from work." Iona dropped her gaze to the tabletop. The last thing she wanted to do was get into a conversation about Scott, him showing up, or why he'd played a role in her coming back. That was something she wasn't ready to share with Freya, who was now on trust-probation.

"So?" Freya leaned forward, her elbows on the table.

Iona took in the shadows under her godmother's eyes, the lank hair and lack of make-up. "I think I just had to let it sink in. Try to put myself in your shoes." She shrugged, not yet ready to let Freya off the hook completely. "While I still think what you and Dad did was awful, disgraceful, I don't think it's unforgivable anymore." She felt the press of tears and, willing them not to come, tossed her hair off her shoulder and focused on the window overlooking the firth behind the house.

Freya dropped her chin to her chest, her breath sliding out in a sigh. "Thank you for that. I know I don't deserve your forgiveness, or hers." She raised her eyes to Iona's. "But I never meant to hurt anyone." A tear slipped down her cheek, and she swiped it away with her fingertip. "It was a moment of self-pity, of weakness, on both our parts." She said. "Your dad was shattered, so hopeless, and it felt like the only way we could..." Her voice faded, and the tortured look on her face melted Iona's last shred of anger.

"I know." She nodded. "I think I understand." The relief on Freya's face was patent, and as her fingers met Freya's, Iona sighed. "It might take me some time to get past this, Freya. But I do want to."

At this, Freya squeezed her fingers. "Take as long as you need, just please don't cut me out of your life." She gulped. "You're all I have left of her."

"You're the one who cut me out of *your* life, actually." Iona worked to keep her voice level as she sat back, releasing Freya's hand. "And I was really hurt by that, because I couldn't understand what I'd done wrong." She let the thought she'd long held at bay ease itself out of her subconscious and releasing it into the warm room felt like a knot untying inside her. "You were just gone, even before Mum was, and then I was alone with Dad, missing you both." Iona sniffed.

Freya squeezed her eyes closed and took a ragged breath. "I know, and it wasn't fair of me. I was such a miserable coward, I couldn't live with myself, couldn't face your dad, or you, after…" She hiccupped. "I should've been there for you." She met Iona's gaze.

Iona nodded. "Yes, that would've been nice."

"I'm truly, truly sorry." She pressed her palm to her chest, her face now flushed.

"I missed you so much." A tear rolled over Iona's bottom eyelid, so she blotted it with her sweater sleeve. "But that was then, and this is now." She shook her head. "And we need to get past all that."

Freya's eyes flashed, a look of naked hope lighting them from behind. "Yes, we can do that, love. We're family, after all."

Iona nodded. "Yes, we are." She tipped her head back and tasted the salt of unshed tears trickling down the back of her throat. "And family is everything."

∾

They had talked until the light had begun to fade, only moving to let Joe outside and for Freya to feed the dogs out in the kennel. Neither of the women had seemed to want to release the fragile bond that they were recreating, and now, with their dinner dishes tidied away, they'd moved into the living room. Freya had lit the fire, which in the dim evening light cast tongue-like shadows on the ceiling.

Feeling a sense of calm returning, and that the fragments of years' worth of unanswered questions were finally coming together, Iona's mind jumped to one last mystery to be solved. "Freya, there's one more thing."

"Sure, have at it." Freya nodded. "No holds barred, anymore."

"I'll be back." She pointed her finger at Freya, who gave a mock salute.

A few minutes later, Iona sat down next to her godmother

and handed her the photograph. "Do you recognize the guy?" She watched as Freya squinted at the picture. "His initials are on the back."

A slow dawning crept across Freya's face, and even in the dark of the room, Iona could clearly see the signs of recognition. She waved the picture at Iona. "Charles Majors. Where did you get this?"

Making a mental note of the name, Iona shrugged. "I found it inside the lining of my cello case, and then, in the letter Beth gave me, Mum wrote about the mistakes she'd made at uni, so I put two and two together."

Freya's eyes were wide. "So, you already know then?" She stared at Iona, who simply nodded and bit down on what she was about to say, not wanting to stem the potential flow of information. "She asked me to tell you everything before I gave you the letter she left here." Freya sucked in her bottom lip. "I was going to talk to you, and give it to you, but then... well, everything fell apart, and..."

Iona fought with the impulse to ask for the letter right now, but seeing Freya, her eyes hooded as she slipped deep into a memory, and not wanting to take them back to where they'd been a few hours earlier, she held her tongue.

"He was a nasty piece of work. One of her music professors." Freya shook her head. "She went out with him for a few months, despite us all telling her what he was like. But when your mum discovered she was pregnant, and he just dumped her like a hot potato, I wanted to turn up on his doorstep, beat three colors of shit out of him, and tell his wife the whole bloody story."

The air left Iona's lungs, as if an anvil had settled on her chest. Her face was instantly hot and her tongue thick.

"She was totally gutted, of course." Freya's voice rose in intensity. "But she still wouldn't hear a word against him. She'd defend him, saying that she'd known what she was getting into."

Freya shuddered. "He made me sick to my stomach. Best thing he ever did for her was to leave her." She eyed Iona, her mouth working on itself. "Are you all right? You're white as a sheet."

Iona simply nodded, her hand over her mouth, and as she locked eyes with Freya, a look of horror swept across the beautiful face. "Shit. Tell me you knew about that." The turquoise eyes were huge. "Iona?"

Iona lowered her hand. She'd never been able to lie effectively, and this moment was no exception. "Not about the pregnancy." She blinked as Freya dropped her face into her palm. "It's O.K. I just…"

Freya pushed herself up from the sofa and walked to the window. "I'm so sorry. I just presumed that when you said that Grace had written about it…" Her voice faded. "I'm such an idiot. Even in death, I'm letting her down." She clamped her hands over her ears.

Unable to sit still, Iona's pushed herself up from the sofa. "So, what happened? I mean, what did she do?" Her eyes bored into Freya's, willing the answer to be what she, Iona, wanted it to be.

Freya hesitated. "Well of course she had to leave uni." She rubbed her palm across her forehead. "Beth was beside herself with worry."

Iona sucked in her breath. Adding to the shock of what she'd just heard, Beth's insistence that she knew nothing of this man was an uncharacteristic betrayal that hurt Iona deeply. "So, what happened to the baby?" The words tumbled from her mouth like cumbersome pebbles as she waited for the answer that she already knew.

Freya met her eyes, her face a mask of pity. "Oh, Iona."

Iona reached for the mantelpiece. The room was beginning to spin, and as she sucked in air, it felt heavy and oppressively warm.

"Sit down, love." Freya had a hand under her arm. "Come

on." She gently pulled Iona to the sofa. "I'm going to get you some water."

Iona sat down, let her head fall back against the cushion, and closed her eyes. The bizarre new reality was rushing through her entire body, taking her breath with it. Grace had had a baby by this man Charles, and that baby was her, Iona. As she tried to control the parade of thoughts and questions, the mixture of confusion and shock collided with the wine she'd drunk with dinner, and just as Freya walked back into the room, Iona leaned forward and emptied herself onto the rug.

∼

Iona lay with a cold cloth on her forehead, and, having cleaned up the mess on the rug, Freya was next to her, stroking the hair away from her face. She could hear the clock ticking on the mantle, marking the passing of seconds that only served to solidify the discomfort of yet another unwieldy truth she'd just been given.

"Are you feeling any better?" Freya was deathly pale. "Do you want to go to bed?"

Iona shook her head against the cushion. "No. I'll be O.K." She sat up gingerly. "Sorry about the carpet." She looked up at Freya, who was swatting the air.

"Forget it. Rugs can be cleaned." She hesitated. "What can I do?"

Iona shrugged. "Nothing, really." She ran her tongue over her teeth, the sourness lingering. "I need to wash my mouth out."

Freya grunted. "Yeah, you and me both." She helped Iona up, followed her to the kitchen, filled a glass with water and handed it to her. "So, how much did you actually know?" She pointed at the table and they both sat down.

"Nothing other than his initials. I just found the photo, and when I asked Beth about it, she denied knowing him." Iona coughed, then sipped some more water. "Mum wrote about how Beth hadn't supported some mistake she'd made, but that was all." She pushed the glass away from herself.

Freya was sticking her thumbnail into a join in the wood of the table. Her hair had fallen loose around the sides of her face, the ponytail now drooping behind her neck.

"So, it was me, right? I'm the baby?" Even knowing it to be true, Iona couldn't help but ask.

Freya nodded. "Look, I have that other letter too. She posted it to me a few weeks after they were here and asked me to keep it for you." She eyed Iona. "Do you want to read it before we go any further?"

Iona shook her head. "No, just tell me, please."

Freya refilled Iona's water glass, got some for herself, and sat back down. "Craig was finishing his Master's, and had only just met your mum when she discovered she was pregnant. When Charles dumped her, Craig was a true friend to her. They spent hours together just talking, going for coffee and walking in the hills and stuff. He really became a confidant, because apart from me and Beth, not a soul knew what was going on." She sipped some water. "Despite all the craziness of those few months, your mum and dad began to fall for each other." She nodded to herself. "He and I helped her work through the consequences of her decision to keep it…" She cleared her throat. "To keep you." She licked her lips. "She was frantic about how much she was disappointing Beth, but Iona, she never considered not having you." Freya's eyes were glistening. "You have to know that. It was only once she started to show that she and Craig came up with the plan."

Iona leaned forward on her elbows. "Plan?"

Freya nodded. "They knew that they wanted to be together. To raise you together. So, Grace left university and a few weeks later, as soon as Craig graduated, they got married at the registry office, packed up, and moved to Orkney. He had this great job opportunity at the maritime energy plant, and the remote location was perfect for an escape." She turned her glass around several times. "She was almost four months pregnant, but so tiny that you would've had to look really closely to see anything." She widened her eyes. "She was so petite."

Iona frowned. "What about Nana Jean? What did she have to say about it?"

Freya shook her head. "They never told her that you weren't Craig's. She had no way of knowing exactly how long they'd been together, so it was easy to keep the truth from her. There was no reason to lie to the community in Orkney either, because as far as everyone was concerned, from the moment they arrived on the island, they were just a young married couple expecting their first baby." She leaned back, jamming her fists into her lower back.

Iona's temple was throbbing, so she ran a hand through her hair, pressing her fingertips into her scalp to ease it. So many questions were tumbling around inside her that the room seemed to be rocking. One that had plagued her for years, but that she'd never asked her parents, bubbled to the surface and when she raised her eyes, Freya was staring at her. "Why didn't they have any more children?"

Freya looked startled, then swept her fringe away from her forehead. "Your dad had mumps as a teenager. It left him sterile." She blinked several times. "That's one of the reasons you were so incredibly precious to him."

Iona let the information permeate, the idea that she'd been Craig's only hope of being a father mitigating, to some extent, them not telling her the truth about her parentage. How hard it must've been for them to keep it secret, and yet, they'd done it admirably—if that was an apt term for deception.

"I'm so sorry, Iona. After everything else, you didn't need to hear this tonight." Freya patted her chest. "I've really screwed things up."

Freya's expression said everything, and as Iona formulated a reply, there was no anger, no resentment or frustration left inside her. Freya had simply been an unwitting messenger, and, as the turquoise eyes sought hers, begging for some form of reprieve, Iona felt herself coming back to life. "This isn't something you did to me. I wasn't totally up-front about how much I knew. I kind of trapped you. And you were going to have to tell me tomorrow anyway, right?" She shrugged. "None of this is your fault, Freya." She tried to smile. "So don't take it on."

"I'd like to think that's true."

"It is true." Iona massaged her scalp. "The burning question I have is why the hell they never told me." This question had been working its way up her insides. *Why had they lied to her for her entire life?*

"They must've agreed not to." Freya shrugged. "They never discussed it with me, and I didn't feel it was my place to ask."

Iona tried to imagine the extremely vocal and opinionated Freya having uncharacteristically respected the boundary that Craig and Grace had obviously set around that sensitive subject —perhaps, for once, accepting that this was somewhere she was not welcome to trespass.

"I wish I knew what to think." Iona lay her palms flat on her thighs. "I don't want to be angry with Dad, but..." She caught herself short. "Jesus, Freya, he's not my real dad." The gravity of the statement felt surreal.

Freya frowned. "Don't say that, sweetheart. He adores you and always considered you his." She shook her head. "Craig was a champion, literally and figuratively. He told Grace that Majors didn't deserve her, but it took her being abandoned to realize he was right. With everything that happened at uni, the mess Charles and she created, Craig never stepped back. He never made her feel less than a worthy, capable, and deeply good human being." She eyed Iona. "He enabled her to retain her dignity, and he never made her feel beholden to him either.

Your mum used to say that even if she told him every single day how much that meant to her, it would still never be enough."

Freya's face was drawn, her eyes flicking about the room. Iona loved this face, albeit altered since the last time she'd seen it. Until recent events, Freya had been the kind of friend who told it to you straight, and now that Iona had Roz in her life, she knew the inherent value in that kind of trust.

Freya closed her eyes as if summoning a memory. "When they were here, Craig still wasn't fully with her about Zurich. She told me that while she couldn't be angry with him, it made the choice feel precarious." She opened her eyes. "She said she would get to a place where it had solidified in her mind but then, when he questioned it, she'd lose confidence in her own logic."

Iona nodded. "I can understand that. I mean, if your husband wasn't on board with something as momentous and crucial as that, it'd make it nigh on impossible to go through with it." Her heart was aching as if she'd been punched in the chest.

"Yes, and when your best friend tells you that it's the ultimate selfish choice, that doesn't help." Freya shook her head, her hair slipping from the remains of her ponytail and tumbling over her shoulder.

"Don't go back over that, Freya." Iona shook her head. "Let it go now." More than anything, she wanted to leave that particular burden Freya carried where it belonged, in the past.

A wave of exhaustion swept through Iona, her head heavy on her neck and her eyelids suddenly leaden. She rolled her shoulders and yawned widely. "Sorry, I think I'm done in." She looked over at Freya, who, picking up the cue, was standing up.

"No, I'm sorry. I kept you up too late." She pulled her sweater down at the front. "Want anything before you hit the hay?" She turned and lifted their empty glasses.

Iona nodded, and nervously shoved the hair away from her face. "Actually, yes. Mum's letter."

Freya looked startled. "Oh, of course. Hang on." She turned and paced out of the room as Iona refilled her glass with water. Freya came back in with the envelope, her face flushed. "Here you go, love." She handed it to Iona. "I'm going to go up, but just come in if you need to talk, O.K.?" Iona nodded, the envelope sending a vibration into her palm. "I will. Thanks, Freya." "No, love. Thank you." Freya moved in and kissed her cheek, then turned and walked toward the stairs.

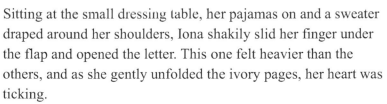

Sitting at the small dressing table, her pajamas on and a sweater draped around her shoulders, Iona shakily slid her finger under the flap and opened the letter. This one felt heavier than the others, and as she gently unfolded the ivory pages, her heart was ticking.

The handwriting was much more erratic now, with several letters oddly top heavy or missing sections, and the lines sloped dramatically down toward the right.

Swallowing hard, Iona started to read.

My darling Iona,

I'm so glad you are with Freya now. She is the only one who could have told you my story without bias, and it is a story best told in person. All I can say is that I hope you can find it in your heart to forgive me for keeping this from you until now.

Rather than go over it again, as I'm sure she's given you all the facts, I want to tell you about a dream I had last night which I think will help you understand where I was at that time in my life.

I dreamt that I was swimming in the sea and the tide was really strong, pulling me away from the shore. I was fighting it as hard as I could, but I could taste the salt of the water. I was beginning to panic, aware of the water filling my ears, when suddenly I remembered my dad telling me that if I was ever caught in a riptide to just curl up in a ball and let it take me. He said it would eventually throw me back to land, like flotsam. But the more I tried to relax, the more tense I became, and then I started to go under. I was saying a prayer, asking to be rescued, and then I felt hands under my arms. I could feel the water rushing away from my face as I was dragged to the surface, and when I opened my eyes, expecting to see my dad's face, Craig was there instead. He was smiling and saying, "It's O.K., Gracie. I've got you."

All the while he was dragging me back to land, I was wondering why on earth he was helping me. Then everything went calm and I was lying on the beach with the sun strong on my face, and I could feel myself sinking into the warm sand. Just as I was about to let myself sleep, I heard Craig's voice. "Wake up, darling. You're safe. You're home, with me." When I opened my eyes, he was crying. I'd apparently been talking in my sleep, but no matter how much I asked him later what I'd been saying, he wouldn't tell me. The more I thought about the dream, the more it seemed a perfect metaphor for what he'd done for me.

Iona, genetics have little to do with being a father, a real father who shows up time and again, who sacrifices for you, puts your needs first, and would throw himself in front of a train for you. That is Craig. That is who your dad is. While I know you may be angry with me, I'm asking you not to direct that at him. After everything that's happened, everything you both have been through, and lost, you must keep him close. He deserves that, and so do you.

As for what happened between Freya and your dad, that's something I've learned to forgive, and I need you to do that too, because you deserve the peace it'll give you. They were in so much pain, they turned to each other, and while it hurt me deeply for a while, I put it away. In the big scheme of things, it was a fleeting moment that didn't warrant me wasting any of my remaining time resenting them, or letting it come between me and your dad.

Go home now, my darling girl. Spend time with him and enjoy the fact that you are his everything, as you will always be mine.

I love you, now and to infinity.

Mum xxx

Blinded by tears, Iona dropped the letter onto the dressing table and felt for the edge of the bed. Pulling herself onto it, her throat on fire with the effort of holding back the wail that wanted to come, she curled up under the heavy quilt and put her fist in her mouth. Panting as she bit into her skin, she tried to conjure an image of her mother: the bright eyes, the small freckled nose, the rippling curls covering her narrow back as she hugged her cello, swaying with the momentum of what she was playing. In her vision, behind Grace, Craig stood looking on proudly, his eyes sparkling and his chin bobbing in time with the music, as always happened when he listened to either of them play.

As a melody began to emerge from the depths of her memory, the crushing absence of not only her mother, but also of Craig, closed in on her. To the last, her mother had kept her secret about Charles and had held Craig in the pole position he'd more than earned, that of Iona's father. Now, more than ever, Iona understood the depth of the man—the love he had for her mother, the way he had so willingly raised her, accepting and loving her as his own. No matter how he'd failed her mother on that one ill-judged night, Iona knew that it was fundamental to her happiness—to both their happiness—to make things right with him.

Gasping, she let the tears come. There was no resisting them, and as they seeped from her eyes, wetting the cotton pillowcase under her cheek, so sleep gradually slid in and took her.

~

A buzzing sound roused her, and as Iona turned onto her back, a thumping inside her head seemed to accelerate. She always got a headache after crying, and as she sat up, shoving the duvet away from her chest, a cold wave of nausea made her shudder.

She reached over and lifted the phone, seeing another text from Scott.

Worried about you. Did it go OK?

The sight of his message lifted her spirit, and through gritty eyes she typed, *Staying with Freya. Have so much to tell you. All OK, though.*

After a few moments, a reply bloomed on the screen.

Want to talk? I miss your face.

Despite her headache, and the weight that was centered on her breastbone, she smiled. *Not tonight. But thanks. Will fill you in when I get back.*

As she watched the ubiquitous dots, her heart rate quickened.

OK. Sleep tight. X

She typed her reply, hesitated for only a moment, then hit send. *Night. P.S. I miss you too. x*

14

The light from Iona's phone was illuminating her face as, sitting in the dark, she scrolled through a list of names in an online directory. Unable to get back to sleep since texting Scott, she had pulled on her sweater over her pajamas, crept downstairs, and stoked the smoldering fire in the living room. Now she sat cross-legged on the rug, a cup of water next to her.

It was 1:45 a.m., and despite the hour, she'd been unable to stop herself calling Roz to tell her everything she'd discovered.

Roz's voice startled her on the speaker. "Can you see him? Is he still listed?"

Iona shook her head. "No. Doesn't look like it. The chances of him still being on the faculty at the uni are slim, after all this time." She shifted her legs, her tailbone beginning to ache. "The signal is bad here, and it's useless trying to do this on my phone."

"Hang on. I'm just opening the webpage now." Roz hesitated. "God, imagine. You must've been in the same music rooms where he taught your mum?"

The thought was chilling as Iona closed the browser and switched off speaker mode. "I probably was. I might've even used the same sheet music or stand, or even touched an instrument that he'd played, too." She shivered.

"Sounds like the old bugger enjoyed having his instruments touched." Roz let out a low laugh. "Oh, sorry. Inappropriate. I realize this is your birth father we're talking about."

Iona pressed her lips together. "Hmm." The notion that anyone other than Craig was her father still prickled, like a cloak of thorns. "It's totally surreal."

"I'm looking at the university site now and there's no Charles Majors listed under faculty." Roz clicked her tongue.

"Can you just Google him? Put in Charles Majors, music professor, Edinburgh University."

"Hold on." Roz huffed. "Bloody internet is so slow in this dump. Oh, the signal is gone completely now."

Iona closed her eyes and waited, her heart picking up its pace.

"It's incredible, all this." Roz hesitated. "I mean, who on earth finds out that their dad's not their dad, then finds out who their real father is, all in a day?"

Hearing it out loud made the whole situation seem ludicrous, and then, with no warning, Iona was laughing—a harsh sound that shattered the peace of the room. She hugged a cushion under her rib cage as she rocked back and forth.

"I'm sorry. I always say the wrong thing. Not that this kind of stuff happens a lot but... Sorry. Are you laughing?" Roz sounded incredulous. "Iona, you're scaring me."

As her laughter subsided, Iona took a shaky breath and pushed the hair from her face. "I'm just... I have no idea what to think or say, either." She tossed the cushion away, then the light flashed on above her, and as she spun around, Freya stood in the doorway, her hair mussed behind her head and her long T-shirt folding around her slender thighs.

"I heard weird noises. Are you all right?" She rubbed her eyes and padded toward Iona.

"I'm sorry to wake you." Iona grimaced. "I'm on the phone with Roz." She lifted the phone back to her ear. "Sorry, Roz. Freya's here. I woke her up." She mouthed "sorry" as Freya moved closer to the fire, crossed her arms, and hugged herself. "I'll call you back later, O.K.?"

"What? You're going to leave me hanging, with all this crap going on? Charming, Miss Muir."

"Look, I've got to go. I promise to ring you soon."

"All right. I'll be here. Probably won't sleep now, anyhow."

"Thanks for being there. Don't know what I'd do without you."

"Yeah, me either, you PIA." Roz laughed.

"Night, Roz."

Freya's expression was telling. She was obviously not happy at having been woken up, but that was being shrouded by her concern. Iona grabbed her hand and gently pulled her down onto the sofa. "I couldn't sleep, so I called Roz and told her about him. About Charles."

Freya nodded, her frown easing. "O.K."

"We did an online search for him."

Freya jolted forward in the seat, holding her hands up as if protecting herself. "Iona, I think that's a really bad idea." Her eyes were flashing as she scanned Iona's face.

"No, listen. It's all right." Iona patted the air, feeling suddenly calm about what she was about to share. "We didn't find anything."

Freya's mouth formed a perfect O shape.

Iona's energy drained away, and she let her head fall back against the cushion and watched Freya, who had stood up and was pacing in front of the fire. She was pale, her eyes darting around as if she were hunting for something vital she'd misplaced, as she wove all ten fingers together in front of her, forming one bony fist. "Are you sure you're all right, Iona?" She halted her progress. "It's been a hell of a day for you, love."

Iona lifted her head. "Yeah, not the easiest."

Freya perched on the arm of the sofa and yanked her T-shirt down over her knees. "Are you going back to bed?"

Iona shook her head. "Not much point, really."

∼

Freya had made tea and stoked the Aga. They'd sat at the table, and finally, the cold that had invaded Iona's feet was ebbing away. She sipped the hot liquid and sighed. "I think I have to find him." She eyed Freya, who was focusing on her mug.

Freya looked up. "Do you think it's wise to go digging around, though?" She frowned. "What if you do find him? What will you say?"

"I have no idea. I just feel as though there's more to this story, and unless I at least try to find out, it'll just be one more thing that separates me from my dad." She blinked. "From Craig."

At this, Freya rounded on her. "Listen. Craig is one hundred percent your father, Iona. You need to remember that."

Knowing the truth when she heard it, Iona nodded. "I know. I'm just struggling a bit here." She held her palms up. "It's all so overwhelming, and perhaps I'm grasping at straws, but I can't stop thinking about possibly finding some extended family, however far removed." She paused. "If I do, I'll be super-sensitive as to how I tell Dad. I'd never want to hurt him, Freya." She eyed her godmother, knowing that with everything Craig had endured, this new information could be the thing that sent him over the edge. Her finding out about Charles Majors could be upsetting enough for him, but if Craig thought he might lose her to some obscure branch of half-family, it would break his heart.

Freya considered what Iona had said, her eyelids flickering. "Well, as long as you're careful of that, and also have a plan, a contingency in case it all goes badly wrong." She set her cup down. "What if he isn't interested in meeting you, or getting to know you?" She leaned back in the chair. "You need to be prepared for disappointment." Freya's voice cracked, and Iona was surprised to see her eyes fill.

"Sorry, I…" Iona stammered.

"It's not you. It's everything. It's a lot for you to deal with, and maybe too much for your dad, after everything else…" Freya stopped herself.

Suddenly, Iona saw light dawning on the somewhat murky situation, a pinpoint at present, but light, nonetheless.

"I was thinking that too, but in some weird way, Freya, this could actually bring me and Dad closer. We've been distant for years. A lot of that was my doing, but there's been something coming between us ever since Mum died."

Freya swiped at her eyes. "I know you were just a child, but you were pretty vile to him for a long time."

The statement knocked the breath out of Iona, the weight of recognition clogging her lungs.

"You blamed him for things that weren't his doing—or his choice, if we're honest." Freya pushed her chair back and walked to the stove. Kicking off her slipper, she pressed the sole of one foot to the door of the lower oven.

"What do you mean?" Iona tried not to sound overly defensive.

"You blamed him for them going to Zurich and leaving you behind." She said. "I know you did, Iona, and so did he."

Iona forced a swallow. The truth was hard to hear, even when given in the spirit of kindness.

"He didn't want to leave you at home. He told her over and over that it was a mistake, but she wouldn't give in. They fought about it several times, but she was adamant that she wanted to say goodbye to you somewhere where you felt safe." Freya's eyes dimmed. "Whatever I thought of her decision, however much I disagreed with what she was doing, that part was not your dad's fault. I told her that when we…"

No longer able to hold back, Iona's damn burst. The first sob escaped her, a howl that truncated Freya's next sentence, as Iona folded at the waist, her hair falling in a dark curtain over her knees. As she gasped for a breath, she felt Freya's arms go around her, easing her upright.

"Oh, sweetheart. I'm sorry, I shouldn't have said that." She pulled Iona in to her middle, her grip tightening around Iona's shoulders. "Just breathe. Take a breath."

Iona sucked in air, her heart thrumming in her ears. All she could feel now was a wrenching emptiness and a yearning to see her loving, good-natured dad. All thoughts of confronting him about his infidelity banished from her mind, she pictured the man who had supported his wife throughout a horrific decline, honored her last wish despite it tearing his heart out to do so, and who had so lovingly cared for Iona, another man's child. Then, forcing its way into her heart, an image the photograph of her mother and Charles Majors materialized, his taut face and dark eyes pulling her in. As she tried to push it away, Iona knew she'd have to move forward on this journey, turn over the clues, such as they were, and see where they took her.

"Am I a totally selfish wretch to want to find Charles?"

Freya was shaking her head. "No, love. You're a really good person." She released Iona, swiping a twist of hair from her cheek. "I'd probably do the exact same thing. I think it's perfectly normal to want to understand your parentage, maybe even have the opportunity to come face-to-face with it, so to speak." She shrugged. "I'm with you on this, as long as you're kind and thoughtful in how you approach it, which I know you will be."

Iona was overwhelmed with affection for this woman who'd been her mother's closest ally for most of her life. The clear eyes were assessing her kindly and, to Iona's relief, without judgment. "Thanks, Freya. I've really missed you."

Freya nodded. "Ditto, kiddo. And I can even talk to your dad about the Charles thing, if you want?"

Iona shook her head. "No. If it comes from anyone, it should be me. I owe him that much, at least."

Freya nodded. "Yes. Absolutely."

∽

Freya had also abandoned the idea of going back to bed and was making toast, the sun having risen over the firth. The morning was tinged with pink, the sky flossy with a thin layer of low cloud, and the water a paler shade of blue than the previous evening.

At the kitchen table, Iona was browsing the internet on Freya's laptop. With some concerted research, she was certain she'd be able to locate this man Majors and potentially, his family. *But what then?* Beyond that point, she had no clear picture of what might happen next, the possibilities ranging from disastrous to, best-case scenario, fulfilling.

Freya set the toast rack on the table and dragged a chair out. "So, any luck?"

"I'm just doing random searches, but I think if I use one of these directory sites that charges you for the full address, I'll get there." Iona dragged a piece of toast out and set in on her plate.

"You're leaving for Orkney tomorrow morning, right?" Freya's hair was in a messy bun, long blonde coils curling against her cheekbones.

"Yes. It's time I sorted things out with Dad." She nodded. "In fact, I'll give him a ring in a bit."

~

Inside the warm kennel building, Freya was cleaning out a large straw-filled tray. Jessie was pacing around her chamber as several of the puppies tumbled over each other on a blanket, the others trooping after their mother in a tiny, black-and-white conga line.

"Morning, Jessie. Your babies are so adorable." Iona hunkered down and gently lifted the puppy at the end of the line. She held the wriggly bundle to her cheek, its coat silky and smelling of milk.

"They're pretty irresistible at this age." Freya set the clean tray on the ground and lifted two water bowls into the sink. "Want to go for a walk in a while?"

Iona set the puppy down behind its siblings. "Yes. That'd be great."

"Did you speak to your dad?"

"Yes. He's fine. Looking forward to tomorrow." Iona shoved the sleeves of her sweater up and lifted a cloth to dry the bowls. "Do you mind if I use your laptop for a little longer?"

Freya nodded. "Sure. But you're not going to spend every waking minute inside, staring at the screen. We're going to get outside and force some fresh air into your lungs. You're peely-wally, as my mum would say. There's no color in your face at all."

Iona rolled her eyes. "I know. I'm as white as fish."

They laughed together, their easy dynamic returning.

With Jessie and the puppies settled, and Joe snoozing in front of the Aga, Freya took another male from his kennel. He was taller at the shoulder than Joe, his snout broader, and his markings gave him white socks on all four feet. He approached Iona slowly as Freya held his collar, letting him sniff Iona's knees, calves and boots.

"This is Iona, Ted. She's one of us." Freya looked at Iona and smiled. "You can trust her."

Iona leaned down and, as she'd been taught, extended her hand, palm down. The dog sniffed her skin then licked it, his tail beginning to wag.

"Hi, Ted, you handsome boy." She ruffled the thick hair at his neck.

"Right. Let's get our coats and take him with us. We can walk down toward the firth. It's a gorgeous path."

Iona nodded absently. Her mind was wandering back to the computer, the search bar blinking at the top of the screen, the name "Charles Majors" stark in the field.

"Iona?" Freya was staring at her. "Ready to go?"

Iona forced a smile. "Yes. Absolutely. I'll just grab my coat."

The land was damp and soft underfoot, the morning dew lurking beneath the surface of the rough grass. The sky had brightened, and with it, the breeze had picked up, making it difficult to talk as they made their way down the gentle slope toward Beauly Firth.

They'd crossed Freya's lower fields of ankle-high grass, showing the striped pattern of a recent cut, then they'd joined the path they were now following, a well-trodden strip with scatterings of flat stones tracing the fence line. The path had taken them through an area of dense trees, the light splintering magically between the branches overhead, making Iona tip her head back to let the rays strike her face.

As they'd emerged, the landscape had opened up to a flatter, meadow-like swath dotted with clusters of low shrubs and heathers that tumbled away toward the flat, sandy shore of the firth. The majestic hilltops of Ben Wyvis hunching across the water formed a dark silhouette on the horizon.

Iona tugged her collar closed and, with a hand shielding her eyes, squinted into the light that was bouncing off the royal-blue water. The last time she'd walked this far from Freya's house, both her parents had been present. Their absence was suddenly tangible, making her long to turn around and see them holding hands and laughing, Grace's hair being whipped across her eyes by the wind, just as Iona's was now.

The lack of them stung as she re-tucked the loose hair back under her hat and sighed. Around her, the knee-high grasses, a tapestry of greens and golds, all bending to the will of the wind, reminded her of a William McTaggart landscape she'd seen hanging in the Scottish National Gallery not long ago. This place had such natural beauty that she felt it filling her chest as she breathed in and out.

Having lost track of time, she checked her watch and tasted salt on her lips as she picked up her pace and moved in closer to Freya's shoulder. Ted was loose, tripping along ahead of them, what was visible of his coat above the grasses being parted by the wind. "Shame we couldn't bring Jessie too." she called into the breeze.

Freya leaned in toward her. "In a few more days."

They'd been walking for almost an hour and Freya, seeming to sense that Iona was enjoying the serenity, simply soaking in the scenery, had kept quiet, only occasionally pointing out a landmark or drawing her attention to a banking bird above them. Eventually, Iona's feet were beginning to complain inside the too-loose boots that Freya had lent her when she'd seen the fashionable leather ones Iona had intended to wear. Despite the chunky hiking socks that she'd added on top of her own, Iona could feel the skin at her heels becoming raw.

She skipped sideways to avoid a pothole and reached for Freya's arm. "This is really great, but I'm afraid I'm getting blisters." She jabbed a thumb at her foot. "Are we turning back soon?"

Freya turned her back to the wind. "Oh, sorry. I get a bit carried away out here." She spread her arms wide. "Let's go home." She nodded, then patted her thigh as she called to Ted, who had wandered a little ahead of them. "C'mon boy. Home now."

As they headed back, Freya slid her arm through Iona's. "You know, there's something I should tell you."

"More?" Iona grimaced.

"No—well, no more secrets anyway." Freya tugged her closer. "Your mum tried to explain something to me when I saw her the last time." The wind whipped her hair up into a golden veil that she shook away from her face. "I wasn't exactly receptive, but I'll never forget what she said."

Iona focused on her godmother's fine profile. "Go on."

Freya sucked in her lower lip, then glanced over her shoulder at Iona. "She said that her illness was like a regression, a Benjamin Button-like existence, her becoming dependent again." She paused as Ted made a wide U-turn ahead and then began trotting back toward them, as if herding them home. "She told me that your dad was trying to hold back time and the inevitable, and he'd been pulling her along with him in that." Freya halted their progress, blinking several times.

Iona simply nodded, unwilling to stop Freya from talking. Each word was a gift that both plucked at and soothed the surface of other questions Iona had been afraid to ask, for so many years.

"She said she loved him for it but that she didn't want that anymore."

Iona forced a swallow. "Right."

Freya looked at her, a frown tugging at her forehead. "Are you all right? I can stop…"

Iona shook her head. "No, please. I want to hear this."

Nodding, Freya gently eased them forward again. "She told me that she'd accepted that she had no control over the illness, and that by giving up any illusion that she did, she might be able to deal with the fear and just appreciate what was around her, right then."

The gentle wisdom of the thought process, and the harsh reality of the colossal fear her mother had been dealing with, quietly and bravely, brought a lump to Iona's throat.

Freya's pale eyes were full of concern.

"I'm O.K. Freya. Honestly." She squeezed Freya's arm. "What else did she say?"

Freya gave a half smile. "She said that if she had to sum up how she felt that day, she'd say she was content, because there were no 'ifs' anymore. MND had shattered her, but her life had also become a simpler score." At this, Freya sniffed, her mouth distorting as the wind yanked away any sound that might've escaped her.

The tortured expression painful to see, Iona eased Freya to a standstill and wrapped her arms around the taller woman.

"It's O.K." She patted Freya's quivering back. "She found a peace, of sorts. A way to deal with it all."

Freya nodded, stepping back and swiping a gloved hand across her eyes. "Yes, I really think she did."

∾

Iona twisted onto her side in the bed. It had been eye-opening, learning from Freya just how much a bone of contention leaving her behind had been between her parents. The fact that Craig had fought so hard for her to join them on Grace's last journey made Iona tingle with guilt.

As the years since her mother's death had passed, Iona and her father had barely discussed the last weeks of Grace's life, as if picking the brittle scab off the subject would only serve to separate them more than was already happening.

For so long, Iona had resented him, labeling him the decision-maker—the one truly responsible for leaving her behind.

Now, having heard Freya advocate for him, say out loud how
hard he'd fought Grace's position—it made Iona's retreating
from him all the more unjust. He had kept the details to himself
all these years, accepted her anger, and in so doing had let her
uphold Grace's innocence in that most hurtful of choices.

As she pictured his face, his open smile, the kind eyes that
glowed with pride at her most minor accomplishment, she
wanted to take back the past few years, reclaim the time that her
misunderstanding, her inability to see the truth, had stolen from
them both.

She closed her eyes. The next day could open a totally
uncharted path for her, and the prospect of more hurt, more
disappointment or loss, was shaking her resolve. *What on earth
might she uncover about this stranger, this person to whom she
was tied by blood?* She opened her eyes and scanned the room,
subconsciously looking for the dark shape of her cello. Realizing
where she was, she lifted the last letter and began to re-read.

～

The alarm buzzed, jolting Iona awake. The letter lay across her
stomach, and as she sat up, it slipped to the floor. She swung her
legs out of bed, picked it up, slid the photo between the pages,
and set it on the bedside table.

Downstairs, Freya had made breakfast and was buzzing
around the kitchen. "Right, get that down you, and don't tell me
you're not hungry," she growled as she placed a plate of scrambled eggs in front of Iona. "You disappear when you turn
sideways."

Iona pulled the plate toward her, wondering how she'd get
the egg past her tight throat. "Thanks. Looks great."

Freya flopped down opposite her. "So, call or text me as soon
as you get to Orkney, and I'd love to know what you find out
about old Majors, too." She ran a hand through her hair.

Iona raised her eyebrows. She wasn't used to seeing the cool, confident Freya looking flustered. "It'll be all right, Freya." Iona tried to catch her godmother's eye.

"I'm just worried for you." Freya set her cup down. "And your dad."

15

The initial stage of the journey to Orkney took around three hours, and as soon as the bus had crossed the Cromarty Firth, as the dwellings began to thin out over the expanse of green landscape and the North Sea stretched darkly to her right, Iona had nodded off and slept for the remainder of the time. She'd then woken with a start as the bus pulled into the ferry terminal at Scrabster.

With time to kill, she'd bought herself a hot drink, wrapped her face against the strong wind, and walked down to the Stevenson Lighthouse at Holburn Head. The lighthouse and keeper's cottage-—bright-white structures, with distinct caramel-colored detailing around the windows, walls, and the base of the light tower—were just as she remembered them. The bright-green door to the lighthouse gleamed in the early afternoon light, a sheen of saltwater making it shimmer.

As a child, she'd called this place Holburn Castle, imagining herself dramatically leaning over the widow's walk that circled the light tower, waiting for her prince to rescue her from the ogre who'd imprisoned her. Her mother would laugh, telling her to grow her hair even longer, like Rapunzel, and give the poor man something to climb up.

The view of the harbor—the cluster of colorful fishing boats moored there, and the handful of cars parked, nose in, along the sea wall—flooded her with memories of childhood trips back and forth from Orkney. When life had been simple, and she'd had two healthy parents.

Now, the water was choppy, the wind whipping up white peaks on the blue-black sea, and as she stared out toward Dunnet Head, the thought of a bumpy crossing made her cringe. She generally had good sea legs, but it had been a long while since she'd traveled this path.

Hearing a squawk above her, she tipped her head back and watched a seagull banking into the strong wind as a flutter of nerves rattled in her chest. As her Nana Jean had often said, it could be a very long hour and a half to Stromness if the sea had its dander up.

Tucking away the wild mesh of hair that had knotted itself across her face, Iona turned her back on the irritated sea and picked her way back along the path to the terminal.

Inside the shelter of the building, she pulled out her phone. She had a missed call from her father and one from Roz. While she'd have loved to call her friend and have a long download of events, she swiped the phone, her finger hovering over her father's name, instead. *Would he sound different, now that she knew his secret? Would she be able to keep her voice level, let events unfold in a reasonable way, or would she let her guard down and rail at him for his deceit, on more than one level?* Scott's words coming back to her, she took a deep breath and hit the number. A few moments later, Craig picked up.

"Hi, love." His tone was warm. "At the ferry?"

"Yep. It leaves in twenty minutes." She scanned the waiting area, taking in the number of people scattered around the various sets of conjoined seats. "Not a busy one today." She sucked in her lip. "Looks a bit rough out there."

He tutted. "You'll be fine. I checked the forecast. It's nothing you can't handle."

She heard the smile in his voice, and, on this, his quiet confidence was calming. "Well, make sure to have some mints and a barf bag in the car." She quipped. "Be prepared."

Having got herself something from the snack bar—and, on an impulse, buying her father a bottle of his favorite Highland Park whisky—she settled herself in a seat by the window. If she was going to be buffeted around for a while, she'd at least keep the horizon in clear view.

Opposite her, a young family was chattering. The couple, thin and sallow, looked to be in their twenties, and the children, rosy-cheeked twin girls, that Iona guessed were around four or five, were shouldering each other to get closer to the window next to their father.

"Sit down, the pair of you," he warned. "I'm not having this all the way there." His profile was sullen as he studied the water.

The young woman rolled her eyes. "Och, leave them. They're just excited." She met Iona's gaze and smiled. "Sorry, it's their first crossing." She leaned over and pulled one of the girls onto her lap. "They'll calm down in a minute."

"Oh, don't worry. I remember when I was their age. It's exciting stuff." Iona smiled back. "How old are they?"

"Five, yesterday. We're going to visit my gran. She lives in Kirkwall."

Iona took in the tired eyes, the pinched mouth and lank hair —in stark contrast to the heartiness of the children's appearance —and wondered if this was simply the mark of concerted mothering. The natural course of energy that a mother expends in caring for her children first. Inevitably, an image of Grace flashed brightly, her face glowing, her hair a mass of long curls, and her cello leaning on her shoulder. Then, another image—

Grace propped up in bed, her collarbones protruding under her translucent skin and her eyes seeming to have taken over her face. The common factor in the two images was her smile—face-splitting and filled with love. Even up to the last days, whether she was imagining it or not, Iona remembered Grace smiling at her. Seeing that trademark smile in her mind's eye, Iona was transported back in time once again.

Six short days after her father told her the news that her mother was leaving for Switzerland, it was time. Iona had been allowed to stay home from school, only leaving Grace's side to sleep, bathe, nibble on the food her nana had prepared, and to bring her mother fresh water in the plastic glass with the straw that sat on the bedside table.

Grace had been mostly silent by this point, seeming to be disappearing into the pillows behind her, her movements increasingly tremulous and her eyes darting around the room, even as she tried to smile for Iona.

That last morning, the one that Iona had been willing away with all her strength, she'd stood in the living room doorway. Her mother lay in the hospital bed, and as Iona hesitated, Grace had crooked an index finger to beckon her closer. As Iona walked over and leaned in, smelling the lilac soap her mother loved, Grace had pressed her dry lips to Iona's cheek and whispered. "Practice."

Iona had nodded, her mother's milky breath warming her skin. "Every day, I promise, Mummy." She'd swallowed over the lump at the back of her throat.

"You…my favorite person." Grace's voice had been almost nonexistent, and the words disjointed. "I'm sorry." She'd gasped.

Iona had buried her face in her mother's sinewy neck, breathing her in, feeling the bone-deep connection between them begin to sever, cut by a blade so broad, so vicious, that not only would it separate them forever, but would likely hack Iona's heart out in the process.

Feeling her mother twitching under the pressure of her chin, Iona had sat up and wiped her eyes. "Can't you stay here a bit longer?" She'd placed her palm softly on her mother's cheek. Grace's chin had been bobbing, seeming to contradict the message she was giving. The bobbing, much like one of those dogs that Iona had seen sitting on the dashboard of a car, gave her a moment of hope that quickly disintegrated when she read her mother's eyes. "Nana." Grace croaked. "Care of you…" She'd pressed her lips together.

Sensing the need to do whatever she could to ease her mother's mind, Iona had lifted Grace's hand and gently squeezed the skeletal fingers. "It's O.K. Nana Jean's here. We'll be all right."

Craig's mother had arrived again from Inverness the previous week and was ensconced in the tiny guest room next to Iona's. She'd become an almost permanent feature in their lives over the previous year. The weaker Grace grew, the more present Jean became, and Iona had been thankful for it.

As she'd locked eyes with her mother, Iona had known that this could be the last time she'd be alone with her for any length of time, be able to hold her hand, touch the tips of their noses together, run her finger over the calluses on her mother's fingertips or move a long curl from her bony shoulder. The knowledge had been like a great hole opening in Iona's middle, its presence leaving her unable to move.

Grace had held her gaze, a single tear breaking loose and trickling down her cheek until it hung under her narrow jaw.

Loosening her hand from her mother's, Iona had scooped the tear onto her index finger and, on an impulse, stuck her finger into her mouth. At this, Grace had smiled. It was an expression Iona knew as well as her own reflection and seeing it had lifted her weighted heart. "I love you, Mummy." She'd lifted Grace's hand and kissed the back of it.

Grace had blinked several times, the tip of her tongue darting in and out of her slightly open mouth. Then she'd forced a swal-

low, her one moveable finger returning the pressure of Iona's.
"Me too. More."

An hour later, when the ambulance arrived to take her
parents away, Iona had been in the kitchen with her nana, filling
her mother's tumbler with water. Her father was upstairs in the
bedroom, his voice a low rumble overhead as he talked to his
wife, and Iona had heard his heavy footsteps tracking above her
as he moved across to the window, then out into the hall.

Panic filling her chest, Iona had tossed the water into the sink
and set the glass on the draining board. Unable to meet her
father's treacherous eyes, she'd silently pushed past him and run
up the stairs, two at a time.

Grace was wearing a pale-pink track suit, her body wasted to
that of a famine victim. Her pale eyes, duplicates of Iona's,
tracked her as she crossed the room, intense and yet gentle as
they took her in.

Iona had leaned over and kissed her mother's cheek. "I will
love you forever, Mummy." She'd whispered. "I will play, forever." She'd swallowed. "For you."

Unable to breathe, Iona had stood up, put everything she
possessed into summoning a smile, then turned and walked out
into the hallway, her heart feeling like it had cracked wide open.

Downstairs, her nana stood in the open front door. Wrapped
in a thick cardigan, she was hugging herself against the cold
while Craig talked to the two ambulance drivers outside on the
path. Iona remembered that Jean's face had been crimson and her
eyes damp as she'd reached for Iona.

"Come here, love," she'd beckoned, the skin around her
mouth forming deep wrinkles, and the midmorning light
bouncing off the thick-lensed glasses she wore.

Iona had shaken her head. The thought of anyone hugging
her, holding her when her mother couldn't, was like scalding
water tumbling down her back.

"Come on, love." Jean had sniffed, circling her hand toward her middle again.

Pushing past her, Iona had bolted through the open door. The gentle hillside that rose behind the house waited for her, a place where she could run, breathe, be alone and far away from the next scene that was about to unfold—one that was more than she could bear to witness. When these two strangers in dark uniforms put her mother into the ambulance and drove her away forever, all Iona would be left with was gaping emptiness, and the sharp cruelty of her father having chosen to leave her behind.

The pain at being excluded from her mother's final days had simmered under her breastbone for years, and the only way she could deal with that ugly feeling back then was to quash it under the distance she'd created between her and her father.

Startling Iona back to the moment, the young woman spoke again. "Where are you going?" She slid one wriggling child back to the ground.

"Oh, Stromness." Iona said "To see my dad."

"Lovely. Time with the folks, eh?" She looked expectantly at Iona.

"Just Dad." Iona gave a half smile. She'd never questioned the title that she'd used to describe Craig Muir all her life, and the fact that it felt less than set in stone now was still surreal.

"Nice." The woman blushed as she lifted an overstuffed bag onto her lap. "Want a sandwich?" She held out a foil-wrapped square.

"Oh, thanks very much, but I've got one here." Iona patted her bag.

The woman nodded and turned to touch her husband's arm. His head had slumped over his shoulder, and his mouth was slightly open, his breathing heavy.

"Typical." She shrugged. "Men."

Iona rolled her eyes in solidarity and picked up her bag.

~

The ferry lurched as it began to turn, and Iona glanced out of the window, seeing the dark line of Stromness's water's edge growing in the distance. Squinting into the light, she spotted where they'd change their heading to skirt the point, passing the links of the golf course before heading north to the harbor where her father would be waiting. She could picture him pacing next to his car, arms folded against the cold, his fair hair being buffeted by the wind. His eyes would be glittering above the high neck of the ubiquitous Arran sweater, and he'd be stomping the ever-present boots below the heavy corduroy trousers he favored. Imagining this, despite her conflict over what he'd done, she felt a loosening in her chest, as if the air was lighter here.

16

Craig had been talking for most of the twenty-minute drive to the cottage, and Iona had let him, enjoying the familiar timbre of his voice and seeing the roads of home unfold as they neared the house.

"It all looks the same." She took in his profile. "As do you."

He nodded, then ran a hand through his hair. "I need a haircut, and I've put on weight." He patted his stomach. "Too many pies from the bakery and not enough walking, these days."

Iona eyed his middle. "Not at all. You look good. But are you not walking as much, then?"

She watched as he negotiated his way around a tractor. He had always been a keen hiker, tackling many of the toughest trails around Orkney. He'd often packed a backpack and disappeared for an entire day, leaving Grace and Iona to wonder about his progress and whether he'd be home in time for tea. The fact that he might have stopped that pursuit, which brought him so much pleasure, was troubling.

"It's the knees." He shrugged. "Damaged cartilage in the left one and arthritis in the right." He turned to face her. "Your old dad's not as young as he was, you know." He winked.

"That's crap," she quipped. "You're just a young man."

Craig laughed. "Well, thanks, but in some books, forty-six is over the hill."

"No way. Fifty's the new thirty." She watched as he checked his mirrors and made a turn. As she took in the slightly deeper lines bracketing his mouth, the definite receding of the hair at his temples, and the new dark spots that were appearing across the backs of his hands, Iona's heart dipped, suddenly feeling vulnerable to his loss. To her, her father had been frozen in time, much the same way her mother had. In her mind, he had been suspended at the age of thirty-six, the age he'd been the day the ambulance had come to take him and her mother away. The idea that he had been aging all this time, unnoticed, shook her. As she tried to imagine what his life had really been like after the loss of his soulmate, the dull sense of betrayal was overcome by a surge of affection. "I love you, Dad." She reached over and patted his leg. "I'm glad I'm here."

He glanced over at her, his eyebrows jumping. "Me too, pet. But should I be worried? Have you robbed a bank or fallen for some drug lord?"

"None of the above. I just love you—warts and all." She said.

His eyes flicked to hers, then back to the road, a frown burrowing its way across his forehead. "Aye, well, that's what we do, I suppose." He focused on the road. "We're none of us perfect."

"No, we're not." Sensing a question in his words, she turned to look out the window. "Far from it."

⁓

Once inside, her father had slung his scarf over the banister and gone into the kitchen, clattering around as he put the kettle on.

The cottage was cozy, and as Iona dumped her bag by the stairs, a welcoming, aromatic smell wafted out from the kitchen.

The living room was tidy, everything in its place, and there was a new, pale-blue blanket folded neatly over the back of the sofa. The alcove by the fire was jammed full of logs, and a pile of books sat on the side table by Craig's chair. As she scanned the room, taking in all the familiar features—the beamed ceiling, the wide-wood floorboards—she caught sight of a vase of flowers on the coffee table. The buttercup-like heads of the marigolds and the tightly packed fronds of the coltsfoot, both resplendent shades of yellow, instantly took her back ten years. Her mother's favorites were just as much a splash of spring color now as they'd always been, whenever her father had brought them home from one of his walks.

Behind her, the Welsh dresser held her mother's treasured willow-pattern plates, and on either side of the tall pine unit, the windows overlooking the hillside behind the house were sparkling. Even the newspapers were folded and stacked in a basket, rather than scattered across the table in Craig's usual manner.

"Have you been cleaning?" she called toward the kitchen.

"I had Muriel come in and help," he called back. "It was getting away from me."

Iona nodded, sensing the touch of the sturdy little woman from town who'd helped them out once a week after Grace's death, until Iona had turned fifteen and insisted on taking on more of the household chores.

"Tea in five." Craig's voice filtered out of the kitchen.

"Great." She walked past the flowers, letting her fingertips linger on the golden head of a coltsfoot, then turned toward her mother's studio. The door was ajar, and as she pushed it open, the smell of rosin hit her, making her stop in her tracks. In the corner, on a stand, was Grace's back-up cello, the old banger, the case battered at the bottom from various drops and accidental knocks.

On the low bookcase by the window were the stacks of sheet music that Iona used to shuffle through, looking for the pieces she could play to her mother here in the studio, then latterly, up in her bedroom.

She stepped inside and closed the door behind her, wanting to commune privately with the slew of memories that were coursing through her. There was her mother, laughing as she played *Penny Lane* while Iona danced, jumping wildly around the room. There was Grace, focusing intently on the music stand that now stood empty in the corner, the tip of her tongue flicking out to her top lip as she concentrated on mastering some complex fingering. There she was, gently guiding Iona's hands from behind as she struggled with a new piece of music, the smell of coconut wafting from her mother's hair and sweet mint from her breath. Iona closed her eyes and held the moments, the myriad precious instances that had taken place in this room, in this house, close to her heart, letting them permeate and warm her insides.

The door opened behind her, making her spin around. "Here you are." Craig stood in the doorway. "Taking it in?" He smiled. "I still do that, too."

Iona walked over to the stacks of music and lifted a pile to her front. She paged through a few until one made her stop, Bach's Cello Suite No. 1 in G major, then pulled it out and set the pile back on the shelf.

"Which one?" Craig was beside her. "Ah, yes. Of course." He patted Iona's shoulder and moved away, toward the cello. "Shall I?" He glanced over his shoulder as he leaned down to open the case.

Iona's nerves fluttered. *Could she do this now, with him in the room? Would it be easier to play if she were alone? Could she, seeing his joyful expression, in all conscience, ask him to go?* She took a deep breath and smiled at him. "O.K. No guarantees how it'll sound, but I'll give it a go."

She sat on the wooden chair as Craig handed her the cello.

"The old banger will have to do." He said as she settled herself.

She carefully rosined the bow and then lifted it to the strings, drew it back and forth several times and then worked the pegs, tuning the instrument, all the time watching her father, who stood at the window staring out at the hillside.

The music sat on the stand in front of her, but Iona knew the prelude by heart. As she started to play, the flutter of anxiety that had been pressing up inside her filtered away, and as the arc of the melody rose and fell, waves of intricate notes building and breaking, she felt her mother's presence come to her as easily as the notes were. Grace's eyes were shining and there was a glow to her skin and, as Iona played, her mother nodded, swaying from side to side in time with the ascending notes, then remaining still, like a held breath, during the plateau.

Blinking, Iona turned the page and began the Allemande section—seven minutes of dramatically scaled, vigorous notes creeping up and down the cello's neck, her fingers flying through the movement as if she'd played it the day before.

Craig stood at the window, his back moving slightly as the momentum of the music took him with it.

When she moved on to the Sarabande, a more melancholy, gentle section, the sheet music began to fade in front of her eyes and so she closed them, letting memory guide her. Once again, Grace was there, turning the virtual pages, leaning over Iona's shoulder and humming as the music's momentum rose and sank. Iona could picture a stage, the heavy curtains folding gently at each side and the lone chair waiting for her mother's presence.

She shook her eyes open to find her father staring at her, his mouth gaping. Suddenly self-conscious, she lifted the bow away from the strings. "What's wrong?" She set the bow down and moved the cello away from her shoulder.

He walked forward, took the instrument from her, and lay it in the case. His eyes were bright as he turned back to face her. "That was more than playing. It was like you were channeling her." He swallowed. "Like she was in the room."

Letting go of all the questions, judgment, the doubt and resentment, everything she'd been holding on to that had weighed her down these past ten years, Iona stood up and wrapped her arms around his neck. "I think she was, Dad."

∾

Craig had lit the fire, discarded the cold tea, and poured them a glass of wine. Now he was rattling around in the kitchen again, and whatever he was cooking was almost ready. As the hands on the mantle clock moved past 6:00 p.m., the darkness of the March sky had fully descended.

Iona nursed her wine, pressing her sore fingertips against the cool wineglass. Her mother would sometimes give her ice water to soak them in after a particularly long practice, and now the similar sensation was soothing. Give or take a few missteps, Iona had played right through to almost the end of the Sarabande without relying on the score. As far as she could recall, she'd never got that far without the music before, and as she studied the flames licking up the sides of the logs in the grate, she sensed her mother again. Closing her eyes, she willed herself open to whatever energy was surrounding her, and as a warmth began to spread from her scalp across her forehead, she took a breath and spoke out loud. "I'm so sorry, Mum. I know I've been a letdown." She opened her eyes. "I miss you every moment of every day."

Startling her, Craig came into the room carrying a tray. "Dinner's up. Thought we'd just eat in here. It's cozier." He set the tray on the coffee table.

Iona pulled herself upright. "Smells great. What is it?"

"Fish pie. Homemade." He grinned. "Haven't made it in a couple of years, so I thought I'd push the boat out."

He bustled out of the room, then came back with his own tray. Settling himself opposite her, he lifted his glass. "Welcome back, pet. It's so good to have you here."

Iona raised her glass. "Thanks. It's lovely to be home."

They ate and talked, covering her stay with Freya—minus the revelation that had caused her little side trip—how things were going in Edinburgh, and Craig's work at the marine energy plant. They'd covered some local island gossip and lastly, the news that a property developer had contacted him about potentially selling the broad strip of land that separated the cottage from the hillside behind.

Iona was horrified at the prospect. "You're not considering it, are you?" She stared at him. "That'd be awful, having some clunky housing development going in there."

Craig shook his head. "No. I didn't really entertain it, but it did make me think."

She set her tray down and folded her legs underneath herself. "Think what?"

He hesitated. "Well, I suppose about how long I intend to live here."

She simply couldn't conceive of the place without his presence. He was, in her mind, as firmly entrenched here as the stone stacks, the rugged cliffs, and the rolling moors they'd walked across all her life. "But where would you go?"

At this, Craig shrugged. "I have no idea, but it made me ask myself the question, which isn't a bad thing."

"So, you're not going to move then?" She exhaled the words.

"Probably not." He scanned the room. "I can't imagine being anywhere else."

She nodded, but seeing the distant look in his eyes, she felt newly sad at the solitary existence he had had for over a decade. As she watched him swipe a finger around his plate and then lick the thin layer of sauce from it, something that would've driven her mother mad, she wondered if in fact he was a prisoner on Orkney, of sorts. Taking her by surprise, she was certain that she needed to open the lid to the secrets that still hovered between them, releasing them into the past, where they belonged. "Dad, I want to tell you something."

He tilted his head to the side, a curious-pup type of expression on his face. "Oh yes?"

Iona's nerves prickled as she shifted forward in the chair. "Freya told me what happened between you."

His eyes widened as he pulled his chin in, the color visibly draining from his face.

"Look, I just want to say that when I found out, I was gutted." She held a palm up to stop him from cutting in. "But I've given it a lot of thought, and got some good counsel from a wise person, and now, I just want to say that I think I understand why you did it." Her voice caught, so she cleared her throat. "I'm not here to judge or condemn you for something innately human." She held his gaze. "Your need for comfort." She felt the prick of tears but blinked them away. "I can't imagine how hard it was for you, Dad. My loss was crushing, but you lost the love of your life, and I don't know if I'd survive that at all." Her vision blurred again. "I don't need you to talk about it, unless you want to. I just wanted you to know that it's in the past, and honestly, I'm tired of living there."

He pushed himself up from the chair and crossed the space between them. "My God, Iona." He pulled her up from the chair and into his arms, his voice rough and full. "I don't know what to say. I'm so ashamed." He spoke over her head, the faint scent of whisky on his breath. "That decision has haunted me for a decade." He sucked in a breath. "It was never meant to happen, and we never meant to hurt anyone, least of all your mother, or you." He released her, stepping back slightly as he swiped his cheek. "A moment of weakness, of self-pity, perhaps." He sought her eyes. "Followed by a lifetime of regret." He dropped his chin. "Can you ever forgive me?" He spoke to the floor.

Iona lifted his hand and sandwiched it between her palms. "Dad, that's what I'm saying. It was crappy, a bad decision among the many good ones you've made. As one flawed human being to another, I'm saying, let's just let it go." She paused. "But let's always be honest with each other from now on."

The moment she'd said it, an image of the photograph flickered behind her eyes. There was more they needed to air, and now that they'd opened the door to honesty, it was the perfect time to be done with secrets, to rid themselves of the shadows that had kept them apart for too long.

∿

As Iona washed the dishes, Craig lifted a towel and began drying. "You must be exhausted. It's a fair trip from Inverness."

"I'm fine, actually." She passed him a wet plate. "Not tired." She smiled over her shoulder.

"Fancy a nightcap, then?" He set the clean plates on the counter. "Someone brought me a very special present, which I'll gladly share a wee bit of." He grinned.

"Just a tiny one. My whisky tolerance is pretty low." She said. "I'm an amateur compared to Roz."

"How is your reprobate flatmate?" He set two tumblers on the table and poured a finger of whisky into each of them.

"She's great. Keeps me sane and drives me insane, all at the same time." She folded the dishcloth and took the glass he held out. "Cheers."

The fire had settled low in the grate, and the living room smelled of woodsmoke as they took up their places on the chair and sofa. Iona sipped her drink, the amber liquid warming the back of her throat. Craig took a sip and set his glass down on top of the pile of books at his side and, sensing her moment, Iona took a steadying breath and leaned forward. "Dad. I wanted to say something else." She held his gaze. "It's been a long time coming, but I need you to know."

Craig frowned, linking his long fingers in his lap.

"Don't worry. It's nothing bad." She shook her head. "What I want to say is that I'm sorry."

"For what?" His voice was low.

"For pulling away from you. And from here." She drew an arc around her. "I ran away from you years ago, distanced myself when you'd done nothing to deserve it." The words were surprisingly easy to say. Having percolated over the past few years, they were ready to be said. "I blamed you for Mum...for going without me and for—well, everything that felt wrong or empty in my life after that." As her throat thickened, she twisted her hair into a rope over her shoulder. "I think I felt trapped in this house with all my grief, and I just couldn't breathe." She watched him lean back, his face draining of color. "It was selfish of me. Can you forgive me for leaving you alone?"

Craig leaned his elbows on his knees. "Iona, I understood. I knew you blamed me, but that was O.K. You needed an outlet for your pain, and if you couldn't direct it at me," he jabbed a thumb at his chest, "where else would it have gone? You'd have bottled it up inside and let it destroy you."

Iona's eyes burned as she took in the look of unselfish resignation on his face, and as she saw it, she knew that this was most likely the same unselfish resignation he'd felt when his wife had chosen to end her life.

"You know, I do understand you feeling trapped, love, but *I* never did—so you mustn't feel like you abandoned me here." He shook his head. "This place was my comfort. The only space where I *could* breathe after she died." He ran a hand over his hair.

Iona nodded. "I read all the letters, Dad."

He locked eyes with her. "Right."

"I know you disagreed with her, about Zurich, about her not wanting to take me." She took a breath. "And I want to thank you for that. I didn't know how hard you'd fought, but I get it now. I get all of it. How difficult everything was for you."

Craig's eyes were full, the reflection of the fire casting shadows across his cheek. "Thanks, love. That means the world. But I owe you an apology too." He frowned. "I should've told you sooner. Perhaps we'd have been closer all this time?" His eyes were hooded.

She uncurled her legs and pulled a cushion onto her lap. There was more she needed to say, and there would never be a better time than now. "It's O.K., Dad. I think I understand. There was no manual for everything you were going through. Me either, so I suppose we did the best we could." She shrugged. Seeing him nod and feeling their bond as strong as it had once been, she pressed on. "Can I ask you something else?"

"Of course."

"Were you ever angry with her, about her choice to end it? I mean, did you ever think that she might've had some sense of a future in front of her?"

He blinked, momentarily taking in the question, then slowly shook his head. "No. I wasn't angry. For a long time, I didn't think it was the right thing to do, to take the decision of living or dying into her own hands. I struggled with the morality of it." He held his palms up. "But it wasn't about me." He shook his head. "She chose right for herself, Iona. There was nothing ahead except pain, fear, exclusion from her own life, and from her life with us, and banishment from her music, being trapped inside a broken body." He leaned back and closed his eyes. "After I got over my own fears, it was clear that there was no other choice for her to make. She knew it, and I did too, eventually." He opened his eyes. "Once she'd decided what she was going to do, she slowed her life down, took in every moment, savored it. The illness moored her to a life she wasn't able to live to the full, but her decision to cut the string set her free, and no one could resent her for that."

Iona nodded, feeling the weight of years' worth of unanswered questions lift from her back. His words, in their simplicity, were freeing her, too. Their sense and sensitivity were not only astounding but liberating. She was overwhelmed with relief, not only for his forgiveness of her childish naivety, but for the realization that for first time since her mother's death, she, Iona, could forgive Grace, too.

Seeing his face contort, his mouth working on itself, she wanted to give him something in return. "You know, I read somewhere that most people die with their personal music still inside them." She waited for him to look at her. "At least Mum didn't have to do that."

Craig looked puzzled, then his face cleared. "No. She didn't." He leaned forward again. "And neither do you, Iona. Stop hiding from it. Go back to university and finish what you started." He smiled sadly. "Don't do it for me, or even for Mum. Do it for yourself."

Iona took in his hopeful expression, the depth of caring in the blue eyes, as the renewed closeness between them, like a warm blanket around her shoulders, made her bold. "Can you tell me about those last few months, Dad?" She focused on his mouth as he sucked in his bottom lip. "I know I was here, but there was so much going on that I missed," she said, her heart rate picking up, "that you protected me from." She dropped her head to the side, a classic Grace movement.

Craig blinked several times and shifted in the chair before locking eyes with her. "Yes, I can do that, love. Where do you want me to start?" His voice was steady and his eyes clear.

Iona sat back, pulling her legs under her. "Early 2009. I have some memories, but they're fading." She sipped her drink as he dragged his hand through his hair.

"That January was brutal for her. No more driving, for starters, and she was constantly cold, so the quilts on the bed multiplied, making it feel like we were sleeping under a mountain of down. But she liked it." His mouth twitched. "There was something calming for her in the weight, but the only problem was that she was beginning to feel short of breath, so it made it even harder for her to fill her lungs."

Iona could picture her mother, the tiny frame forming nothing more than a small bump under a princess-and-the-pea-sized pile of bedding.

"By early February, she was short of breath, even when resting. One night she woke up scared because she couldn't breathe. We had to use the breathing mask, which she felt was a major setback. I tried to comfort her, but her eyes said it all." He swallowed. "According to the doctor, she was officially in the advanced stage by then." His voice caught, sending a zap of pain through Iona's chest.

"It's O.K. Dad, you don't have to…"

He shook his head. "No, it's good. It's important we do this." He gave her a watery smile. "There are some good memories of that time too, you know." He nodded. "You'd been learning to knit. Mainly long skinny scarves and weird-looking squares." He gave a soft laugh. "Your pièce de résistance was a pair of three-fingered gloves."

Iona let out a laugh. "I remember those."

Craig nodded. "You had fun with it. My mum spent much of that month here, teaching you and, God bless her, taking care of the rest of us into the bargain. I honestly don't know what we'd have done without her."

Despite having known, deep down, that the knitting exercise was an intentional distraction to keep her from hovering at her

mother's door and worrying about every noise or stretch of
silence surrounding Grace, Iona had gone along with the
scheme. Her Nana Jean had been patient, coaxing her and trying
to teach her how to control the tension, add and reduce rows, and
follow a pattern, but Iona had never quite got the hang of it.
She'd eventually give up, hand whatever project she'd been
working on to her nana and ask her to please fix it. Jean would
tut as she undid the mess Iona had created, picked up dropped
stitches, and tidied uneven edges, then she'd hand the corrected
item to Iona, smile and say, "See, I told you you could do it."
The warmth of her nana had lingered long after her death, and
Iona could still feel the safety that came from being held in those
capable arms.

Craig cleared his throat. "By June, she had little energy. We
eventually moved her down to the studio, onto the dreaded
hospital bed, just during the day." He grimaced. "She insisted on
coming upstairs at night, which I was glad of. Not having her
next to me would've been be too hard."

Iona pressed her eyes closed, the image of the foreign-
looking bed set up in the small studio downstairs seared on her
memory.

"The breathing machine was easy enough to move, and as
she was sleeping most of the day, she seemed happier to be
downstairs. It was easier on your nana too, having her on the
ground floor." He paused. "When she was awake, she was generally staring out the window. She told me that the hills were the
only view that she ever needed to see." His eyes filled as Iona
leaned forward, a tightrope of shared loss connecting them
across the room.

"She asked me to put on her classical mix CD one day. It was
the first time in weeks that she'd wanted to listen to music. I felt
it was a good sign." He nodded to himself. "I'd have taken
anything, right then."

Sensing his need for a break, Iona stood up, took his glass

from his hand, and went to the cabinet to refill it. As she pressed it back into his hand, a vivid memory flashed brightly.

She remembered, around this time, having crept downstairs early one morning and seeing her father lying next to her mother in the hospital bed. Neither of them had noticed her as she'd hesitated in the doorway, and he had stroked Grace's hair, whispering in her ear as Iona backed away. While there was nothing she'd rather have done more than launch herself in between them, it was too private a moment to intrude upon.

Craig sipped his drink and circled his shoulders as Iona settled back on the sofa.

"By that July, she was mostly in bed during the day. Almost silent. She had bad tremors, and arm and leg weakness. She was wasted to a skeleton." He shook his head slowly. "But I still saw the resolve in her eyes—the certainty in her decision." The light from the fire cast a warm glow across his face—an odd contradiction to the chill in his tone. "I admit, I was still tortured by it. I kept asking myself, can I do what she asks of me?" At this his voice broke, so Iona got up and moved over to his chair, slipped down onto the rug in front of him, and crossed her legs.

"I'm here, Dad. It's O.K."

A few moments later, having gathered himself, Craig looked down at her. "By the time we took the trip down south that September, I was worried it was going to be the end of her." He shook his head. "But she was determined."

Iona nodded, picturing the little car as it had pulled away from the cottage, leaving her bereft—an inconsolable mess for her nana to deal with.

Craig cleared his throat. "For some weeks after that, she seemed to level out—I mean, the deterioration slowed down." He shrugged. "Or perhaps that was just my wishful thinking." He shifted in the seat. "She'd tell me, 'See, I was right to go. It did me good.'" He smiled at Iona. "Typical of her."

Iona nodded, her heart tearing a little.

"Before we knew it, it was your eleventh birthday and she was determined to make it special." He hesitated. "Do you remember it?"

Unable to speak, she simply nodded. The memory of that birthday was vivid, them all eating cake up in her parents' bedroom because her mother was too tired to sit at the table. The two big 1-shaped candles that dripped wax onto the bedding, Nana Jean tutting at the mess, and Grace saying, in her broken voice, "Jean, leave it. What does it matter?"

Her father had brought the record player upstairs, and they'd listened to Brahms, Sonata No. 1, while her mother closed her eyes and let her quivering head rock gently from side to side. Iona had dug deep, swallowing down her tears as she noticed her mother's fingers moving, their skeletal tips pressing into her thigh as she marked through the piece she was hearing. That picture had stayed with Iona long after the candles were blown out and the house had returned to its customary quiet.

"It was March ninth." Craig's eyes turned glassy. "I'll never forget that date." He lifted his glass to his lips and let it hover there. "I knew when I woke up that day that she was done. The way she was swallowing my name, the size of her pupils when I sat on the edge of the bed. The way she wouldn't look away from me. I knew." He blinked. "I'd been preparing myself for that moment for months, but when it came, I'm ashamed to admit that I felt paralyzed." He sipped some whisky. "I knew I needed to be unfaltering, her advocate, her champion, but all I could think was that I was soon to be her widower."

He leaned forward, balanced the glass on his knee, and rubbed his eyes. "I also knew that the trip to Zurich, that one-way journey she was asking me to take her on, was my final act of love, so despite everything I was feeling, how gutted I was, I vowed to do it for her."

Iona reached up and squeezed his fingers.

"It was only a day later when I told you that your mother was

leaving home in a week." He scanned her face. "You were shattered, not understanding and asking if you could go too. It was
all I could do to keep it together as I said no to you." He leaned
over and set his glass on top of the pile of books. "I knew that
she wouldn't bend on that decision, so I decided to stop trying,
even though it broke my heart." He slowly shook his head. "I
was so sure of the mistake she was making."

Iona let her hand drop to her knee. That particular memory of
her father, the conversation they'd had as the fire popped in the
grate behind him and a meaty smell that had hung in the air, was
as vivid now as the day it happened. As she replayed the scene in
her mind, she felt again the shock—the painful snapping of the
father-daughter tie—but now the shadows surrounding that day
were finally lifting, a soft light hitting the baseless judgment
she'd made.

"You had no choice, Dad. I see that now." She tried to smile.
"It was an impossible situation."

The tension in his face eased slightly as she got up from the
floor and stood with the fire at her back, letting the heat settle the
surging adrenaline that was sending unnerving tingles down the
back of her thighs.

As the clock ticked on the mantle, the only sound in the
charged room, she took in her father's familiar profile and tried
to put herself in his shoes. As she let the reality of his agonizing
position sink in, the only thing she wanted was to alleviate any
more suffering this good man might have to go through.

He was chewing his lower lip as he stared past her, into the
flames.

"We got to Zurich on March the eighteenth. The journey was
mercifully easy, and the people there were extraordinary, but
then that's to be expected. Only the most deeply compassionate
human could possibly entertain that kind of occupation." He
shook his head. "It blew my mind that this most profound service
to humanity was a daily event for them. What kind of people

have that amount of selfless strength?" He frowned and searched her face. "I know I don't."

At this, Iona turned to face him. "But you do, Dad. You proved that." She held his gaze as he dropped his chin to his chest and sighed.

"Thanks for saying that, love."

She walked across the room, sat back in the chair, and leaned forward, her elbows on her knees.

"Her room was very comfortable." Craig forced more energy into his voice. "There was a lovely bed—which, to her obvious relief, wasn't a hospital bed. There were tall windows with curtains that let the light in, and soft rugs on the floor." He blinked, as if the image was flickering brightly behind his eyes. "I had a bed too, next to the window, and there were watercolor paintings on the wall of mountain ranges and waterfalls." He glanced over at the darkening window. "She stared at one picture, and when I leaned in, I'm sure she said, *Where's Heidi*? Her eyes were laughing, so I let myself laugh too." He snorted softly. "I put her wedding ring back on her and sat our family photo next to her bed, as she'd instructed me to months before, when we talked about that day. I helped the nurse put her into her pajamas and tied her hair back with a red velvet ribbon."

A dangerous force was building in Iona's chest, the strength of which threatened to suck the breath right out of her. As she focused on her father's voice, she closed her eyes, preparing for his next words, a mixture of hope and dread now filling her.

"When I cleaned her teeth, there was something in her eyes, something like release. I had to leave the room for a few minutes, and when I came back, she was asleep. The breathing machine was ticking as her chest made these tiny hitches under the covers." His hand went to his own chest. "As I watched her sleep, the lines smoothed from her beautiful face, the tension went out of her, and finally, I knew it was the right choice. I knew that the next day she would close her eyes on the world as someone who could still tell me she loved me, still squeeze my finger, see the love in my eyes and take that with her. She'd chosen the end point to her suffering, and who was I, who was anyone, to deny her that?" Craig let his head fall back against the chair. "My wife. My Grace."

As her name left his lips, Craig's face dissolved, pulling Iona back to his side. She knelt down, wrapped her arms around his neck, and buried her face against his shoulder as their sobs melded into a symphony of gentle pulses, passing back and forth between them.

"Thank you, Dad. Thank you for telling me," she sputtered as his arms went around her, and he began to rock her gently back and forth.

∾

That night, with two aspirin for her thumping head and a cup of cocoa, Iona lay in her childhood bed. Having spoken to Roz to bring her up to date, Iona was on the point of texting Scott when her phone rang. Startled, she hesitated for only a moment before answering.

"Hey." He sounded tired. "Just checking up on you."

"Thanks for that." She slipped further down under the duvet. "I'm still alive."

Scott laughed softly. "Glad to hear it. So, how was your day?"

Iona considered the rollercoaster she'd been on since seeing him, the heights and depths of years of hurt that she and her father had navigated, all the unanswered questions and unfaced fears they'd both addressed.

"Gut-wrenching. Enlightening. Freeing." As she said it, the last word hummed around her, its truth like a bright light in the dimness.

"Wow. Well, I've got all the time in the world." She could hear the smile in his voice. "I'm listening, fair Iona."

～

The following morning, Iona stuffed her waterproof jacket into the mini backpack Craig had lent her. After the best night's sleep she'd had in weeks and a bigger breakfast than she was used to eating, they were almost ready to head out to Yesnaby Castle. Despite her father's concern about the coldness of the day, she'd insisted that she'd be fine to walk the mile or so from the closest parking area across the open fields to the amphitheater of cliffs that hugged the ancient stone stack—a favorite of Iona's since childhood. "A bit of cold's not going to stop me," she'd teased. "I'm an Orkney lass."

Laughing, he'd suggested they stick to Yesnaby Castle rather than walk all the way to North Gaulton, as she'd originally intended, and Iona had conceded, deferring to his superior knowledge of the unpredictable island weather.

Now, she tucked her gloves under her arm, checked her phone for messages, and texted Roz. *Heading out for a walk. Will call tonight.* Within moments Roz replied. *Have you asked him about CM yet?*

Iona bit her lip. *Not yet. Today. Maybe. x*

Craig thundered down the stairs. "All set?" His hair was wet, and his face flushed from the heat of the shower.

"Yep. Just going to fill some water bottles." She nodded toward the kitchen.

He raised a hand. "I'll get them. Two seconds." He walked away from her.

Just as Iona was slipping her fleece on, Craig's phone buzzed on the coffee table next to her. She glanced down, squinting to see the screen and, as the phone buzzed a second time, juddering on the wood surface, she saw the name *Janice* appear. She reached out instinctively, wondering if she should answer it, then halted.

In the past few years, when she'd tried to imagine her father meeting someone new, allowing himself to be with or potentially love someone other than her mother, it had been an abrasive image, but now, as she looked at the name flashing on the screen, the idea felt less uncomfortable. The thought of him being alone any longer was far more upsetting than the idea of him having someone new in his life.

Wanting to create some credible distance from the phone, she moved over to the front door and began fiddling with the strap on the pack.

As Craig walked back into the room carrying the water bottles, she pointed at the table.

"I think your phone was ringing."

"Oh, right. Thanks." He shoved both bottles into his backpack, lifted the phone, and slid it into his back pocket.

"Not going to check who it was?" She slung her pack over her shoulder.

"Not now. Come on. If we're going to do this, let's go."

Iona followed him along the narrow path to the front gate, watching his steady gait and solid shoulders. The way he moved momentarily reminded her of Scott's broad frame, the thought of which warmed her face.

As she helped him stash the packs in the boot and then slid into the passenger seat, she put the idea of asking him about Janice to the back of her mind. The very least she could do, after everything he'd done for her, was to give him the gift of privacy. Something told her that Janice would come up anyway before she, Iona, went back to Edinburgh in three days.

In the car, Craig chatted about the island, bringing her up to date on more of the changes in the community since her departure: a wedding between a widow and widower, both named Finlay, who'd been next-door neighbors for two decades, a ceilidh that had gone awry, culminating in a fistfight and two arrests, and then the passing of dear old Mr. McHugh, the man who'd run the newsagents' in the village for over thirty-seven years. Iona listened, letting her father's voice lull her into a half-sleep as she watched the familiar countryside slip by until she was aware that he had stopped talking.

"Are you asleep? Am I that boring?"

"Sorry. It's just so relaxing being here and listening to you." She said. "I've missed you, Dad." No sooner were the words out than the photograph of Grace and Charles Majors flashed brightly behind her eyes, and a nut of dread took hold as she considered when she might broach the subject with Craig. *Now that they had regained so much of their former closeness, could they safely navigate this new, dangerous territory, or would it tear them apart once and for all?*

The car park at Yesnaby was quiet, with just a handful of other cars dotted around the gravelly space. As a child, Iona had loved to climb onto the flat concrete slabs that were scattered around, which Craig had told her were leftover pieces of old, World War II look-out buildings. Seeing them now, she grabbed her pack and walked over to one, stepped onto the slab, and spread her arms wide. "Hey, Dad. I'm king of the castle," she called at his back, the wind whipping her words away as her hair wrapped itself across her face. She shoved it away and saw him turn to face her, a smile shattering his look of concentration.

"That you are, m'love."

The walk over the fields was challenging, the ground soft under their boots, and the buffeting wind made their progress slow. When they'd been walking only ten minutes, Craig leaned in and spoke close to her ear. "Sure you want to keep going?" His face was pink, his woolen hat pulled down so far that it covered his eyebrows.

"Yes, it's great." She nodded. "Just what the doctor ordered."

She re-tucked her hair inside her hat and slipped her arm through his. "Lead on, MacDuff."

Walking with their arms linked slowed them even more, but neither made to break the connection, and within a few minutes the cliffs were visible ahead.

"There's the cliffs," Iona shouted, pointing. "Still here." She smiled at her father as he nodded.

"As ever."

Making their way carefully along the coastal path, they followed the line of the cliff-edge, or as close as Craig would allow them to get to the heart-stopping drop to the sea. The path had several sections that were treacherous, the ground loose beneath their feet, so Craig walked in front of her, painstakingly checking his footing before beckoning to her to follow.

Out to sea, the dark water roiled, white-topped waves thrashed into long coils, and clouds of sea foam rose from the surface. Iona filled her lungs with the salty air that misted her face. The temptation to close her eyes was strong, but having walked this path numerous times, she knew better than to give in to it.

Edging forward behind her father, flicking her glance from the backs of his heels to the stunning view to her right, Iona lost herself in the simple motion of walking, the sound of the sea birds squawking overhead, and the briny scent of the island that she loved—that was so deeply ingrained within her.

As they approached Yesnaby Castle, Craig halted on the trail. "Here we are." He pointed down at what the locals called Old Red, the sandstone sea-stack, with ragged cliffs rising around it on three sides. The blowhole at the bottom left side of the stack, which split the lower half into two sections, and the uneven layers of stone that jutted out from the front, had always reminded Iona of a man's face, his long hair dangling down his neck at the back, all topped by a mossy-green crown on his head.

"The old man's looking good today," she called at Craig's ear.

He nodded, taking her hand and wrapping it around his lower arm. "Just keep a hold of me. O.K.?" He scanned her face.

"O.K." She grinned. "Old man."

As was their habit, her father led her to a flat grassy area, close enough for them to see the stack but far enough from the cliff-edge not to send his blood pressure soaring. Iona positioned herself as close as she could to the spot she always sought and sat on the damp grass. She extended her feet out in front of her and closed one eye. If she moved a little to the right, she could hold the stack perfectly between her feet, one battered hiking boot on either side of it, like rumpled leather splints.

As she looked over at him, Craig was swiping at his eyes, the wind buffeting his coat-sleeve. Iona reached over and tapped his shoulder, expecting to see him smile at her, but when he turned, she saw that his cheeks were wet.

"Dad?" She reached her hand out to him. "What's up?"

Craig shook his head. "Nothing. I'm just getting sentimental." He shrugged and then, to her relief, smiled. "You're so like her, Iona. Sometimes it still takes me by surprise."

At this, Iona pulled her legs in and shifted closer to him. He'd brought a flask of hot tea and some biscuits, which he was pulling out of his pack.

"Want some tea?" He titled the flask toward her. "Might have to be a quick one, if this wind gets any worse." He grimaced.

"Sure. Let's live on the edge." She held the plastic cups still as he poured the steaming liquid into them.

"Cheers." She tapped her cup to his. "Thanks for bringing me out here."

Craig sipped some tea, protecting the cup from the wind with his gloved hands. "Pleasure, pet. Pleasure."

They were quiet in the car on the drive home. Iona's face was raw from the salty wind, but as she pushed her feet out, holding them under the warm air that was pumping into the car, her whole body tingled, exhilarated. The view over the mystical stone stack, the sea crashing angrily below, the screeching gulls banking overhead, the thick swaths of bending grasses, and the bright pink patches of sea thrift they'd passed, another favorite flower that Grace would fill vases with in the spring, all spun around her mind, filling her senses and making her feel more alive than she had in years.

Craig was now humming along to a Phil Collins song on the radio, and as she took in his profile, the strong nose and jaw, the thatch of fair hair that flopped over his forehead, the prominent Adam's apple that bobbed over and under the collar of his thick sweater, Iona couldn't remember feeling this close to him since her mother had died.

Overcome with a sense of well-being and a security generated by the honesty of their conversation the previous day, she twisted to face him. "When we get home, I'd like to talk to you about something else."

"O.K." He glanced over at her. "Once again—should I be worried?"

"No." She shook her head "Not at all."

They sang along to the radio for the remainder of the journey and, back at the cottage, laughed loudly as they jostled, their shoulders pressing against each other's to get through the narrow front door. They'd been gone less than four hours, but the light of the day was already fading and the temperature dropping toward the cold of evening.

Iona hung up their coats and stowed their boots outside in the little mudroom off the kitchen, while Craig stoked the fire. Shivering, she moved up close to the mantel, holding her palms out, as her father placed logs in an expert pile above the pinkish glow of the embers. Within seconds, sparks grabbed the dry wood, eventually pulling into tall, orange flames that licked the tepee of pine.

She rubbed her palms together. "Oh, that feels good. Thanks."

He slung an arm around her shoulder. "Welcome, love."

Iona stared into the flames, mulling over the question she was burning to ask him, momentarily anxious that while this instant might not be perfect, there might never be a better time.

She moved away from him and sat down on the fireside rug. Craig sank into his chair, crossed his long legs at the ankle, and sighed contentedly.

She took a breath and leaned forward, locking her arms around her knees. "Do you remember Mum seeing one of her professors, Charles Majors?"

Craig's eyes snapped to hers, the look of relaxation gone. "What?" His brow folded as he squinted at her.

Iona felt a stab of doubt at her timing, wondering if she could back out of this somehow, but her father's eyes were locked on hers, his mouth now pinched tight.

"Sorry, I don't mean to upset you." She held her palm up as Craig, jerking himself upright in the chair, crossed his arms over his middle.

"Why would you ask me about him?" His eyes had become hooded, his face having lost the healthy color the wind had engendered.

Wanting to slap herself, Iona shifted, extending her legs out in front of her. "I found a photo in the lining of Mum's cello case." She said. "It was of the two of them, dated nineteen-ninety-eight."

A trickle of color had begun to reclaim Craig's cheeks. "Oh, right." He raked the hair from his forehead. "Yes." He stared into the flames again. "Not the happiest time, for your mother."

Iona felt her resolve slipping away. *Should she let it go? Would this be too painful for him to talk about?* Just as she considered leaving things as they were, letting a secret truth remain an incomplete conversation, certainty flooded her insides. "Dad, I know about them, about Mum getting pregnant. About him being my..." Her voice faltered as Craig closed his eyes. He let his arms drop to his lap, and his hands gradually formed two fists, one on each knee.

"Dad?" She swallowed. "Can you look at me?"

After a few moments, he opened his eyes. His mouth was pulsing, as if unwanted words were battling to get out.

"Dad?"

Craig looked at her, his face a mask of misery. "What do you know?"

Iona blinked, there was no going back now. "Mum told me about it in the letter she left for me at Freya's." She swallowed. "You knew she'd left me more of them, didn't you? One with Professor Douglas and another with Beth." She watched his jaw pulse as he nodded, his eyes fixed on the fire.

"I thought she might have."

Battling to keep her voice balanced, Iona continued. "I know everything. That she was pregnant when you two got together. That Majors basically abandoned her. That..." Despite her efforts, her voice hitched.

He held up a hand. "Please, just give me a minute." He pushed himself up from the chair and went into the kitchen.

Iona's heart clattered as she heard water running, the clink of glass. Then a few moments later, he came back into the room holding an envelope away from himself, as if it were burning his fingers.

Iona caught her breath. While not surprised that her mother would leave a final letter with him, the sight of the handwriting still brought a lump to her throat.

His eyes darted around the room as he flapped the envelope at her. "This is for you." He stepped forward and slid the cream bundle into her outstretched hand. "I wasn't sure when to give it to you." He stepped away and sank back into his chair, his shoulders rolling forward. "But now seems like the time."

Iona felt the weight of the envelope on her palm as she scanned his weary face. "Dad, listen. I know you think this is some kind of how-could-you confrontation, which is absolutely not my intention, but I had to tell you."

Craig flopped back into the chair. "There's no point denying, I'm relieved that you know." He eyed her. "But what I need to know is, are you very angry with me?" His eyes were scanning her like a searchlight looking for land over dark water.

His pained expression was heartbreaking, and rather than the shock, or defensiveness, that she might have expected, all she saw was fear. She set the envelope on the arm of the sofa, shifted onto her knees, and shuffled over to him. "No. I'm not angry. I was initially, but now, quite the opposite, actually."

His face loosened, the tension around his mouth easing.

"I just wanted to tell you how much I love you and appreciate you, and how much I admire you for being there for Mum, even when he wasn't." She paused, filtering the myriad thoughts that were filling her head. "You are my dad, and I couldn't have asked for a better father." His features blurred before her.

He placed a callused hand over hers. "I've been so afraid of this conversation. I've imagined how it would go, over the years, and it was never good."

She nodded, shifting back onto her haunches.

"I wanted to tell you, so many times, but your mother just wouldn't hear of it. She made me swear on my life never to tell you, and despite what I felt in my heart," he jabbed himself in the chest, "I kept my word."

Since discovering the photograph, then finding out from Freya the extent of Grace's relationship with Charles Majors, with everything she'd learned and each subsequent word she'd read about that time in her mother's life, Grace's motivation in keeping this from her had become clearer. She had done what she'd done, swearing Craig to secrecy, because she'd believed she was protecting him from losing Iona to the truth, whereas what she had actually done was drive a wedge between them—Craig being bound by his word even after her death. Iona was struck by the cruel irony of that.

"I think Mum was afraid that if I found out about him, that you and I might…" She stopped.

He was staring at her, his mouth slightly open.

"That it would come between us." She searched his face. "But I think it was unfair of her to make you swear to keep it secret. It was a heavy burden she left you with." She watched as his eyes flicked around the room, as if searching for something specific to land on. "The saddest part for me is that she didn't trust the love we had for each other. That she didn't know that there was nothing you could tell me that would've stopped me thinking of you as my father."

Craig's eyes were now locked on hers, his fingers plucking at the front of his sweater. "Do you mean that?"

"Of course I do."

His eye brimmed. "It's all I ever wanted to be from the first time I heard your heart beating and saw your little fists on the ultrasound. I knew you were meant to be mine." He gulped. "You were always my daughter."

Iona nodded, forcing a slow breath. "I know that, Dad."

Craig leaned forward and reached for her hand. "Iona. Can you ever forgive me?"

She squeezed his fingers. "There's nothing to forgive. You literally saved me, and Mum. You gave us both your love and a life we might never have had if you'd been anything less than the man that you are." She paused. "No one could've been more of a father, or a better example, than you." She caught her breath. "I don't deserve you."

～

Two hours later, they sat opposite each other. Discarded plates of pasta lay on the coffee table, the fire was burning low in the grate, and the unopened letter burrowed its presence into Iona's thoughts from the cushion next to her. She wrapped her hands around her mug of tea and stared into the glowing embers.

"You look exhausted." Craig frowned. "You should turn in."

She yawned, feeling the tension in her jaw. "Yes, I think I will, if you don't mind."

"Of course not, love. It's been quite a day for us both." He hefted himself out of the chair. "And we still have tomorrow, and the next day too."

Standing up, she lifted the envelope and tucked it under her arm. "Goodnight, Dad." She stepped in as he came toward her, stood on tiptoe, and kissed his cheek. "Thanks for telling me everything."

He nodded. "It was time, Iona. Well past time, in fact."

Upstairs, Iona quickly showered and pulled on her pajamas. The warmth of the living room had not carried up the stairs, and she shivered as she slipped under the covers, the chill of the sheets making her draw her feet up toward her. The letter sat on the bedside table, and as she lifted it, her heart skipped at the prospect of seeing her mother's words, likely the last that Grace had ever written to her, unfold.

Settling back, she slid her finger under the flap and opened the letter. The heft of the number of pages gave her a lift as she unfolded them and began to read the spidery, erratic writing.

February 14th, 2010

My darling girl,
It makes me happy to think of you being with your dad when

you read this, and knowing that he is there with you to answer your questions helps me say what I want to say.

Today is your birthday, and I can't believe our baby is eleven. It seems like yesterday when you first sat up on your own, used a spoon to eat rather than your fist, walked, and slept through the night. Where have the years gone?

I wish I could bake you a cake, wear the pink dress, make it the same as, or better than, any other birthday, but this one will be quite different. We'll make the best memories for you that we can, even if they're different ones than I'd like.

Iona clasped the letter to her chest, let the flipflop of her heart settle, then turned the page.

I tried to play Bach's No. 1 this morning. I managed the first movement but then had to stop, as it's sacrilege not to do it justice, and I couldn't bear the way I was sliding notes.

The future that offered so much richness for me just by being a part of my family, of the world, and music, has felt truncated, like a beautiful sonata with no ending. Then, this afternoon, I heard you practicing Britten's No. 1. It was flawless. As I let it soak into me, I felt privileged to be connected to you, and when you finished, I could hardly breathe. I know it's extreme self-flattery, but I think I heard a little of myself in your playing. You're so much more talented than I ever was, Iona. There are no limits to what you can achieve. You, my little daughter, took my breath away today, quite literally. Never doubt your talent, because it is as blatant as the sun.

· · ·

The guilt that surged into Iona's throat tasted bitter. *How could she have let her mother down so badly?* Blinking, she continued to read.

I've been afraid that if I let go, allow myself to let the riptide that is MND take me where it would, everything would disinte-grate. But then hearing you play, I realized that I was wrong— everything will go on regardless. I don't have that much power. Your dad will go on. You will go on, Iona. Only I will cease to be.

About your father. Today I can still speak to him, albeit an odd sound now, but soon I'll lose the ability to do that. Such a fundamental process, to have a thought, then say it out loud, and yet that simple neural activity will soon stop. This is more fright-ening than the loss of movement, or any other function, for me. He and I have always communicated at a foundational level, with such honesty, that eye blinks or nods just won't be sufficient for everything I need him to know. When I can no longer speak to him, or to you, sweet Iona, to tell you both how much I love you, or how you have made my life so extremely perfect, then it'll be time to go.

I chart my progress, or regression rather, in other people's eyes. Only you seem to keep my image intact, seeing me as I was and not as I am. Perhaps that's a gift that children have, because Craig isn't capable of it. Jean cries, not knowing I can hear her downstairs, while you play for me and paint my toenails with glitter.

Iona fingered two warped suns that overlapped each other at the bottom of the page, the outline of teardrops long-since dried. As she swallowed, the scene was clear as day—Grace propped up on pillows while Iona giggled, trying to paint her mother's toenails as, scandalously, more of the varnish ended up on the sheets than anywhere else.

He and I talked about Zurich again last night and it ended badly —no pun intended! He said that I mustn't give up, that I need to keep fighting, and I told him that's exactly what I AM doing. The idea of losing control of my speech and limbs is bad enough, but to relinquish the ability to steer the course of my own life is terrifying, and in making this choice, I am fighting to retain the last shred of my dignity. When I told him that, something changed in his eyes. It was as if a light went on. He was quiet then, just holding me close and stroking my hair. I thought we might've had our last fight about it, but then he brought you up again.

I might be wrong, Iona, and heaven knows it wouldn't be the first time, but I feel so strongly that taking you with us to Switzerland is crueler than not. To expose you to that place, the strangers, the environment so totally foreign to you, in every sense, just seems torturous. Here you are safe, you have your room, your things around you, and Nana Jean close at hand. In Zurich, there would none of that to comfort you.

This is certainly not the symphony I'd have written for my life (I never was a big fan of requiems, as you know), but there is still beauty in it. In my family. I've loved my life, Iona. Of course I've regretted parts of it, but lately regret has felt like a wicked waste of my remaining time. My life was simply my life—who I was and would ever be. The best part of a person stays behind and Iona, you are the best part of me. You and your father are my love-legacy to the world.

My darling daughter, I hope you see things that make you hold your breath. I hope you fall passionately in love. I hope you step outside your comfort zone, often, and I hope you stay as wonderfully kind and open-minded as you are today. I hope you make mistakes you can learn and recover from. I hope you love

your life, and travel far, finding your own treasure. If you do
wander, I hope you always remember where home is, and I hope,
wherever you land, that you keep your father close.

My greatest hope is that you will learn to forgive me for the
last choice I was able to make for myself. You are everything,
and I will love you for eternity.

Mum x

Iona folded the letter and, with quivering hands, slid it back into
the envelope. As she switched off her lamp and slipped down in
the bed, her mother's words surrounded her, teasing emotions
from her that she'd been keeping at bay for more years than she
cared to remember. The loss, pain, and dearth of her mother's
presence in her life, and the misplaced resentment toward her
father, had been weights buried inside her soul, and as she
gulped past what felt like the last walnut of grief she'd been
cradling, gradually her breaths began to come more easily.

Wiping the back of her hand across her eyes, she spoke into
the darkness. "I needed that more than you'll ever know, Mum."
She kissed the tips of her fingers, reached out and touched the
envelope. "And I'll take care of Dad too. Don't worry."

Smiling, she texted Scott and Roz, then rolled onto her side
and pulled her legs up to her chest.

"Goodnight, Mum. I love you forever."

17

The following morning was bright, with a few cottony clouds scattered throughout the cerulean sky. Iona had dressed quietly and slipped out for a walk without waking her father, and now, having circled the center of Stromness, revisiting the familiar winding streets of terraced houses and the labyrinth of steep passageways leading down to the picturesque waterfront, she was heading back to the cottage.

Passing the museum, she stopped to read a sign about a new exhibition of Orcadian tools dating back to the Stone Age. Proud of the remarkable place she hailed from, she walked on, leaning into the breeze, and with every early riser she acknowledged, her sense of belonging deepened. No matter what happened now, wherever she might go, this would always be her home, and her relationship with her father was back on solid ground, so nothing would threaten that again. The knowledge that they were finally, after all these years, sharing their deepest truths, had brought her back to him literally and figuratively.

Turning onto the street leading to the cottage, anticipating the day ahead with him, Iona felt released. Even breathing was easier now.

Craig was up, reading the paper at the kitchen table. "Go for a walk?" He nodded at the pot on the counter. "Coffee's hot."

"Great." Iona dumped her jacket over the back of a chair and filled herself a mug. "What's on your agenda today?" She sat down opposite him.

"I'm off work and at your disposal." He curved his arm across his waist and dipped his head. "What's you pleasure?"

Iona sipped the extra strong, dark coffee. He always made it this way, and Grace had often teased him, saying that she almost needed to chew it. As she thought of her mother flitting around the kitchen, humming Bach, nagging them both to hurry up, finish their meal, get to school, etcetera, Iona smiled.

"What?" Craig looked quizzical. "What's funny?"

"Oh, nothing, I was just thinking about Mum." She set her cup down. "It's strange, but since I've been back and we've talked about everything, I can think about her without it hurting so much." She focused on his eyes. "Do you know what I mean?"

Craig nodded, turning his cup in circles by pushing the handle away from himself. "I do. I dreamt about her last night, and for the first time in ages, I didn't wake up with a pit in my stomach." He eyed her. "Perhaps we're finally letting her go?"

"Yes, I think you're right." She nodded. "I suppose it's time."

Craig nodded, his eyes locking on hers. "Iona, I was wondering if you'd thought about tracking him down." He dropped his chin.

Iona's eyebrows jumped as she shifted in the chair. "Who?" Her voice faltered, giving away her surprise.

"Charles Majors." Craig leaned back, pushing his empty cup away from himself. "Have you given it any thought?"

A mixture of adrenaline and nerves made her stammer. "Um." She bit her bottom lip, questioning why she hadn't given it much more thought since initially discovering the truth at

Freya's house. "Well, I suppose I might have, briefly." She said. "But I really don't need to, Dad. I'm totally fine with the way things are."

Craig shrugged. "I am too, but I think you should consider it. Whatever way you look at it, and however everything came about, you and he are related. There are blood ties there." He frowned. "There's no reason to deprive yourself of the potential of that relationship." He pressed his palm to his chest. "Not to protect me, anyway."

Unsurprised at his position, and once again overcome by his selfless magnanimity, Iona nodded. "O.K., I'll think about it some more." She said. "You really are amazing, Dad."

Craig's face colored. "Oh, I don't think so." He stood up, avoiding her eyes.

"Well, I do." She stood and followed him into the kitchen, and addressing his wool-clad back, she whispered over a knot of love and gratitude, "I really don't know what I did to deserve you."

～

Their breakfast cleared away, Craig suggested they take a drive to Skara Brae. Just twenty minutes due north of Stromness, dating back to 3200 BC, the prehistoric settlement had been discovered in 1850 only after a great storm had battered the bay, blowing away the sand to reveal the stunningly preserved village ruins complete with furniture, tools, and a network of corridors that linked the dwellings.

"We could pop up there for a walk, then come back to town for a pub lunch." He tapped the tabletop. "It's been a few years since we were there."

Iona raised her arms above her head, stretching out her neck. "That's a good idea. There's something magical about that place." She nodded. "Doesn't matter how many times I see it, it still stops me in my tracks."

Craig nodded. "Yes. I know what you mean." He shoved his chair back and stood up. "So, Skara Brae it is, then."

As Iona lifted the newspaper and began scanning the front page, Craig's phone rang in his pocket. She tried not to stare as he dug it out and scanned the screen. Without answering, he put it back in his pocket, a distinct flush appearing on his ruddy cheeks.

Iona folded the paper and set it on the table. "Dad, who's Janice?" she asked, amused by the startled look he flashed her. "Is she a new friend?"

Craig paced over to the stove and began moving pans around the surface, as if shifting chess pieces on a board. His back was to her, but she could sense the frown that had folded his brow.

"It's O.K., you know. Life goes on, and it's been years." She got up and stood next to him, leaning her head against his solid shoulder. "You can tell me about her, if you want."

She felt him relax, the tension slipping from his back. He let his head drop until it made contact with the top of hers. "Are you sure?"

Iona lifted her head and gently poked his shoulder, making him turn to face her. "I'd really like to hear about her." She smiled. "Honestly."

Craig led her to the table, pulling out a chair for her. "She's from Ayr. She came here to attend a conference on tidal energy last June. We were in the same breakout group at lunch, and we just hit it off." He shoved the newspaper to the edge of the table then moved it back to the middle. "She's awfully intelligent. Much cleverer than me." He nodded to himself. "I've never met anyone more curious and passionate about what we do. The renewable and maritime and environmental expertise she has is astounding for someone her age." He cleared his throat. "I mean, she's not that young, she's forty." He studied Iona's face.

"Go on." She consciously kept her expression open, receptive.

Her father's work in wave and tidal energy testing, studying technologies that generated electricity in the purpose-built, open-sea testing facility in Stromness, had always fascinated her. His ability to work in a field that excited him so much, his enthusiasm for it bleeding into the conversation over many a family dinner, was a gift they'd all recognized as *his* personal music.

Seeing him hesitating, she dipped her chin.

He pulled his shoulders back and ran a finger under the collar of his sweater, his nervousness endearing. "Well, she came back a couple of times for research projects she was working on, and then in November, an opportunity came up for a job at the center." He paused. "By that time, we'd become friends."

"Friends. That's nice." She teased.

Craig narrowed his eyes, a smile tugging at his mouth. "Now listen to me, madam. Friends, I said."

"Right. That's what I said, too." She widened her eyes.

"Anyway, she took the job, and when she got here, I helped her find a place to live, get settled in, so to speak." He leaned back in his chair. "She rented a wee house on the other side of the harbor, and we saw each other a couple of times for dinner, and then we started walking together at the weekends." He eyed her. "She's a keen walker."

Iona nodded. "That's great. She could've come with us yesterday."

Craig shook his head. "No. Yesterday was about us. I wanted you to myself."

"Yes. It was a perfect day." She said. "So, am I going to meet her?"

He shifted in the seat, his face coloring again. "Do you want to?"

"Of course. If you'd like me to?" She studied his face,

suddenly concerned that this was perhaps a step too far, but to her relief, he nodded enthusiastically.

"Yes." He leaned his elbows on the table. "I think you'll like her."

~

The Ferry Inn was busy for lunchtime, with only two tables available as they walked into the harbor-side pub. The mesh of voices and the homey food smells were familiar as Iona scanned the room, looking for a face that might scream the name Janice, or a particular feature that would identify the mystery woman her father had been seeing for some months.

On the way there, Iona had been trying to picture the face, the eyes, the body type that had drawn her father back from his loneliness, but coming up blank, she'd determined that it was perhaps better to have no preconceptions.

Craig led her to a table. "Sit here. I'll get us some drinks." He shrugged his coat off, tossed it onto a chair, and eased his way to the bar.

Iona sat with her back to the wall. The leather banquet curved around the corner behind her, and the wood-paneled wall above its high back had a ship's wheel and several portholes set into it. She looked up at the ceiling, taking in the draped sails and sections of net that were artfully strung overhead. She'd loved coming here with her parents for Sunday lunches, sipping a glass of orange juice and watching the familiar faces of the community milling around them.

Her phone buzzed in her pocket, startling her. She hadn't spoken to Roz for a day or so and seeing that Craig was still waiting to be served, she answered the call. "Hiya. Sorry I haven't called. It's been a bit of a whirlwind since I got here." She watched a young man walk in the door, scan the room, and then wave to his friend before joining him at a nearby table.

"How's it going? I've been dying to know." Roz sounded breathless. "The suspense is killing me."

"Sorry. A lot's happened, and I'm still reeling a bit." She saw the door opening again and an elderly man walking in, with a flat hat and gnarled cane. "I'm at the pub with Dad. We're waiting for his friend to arrive."

"O.K., wait a minute, before you tell me about that, did you ask him about Charlie boy?"

Iona cupped her hand around her mouth. "Yes. We talked about everything last night. It was difficult to start with. I was scared, but it went fine. He was amazing." She watched her father lean over the bar to order. "This whole trip's been amazing, actually."

"God. I hate that I'm missing all the juicy stuff," Roz huffed. "I want details."

Flicking her eyes between her father and the door, Iona quickly summarized her conversations with Craig and their abject honesty with each other.

"That's great. You've both been needing this for ages." Roz sounded genuinely happy. "So, what now?"

Iona shrugged. "I still have to decide whether to track down Charles. Dad thinks I should." She nibbled at a hangnail around her thumb. "I'm sort of wavering, though."

"Why? I thought you were all about getting to the truth. If I had a mysterious father out there somewhere, I'd be right up in his face, being a huge pain in the arse. I mean what's the worst that can happen? He says thanks very much, but I'm not interested in getting to know you. What've you lost?" She paused. "Nothing that you haven't already lived without for twenty-one years."

Iona stacked the three warped beer mats into a pile in front of her. "Yeah. I know. I'm just worried that I might let rip about him being such a waste of space, basically abandoning my mum at her most vulnerable." Iona felt a flash of anger toward the parent she'd never met.

She glanced over to see Craig paying for the drinks, laughing with a man sitting at the bar. "Listen, he's coming back. I'll have to go."

"Bugger. Can we talk more later? I want to tell you about my date last night."

"What? Now you tell me." She let her jaw go slack. "Who is he? Speak fast."

"His name's Jim."

"And?"

"Oh no, we're not talking about that until I hear all your stuff first."

"All right." Iona laughed. "Deal."

"You sound good." Roz's voice was warm.

"I really am."

Craig squeezed in behind the table and sat next to Iona. He set a glass down in front of her, his eyes glinting. "I got you your usual."

"Great, thanks." She rolled her eyes. "I'm nine again." She sipped the orange juice. "Hmm, delish."

Craig was laughing softly as the door to the pub opened. A tall, willowy woman with chin-length auburn hair stood in the doorway. She wore a tan-colored mackintosh, her jeans were tucked into long leather boots and a floral scarf was wound around her throat. As she combed her fingers through her hair, she spotted Craig and waved.

Craig waved back, half rising behind the table. "That's her. That's Janice." He looked down at Iona, his face awash with nerves.

Iona put her hand over his. "It's fine, Dad. Just relax."

Janice walked toward them, tugging her coat off as she moved. Craig eased out from behind the table to greet her, then leaned in to kiss her cheek.

Iona watched her father's body language speaking volumes as he turned to face her, his hand under Janice's elbow. "Janice, this is my daughter, Iona. Iona, this is Janice."

Janice stepped forward and extended an elegant hand. She wore a gold ring with a Celtic design, on her middle finger, and her nails were plum-colored. "It's lovely to meet you, Iona." She smiled, revealing a tiny gap between her two front teeth. "Your dad has told me so much about you."

Iona shook Janice's hand, noting the firm grip. "Lovely to meet you too. And sorry about that." She jutted her chin toward Craig, who was sliding back into the seat. "I hope he didn't bore you to tears."

Craig let out a laugh. "If I did, it's my prerogative."

Janice smiled at him and then sat opposite Iona. Janice's eyes were a deep blue and the scattering of freckles across her nose and high cheekbones made her look younger than her years. There was a warmth to this face that instantly drew Iona in.

"So, how's your visit going?" Janice took the glass of wine that Craig had pushed toward her.

"It's been great. We've had loads of time to catch up, go on lovely walks, and just spend time together." Iona leaned in, her shoulder touching Craig's. "It's been long overdue."

Janice ran her finger around the base of the glass, her eyes flicking between them. "Well, sometimes these things just take their own time, don't you think?" She met Iona's gaze. "The important thing is that they happen."

The message was clear, and Iona could see why her father had taken to this woman. There was an honesty to her, an aura of authenticity that was both attractive and refreshing.

"So, Janice, Dad tells me you're an eco-fiend like him?" Iona grinned. "How did you get into that field?"

～

Lunch had gone well, the conversation easy, taking on a natural flow. Craig had them laughing at stories of testing projects gone wrong, and both he and Janice talked about their colleagues, a group of environmentalists and academics who kept them on their toes.

Seeing how the two interacted, the ease with which they shared stories and finished each other's sentences, was touching. Craig's face had taken on a glow, and each time Janice laughed, he'd reach out and touch her arm, obviously wanting to be connected to the joy that was emanating from this woman.

When Janice eventually asked Iona about her music, for an instant she wanted to defer but then, seeing her father stiffen slightly, she took a decision that she hadn't been aware was percolating.

"It's been a while since I played properly. It reminded me so much of Mum, it just became too hard." She glanced at Craig, whose mouth had gone slack. "But I think it's time I get back to it. I know she'd want me to and, to be honest, I miss it badly. It's like having lungs but not breathing properly."

Janice took in what she'd said, her eyelids flickering as she studied her empty glass. When she spoke, Iona heard a depth of compassion that touched her deeply. "I think when you're gifted in the way that you are, and your mother was, there's some kind of cosmic obligation to use that gift." She said. "After all, it's people like you that have to balance out all of us ordinary souls that exist in the world." She pressed her palm to her chest. "I'm so happy that you're ready to take it up again, Iona." She looked over at Craig, whose eyes had filled. "And I know someone else who will be too."

While Craig went to the bar to pay the bill, Janice hugged Iona goodbye before heading back to work. She held Iona tight, and dropped a light kiss on her cheek. "Thanks very much for meeting me. I know it probably wasn't high on your to-do list for this visit." She stepped back. "It means a lot to me." Her face colored slightly. "As does he."

Surprised that she had to hold back tears, Iona reached out and squeezed Janice's fingers. "That makes me very happy."

When Craig came back, both women were dabbing their eyes. He looked momentarily concerned, glancing back and forth between them, until Iona and Janice laughed simultaneously.

"Just ignore us." Janice laid her hand on his arm. "We're fine."

Craig looked relieved, helping them on with their coats.

"That's all right, then." He steered Janice toward the door, while holding Iona's hand behind him. "Can't have my ladies upset."

~

Back at the cottage, while Craig checked his emails and then built a fire, Iona had begun cooking. With just one day left of her visit, she wanted to make her father's favorite meal, and as she stirred the rice, Craig asked her shyly what she thought of Janice.

"I think she's absolutely lovely." She nodded enthusiastically. "And I think she's a bit besotted with you."

Craig swatted the air. "Oh, I doubt that."

"Um, I think she is, Dad, and it's wonderful."

Craig hugged her, his relief transmitting itself through her arms and straight to her heart. Then he stepped back from her with an odd look in his eye. "Stay there. I've got something for you."

He was gone only a few minutes before coming into the kitchen, holding a sheet of paper.

"What's that?" She put the lid on the pot and turned down the heat.

"It's something else your mother wanted you to have." He

looked sheepish as he passed the paper from one hand to the other.

Iona's eyebrows jumped, her heart rate picking up. "So, what is it?" She wiped her hands on a dishcloth and gently took the paper from him. It was a sheet of music, the lines of the staves carefully hand-drawn, and the notes on both the treble and bass clefs meticulously marked in black pen. Her mother's distinct handwriting at the top made her catch her breath. She held it up and read out loud. "Iona's Star—because she was mine."

Craig stood behind the kitchen table, his big hands clasping the back of a chair. His mouth was pressed tight, and his eyes were glued to the tabletop.

"When… I mean, where did it come from?" She turned the paper over to see the back also covered in clusters of notes, and as she began to follow the melody in her mind, hearing the gentle climbing scale, the underlying chords, Craig cleared his throat.

"She wrote it for you, around the spring of 2009." He shoved his hands into his pockets. "But then she asked me to keep it for when you were older." He shrugged. "I put it away, and when you went to university, I meant to give it to you then. I don't know why I didn't, but I suppose I thought you weren't ready." His eyes lifted to meet hers. "I think you are, now."

Iona blinked, taking in his obvious discomfort. She could understand why he'd withheld this gift; her demeanor and her tendency to hide from all things that reminded her of Grace had been raw and ever-present since her death.

She turned the paper back over and re-read the title. "Iona's Star."

"Yes. She always said you deserved to have one named after you." He smiled. "I was meant to arrange it, with the international star registry, but then, with everything else going on, it just didn't happen."

She shoved a strand of hair behind her ear and nodded. "It's understandable. I wasn't exactly receptive."

Craig nodded. "True. But that's why I'm so glad to give it to you now." He moved around the table and opened his arms wide. "Not angry?" His voice was husky.

She hugged his middle. "No. Not."

Craig stepped back and took in her face. "Would you play it for me?"

She lifted the paper to her chest. "Of course."

18

Their last day together had been relaxed so far, the weather kind, the sky staying clear, and, for the first time since Iona had arrived, the wind dropped to a gentle breeze. After breakfast, they'd walked far out onto the moor, and Iona had taken several pictures with her phone, explaining the selfie phenomenon to Craig, who claimed not to understand people's obsession with photographing themselves.

Despite him rolling his eyes repeatedly, she'd persuaded him to press his cheek up close to hers, and she'd taken a few of them with Hoy visible in the background, which she'd then texted to Roz and Scott.

"There's some great ones in there, Dad." She'd flicked though the shots. "I'll email them to you."

"O.K., love. Can't wait." He'd winked.

Iona had spent much of the previous night awake, running through myriad scenarios where she might come face-to-face with Charles Majors. Now, as they headed for home, she was suddenly certain that the only way she wanted to look for her birth father was with the man who had been her true father her entire life by her side. As her time with Craig was drawing to a close, she had to ask now what she'd been working up to all day. Taking a moment to compose herself, she linked her arm through his and drew him close, the lemon scent of his soap safe and familiar.

"Dad, I need to ask you something."

He wrapped his big hand over hers. "Ask away."

Iona swallowed. "Would you help me look for him?" She looked up at her father's profile, searching for a twitch of pain, a flash of regret at his having put this notion in her head. Instead he smiled at her.

"Of course I will, love." He dipped his chin. "Of course."

Relieved, Iona leaned her head against his arm and steered them toward the cottage.

~

Craig's old laptop sat open on the kitchen table. Iona was pacing behind him as he shifted his chair closer to the table and waited. The flashing symbol on the screen ticked in time with her heart as she willed the page to load.

"Come on, come on," she whispered.

"Oh, here we go." Craig leaned in, peering at the screen. "There's a few listings, one for a musical instrument repair service. That's not likely. Um, a list of reviews on Major's music store in Dunfermline—again, probably not likely."

Iona chewed the cuticle around her thumb. "Anything else?"

"There's a prizewinning fisherman by that name." He grimaced. "Oh, wait. Here's something. It's an article from the Herald, but it's dated 2015."

"What's it about?" She walked to the window, the thickness of the encroaching night obscuring all but the outline of the moon, masked by a heavy layer of cloud.

"Perhaps you should read it yourself." His voice was soft, kicking Iona's anxiety level up a notch.

"What's wrong? Just read it to me, please." She flopped onto the chair opposite him. "Please," she whispered.

"If you're sure." He frowned.

Iona nodded, wrapping her arms around herself. "I'm ready."

Craig focused on the screen. "A local man and his wife were tragically killed in a house fire in the early hours of yesterday morning at their residence in Leith. Professor Charles Majors, formerly a prominent member of the faculty at Edinburgh University's Reid School of Music, and his wife Caroline were apparently asleep on the upper floor of their home when the fire broke out in the kitchen. Local fire chief, Sgt. David Walcomb, stated that the source of the fire appeared to have been electrical in nature and that an investigation is currently underway to determine the exact cause. Fire crews reached the scene approximately eleven minutes after a neighbor reported seeing flames on the ground level of the home, but were unable to stop the fire reaching the second floor. 'By the time we found them, we were unable to revive the residents,' said Walcomb in an interview at the scene on Thursday evening. The medical examiner's report will establish cause of death, which at this point appears to have been smoke inhalation."

Craig halted. "Are you all right?" His voice was loaded with concern.

Iona felt as if she were floating, images of red-hot flames licking up the front of a stylish waterfront home crimping her insides. As she blinked to blot the vivid pictures out, she hoped with all her strength that those poor people had slept away, unaware of their untimely end and escaping the horror of burning to death.

Breathing rapidly, she tried to refocus on what Craig was saying. "Yes, I'm O.K. Is there anything else?"

Craig shook his head. "That's it, love. I'm sorry." He closed the lid of the computer and stood up, his grey cords sagging around his hips. "So, they died in a fire." He looked incredulous as he repeated the information. "What a hellish way to go. I'm so sorry, Iona. I mean, I'm sorry you had to find him just to lose him again." He scanned her face, his mouth pinching.

An ocean of conflicting emotions roiled around inside her—a mixture of disappointment, relief, shock at her relief, and then sadness at the potential of something being gone before it had begun. As she sifted through the tide of feelings, she took in Craig's expression—his frown, the lines around his eyes, each one carrying his hopes and fears for her, the way he was leaning toward her like a runner at a starting gate, as if he was wanting to reach out and hold her but afraid to at the same time. Suddenly, all seemed clear, and Iona knew what she needed—and wanted to do.

"It doesn't feel like that, Dad. It's a very sad story, of course, but I don't think I feel loss because I didn't know him to lose him. Does that make sense?"

He nodded. "It does. But it's tragic, nonetheless." He moved to the cabinet and poured them both a drink. "Do you want to talk about it?" Craig set a glass in front of her and settled back in his chair. "It's fine if you do." His kind eyes held hers.

Iona shook her head, the sense of a door closing once and for all saddening, and yet unlocking a vice around her heart. "No, I don't think I do." She sipped some whisky. "Does that make me callous?" Her brows drew together.

Craig frowned. "Of course not." He swirled the amber liquid around the glass. "But I think you may be a little shocked. Perhaps you'll feel differently once it all sinks in." He sipped his drink. "You might find that you need to know more, at some point."

As she watched him, Iona considered the past few weeks and all the monumental knowledge she'd gained. All the new fingers of light that had illuminated the darkest corners of her past, the places she'd been scared to look for so many years, and where, in among all that, this new, somewhat hollow nugget of knowledge fit. The image of her mother and Majors flashed behind her eyes, the coldness of his expression in stark contrast to the glow of Grace's smile. No, despite her pity for his hideous end, there was nothing in her that wished that man back into her life. "No, Dad. I think I know everything I need to."

~

They spent the rest of the evening watching TV in companionable silence, and then, feeling heavy with what her Nana Jean had termed a healthy tired, Iona went to bed. No sooner had she slipped under the covers than her phone buzzed.

How was your day? Scott's message flashed, and a smile split her face.

Great. Both sad and perfect, she typed.

Wow. Can't compete with that ;)

She hesitated, then answered quickly before she could change her mind. *You don't have to. You're a shoo-in.*

The bubble of his pending reply hovered as her heart ticked.

Glad to hear it. Want to talk?

Yes.

She thumped her pillows, settled back, and waited.

~

The following morning, after plying her with a cooked breakfast, Craig was driving her to the ferry terminal. He'd put a pair of glasses on, and Iona was distracted, not having seen them before. "Since when do you wear glasses?" She pulled a face. "Old man."

Craig had tutted. "Cheeky bugger. I only wear them for driving, and only occasionally." He shoved them further up his nose.

Iona twisted to face him. "Thanks for everything, Dad. It's

been so wonderful." A swell of sadness at the prospect of leaving him filled her throat. "It won't be as long until the next time."

"It's been great having you, sweetheart."

Suddenly desperate to share the last piece of her innermost self that she'd been keeping safely locked away, she raked her hair into a ponytail, then released it across her shoulders. "You know, there's someone I meant to tell you about." She felt her face warming. "A guy."

Craig flicked a glance over his shoulder, a glint of mischief behind his eyes. "Oh, really? I'm glad to hear it." He grinned. "Will I approve?"

"Yes, I think you will." She said.

~

As they hugged in the car park, Craig crushed her to him, her ribs flexing under the pressure of his arms, then he held her at arm's length and scanned her face. "Did you mean what you said about getting back to your music?"

Iona nodded. "Yes, I did."

His face folded into a smile. "Whenever you're ready, let me know. I want to support you, help out with rent and stuff again." He cupped her cheek. "I'm so happy you've made this decision."

"I'll talk to the university on Monday. It might not be possible until September, but I'll get the wheels in motion." She hoisted her bag onto her shoulder. "Maybe Mr. Halloran can put in a good word for me, plead my case for readmission?" She shrugged. "I just know that I want to play again. I need to."

Craig sounded choked as they said their final goodbyes, and, having given him her best smile, Iona walked away, heading for the ferry.

~

When she arrived back in Edinburgh, Roz was waiting for her at the bus station. Iona spotted the Mini on the opposite side of the road and her friend's scarlet cap bobbing out of the driver's window as she waved wildly.

Hitching her bag onto her shoulder, Iona dashed across the street. "Hiya." She opened the door, tossed her bag onto the miniature back seat, and jumped into the car.

"Hiya yourself." Roz grinned. "Welcome home." She pulled away from the curb.

Iona slipped off her gloves and held her cold fingers up to the anemic heater. The early evening sky was grey, reflecting the color of the flinty buildings along the route to the flat.

"I'm not speaking to you." Roz pouted as she stood on the brakes to let a woman cross in front of the car. "Two poxy phone calls in over a week." She poked Iona's thigh. "Pretty pathetic."

"I know. I'm sorry. It was just so all-consuming. The time with Freya was good, then awful with the whole Dad thing, and then it was good again." She shrugged. "When I found out everything about Charles Majors, that sent me off on a massive tangent." She pulled her hair away from her face and secured it with a band she'd had around her wrist.

Spotting a rare parking space up ahead, only feet from their building, Iona pointed. "Quick. Over there."

Roz stepped on the accelerator, pulling up close to a black Mercedes that was indicating. "Don't you dare," she shouted as the car halted next to the space and began reversing in. "Bastard." Roz thumped the steering wheel.

"You snooze, you lose." Iona tapped the dashboard. "Come on, let's drive around the block and see if there's another one somewhere."

The flat was chilly as ever as Iona dumped her things in her room. Roz was shouting something from the kitchen as Iona gently eased her door closed rather than immediately joining her. She dumped the contents of her bag onto her bed, sifting through the pile for the small framed photograph of Grace that, as she was leaving the cottage, she'd asked her father if she could take. He'd gladly agreed, saying that she could take as many as she wanted.

Now, she rubbed her sleeve over the glass to remove a smudge and set the delicate frame on her bedside table. Having not had any pictures of her mother around her since leaving Orkney two years before, she could taste the rightness of having brought this with her.

The cello case was dusty, so she pulled a T-shirt from her drawer and carefully wiped the black figure-eight. Satisfied with the front, she leaned it against the bed in order to get to the back, and then hauled the case up onto the bed and opened the lid. Nestled in its crimson-lined bed, the cello was gleaming, the rich cherry-red of the wood begging to be touched.

She ran her fingers over the strings, tracing a line from the neck, over the fingerboard to the bridge, then she followed the outline of each f-hole, finally letting her fingers linger at the waist of the beautiful instrument.

She lifted it from the case and sat down on the edge of the bed, resting its elegant neck on her shoulder. Within a few moments, she had it in tune, had rosined the bow and, having no doubt about what she wanted to play, had propped the sheet music for "Iona's Star" up against the base of the bedside lamp.

She picked up the bow and began to play. The opening notes sounded like a choir of gentle baritones, voices hovering low on the scale, bringing to mind the cool tones of winter. As she played, Iona imagined walking down a snow-covered lane. She pictured icicles hanging from fairy-tale pitched roofs, water droplets trickling down tree branches toward their tips, and she imagined the clean smell of newness in the air.

She slid the bow deftly back and forth, her elbow drawing elegant arcs and her eyes flicking over the music, her mother's handwriting appearing to glow on the sheet.

As she got to the end of the page, she reached out and flipped it over, scanning ahead on the staves. The second section wound its way through a series of mellow chords, gradually rising, drawing Iona's back up straighter as she met the technical requirements of the piece. As she continued, the music built with a natural momentum that culminated in a bright, alto crescendo, the combination of the closing notes sounding like fireworks popping in the night sky, leaving tiny sparks of musical light falling to the ground as the melody drifted to a sweet and satisfying finish.

Not wanting to stop yet, she closed her eyes and, working from memory, repeated the first section. With the bite of the strings under her softened fingertips, and the air rich with the beautiful melody her mother had created, she felt the music finally bringing her home.

As she finished playing the piece for the second time, she opened her eyes.

Roz was standing in the doorway, her palm clamped over her mouth. Her eyes were full of tears, and then she let out a whoop. "That was incredible." She swiped at her face. "What was it?"

Iona lifted the music and held it out. "Mum wrote it for me, a few years ago." She stood up and laid the cello back in the case. "Dad gave it to me the other day."

Roz was staring at the page, looking confused. "When did she write it?"

"When I was ten or so. He kept it until he felt I was ready for it." Iona gave a half smile. "He timed it perfectly."

Roz nodded. "It's beautiful, Iona." She held the paper out. "You sounded incredible."

"Thanks. I'm a bit rusty, but it feels right to be playing again. It's funny to think that simply going home, the very thing I've been avoiding for two years, was all I really needed." She set the cello case against the wall.

Roz laid the sheet of music on the bed. "I won't say I told you so, but..."

Iona smiled as her friend's forehead folded into a frown.

"Are you sure you're all right? I mean about the whole Charles Majors, finding out about your real father, but losing him before you got a chance to meet or get to know him, thing." Roz asked.

Iona considered for a few moments, then nodded. "Honestly, I'm kind of numb about it." She blinked. "Maybe I'm just so shell-shocked by everything that's happened that I'll feel different someday, but for now, it just feels like a door that closed before I got the chance to walk through it." She shrugged. "One thing I know for sure. I *do* know my father, and he lives on Orkney."

~

They sat in the kitchen, the dim light casting an orange glow over the tabletop.

"It really wasn't Dad who chose to go to Switzerland without me. It was Mum. She insisted on it, and it was Mum who swore him to secrecy about Charles, too. Poor Dad."

Roz's mouth was gaping as she plucked at the placemat. "So, he's got a girlfriend?"

Iona snorted. "After everything I've just told, that's where you're going?" She tossed a sugar packet at her friend. "Honestly."

Roz pulled a face. "Well, it's about bloody time. He's been living like a monk for years." She glanced at Iona. "So, what's she like?"

Iona lifted their empty cups and began washing them in the sink.

"She's lovely. A redhead. Tall, kind, clever. She works in the same field as Dad, which is perfect, and she seems to adore him."

"Nice."

Iona set the cups on the draining board. "She's warm and insightful. She let me know that she knows our history, mine and Dad's, but without seeming to be intrusive." She shrugged. "I liked her a lot."

Roz nodded, brushing some crumbs onto the floor.

"I even blurted out that I was going to go back to music. I don't know why it felt right to come out with it right then. I mean, Dad and I hadn't even talked about it at that point." She shook her head. "I just knew it was what I was feeling and blah —out it came." She fanned her fingers under her chin.

Roz's eyes had widened. "So, it's official? You're going back to uni?"

"I'm going to go in on Monday, speak to the head of Reid and see what she says. They might make me repeat some courses, or it might be a lost cause altogether, but I'll never know unless I try. Right?"

Roz was up and had crossed the room. She flung her arms around Iona. "God, I'm so happy. It's been awful having you sort of suspended in time." She stepped back. "Plus, it'll be far easier to pull interesting men when I tell them my flatmate is a sexy cellist."

"Roz, you're the limit." She swatted Roz's arm. "So, what about this Jim guy? I still want all the juice on him, and what's going on there. How was your dinner? Have you been out again?"

Roz's face bloomed pink. "Yeah, don't hold your breath. It's not that interesting."

Iona watched as Roz fluffed her feathery hair, ran a finger over each eyebrow, and appeared to be avoiding meeting Iona's gaze.

"Roz? Tell me everything, right now."

Roz shuffled her feet. "I went to the Braeburn with him, the other night." She bit at a hangnail. "Great food."

Iona squinted at her friend. "Hey, now you know all my secrets, tell me about this man. I want details."

Roz swatted the air dismissively. "He's nice. Quiet. Well, quiet compared to what I usually end up with." She grinned. "He's intelligent, well-traveled. In that he's actually been out of Scotland." She slapped her thigh. "No, seriously, he's been everywhere. Used to volunteer for an aid group in Africa." She widened her eyes. "He's older than me so, mature, you know. A grown-up."

Iona saw the spread of another blush on Roz's cheeks.

"So, has he kissed you?" She leaned forward and set her mug down.

Roz pressed her lips together.

"Roz. Have you…Oh my God, you've slept with him already?" Iona yelped.

Roz burst out laughing. "Settle down, Reverend Mother. We're consenting adults." She sipped her wine. "We've been out lots, anyway." She mocked offense.

"What do you mean, lots?" Iona frowned.

Roz eyed her over the rim of her glass and then slowly shook her head. "Actually, I've a confession to make." She twisted her mouth to the side.

"Go on." Iona sat back and crossed her arms over her stomach. "I'm listening."

"We've been going out for a few months." Roz had lost the characteristic smile and looked positively guilty. "We started seeing each other before Christmas. I just didn't tell you."

A tiny needle of hurt prickled under Iona's ribs. "Why wouldn't you tell me that?" She scanned Roz's face.

"Because I didn't think it was good timing. You were going through some tough stuff, and I didn't want to rub your nose in anything."

"Oh, Roz. You didn't have to hide it from me." She rose from the seat and stood in front of Roz's chair. "I'm sorry you felt that way, or if I made you feel that you had to hide it."

Roz shook her head. "No, it wasn't like that. I just thought about everything you were dealing with and then tried to put myself in your shoes, to think how I'd feel if the roles were reversed."

Iona grabbed Roz's hand. "You daft tart. I'd have been delighted for you."

Roz squeezed her fingers. "Well, if it had been me having a hard time, and you'd brought some hunky, musical hoo-rah back here, I'd have been pissed off." She smiled again. "You know it's true."

"You're the best friend anyone ever had, and here's to you and Jim, who I suspect I'll be seeing a lot of now." Iona grinned, lifting her empty hand in a toast. Seeing the light behind Roz's eyes, Iona dug into her heart, ready to feel the familiar vacuum that had filled it for years, but instead, Scott's presence was there, seeping in like mercury, a silver flood full of promise. "While we're sharing everything…" She hesitated. "I meant to tell you about what happened with Scott." The rush of words a powerful release, Iona let out a laugh at Roz's comical slack mouth.

"You cow." Roz batted her arm. "I bloody knew it."

～

The next day, Iona had a lunch shift at work. After calling both Beth and Freya to thank them again for having her, and then Craig to say hello, she'd dashed to the supermarket to grab some provisions. When she'd unloaded everything, she'd ridden her bike to the restaurant in the pouring rain. As the water pelted her face, her hair sticking to her back like long wet fingers, rather than cowering against the cold spring shower, she'd shoved her chin out and laughed aloud, a warmth spreading from her middle along her limbs to her toes and fingertips.

By the time she got to the Bonnie Prince, she was drenched, and Scott grimaced as she walked in the door, his eyes scanning her bedraggled appearance from head to toe like a searchlight.

"What a sight." He beamed. "Great to have you back, Muir."

"Thanks." She shook her head like a dog, water flying from her hair. "Ah, Edinburgh." She bounced her shoulders. "It's bracing, I can tell you."

Scott chuckled. "You sound in good fettle." He gestured toward the bar. "There's a pot of coffee in the back room. You should warm yourself up before you catch your death."

Iona folded her soaking coat over her arm and gathered her wet hair behind her neck, aware that he was watching her, his dark eyes alight with something other than the usual lightly masked humor.

"So, what's been going on here?" She mocked alarm. "Place looks like a bomb's gone off." She pointed at several tables that were loaded with boxes of glasses, piles of plates, and a mess of unfolded napkins heaped in a big basket, then she passed him and headed for the back room.

Scott followed her. "Prepping for a party tonight. Don't suppose you can do a double shift, can you?"

"You'll be lucky," she raised her eyebrows. "Time and a half?"

"I didn't miss you *that* much." He squinted at her.

"Missed me, did you?" She gave him a half smile. "Glad to hear it."

She dried her hair with a towel, changed into the clean white shirt she kept in her locker, and brushed her straggly hair up into a tight knot on the crown of her head. Glancing in the mirror, she wiped the smudged mascara from under each eye, suddenly alarmed that Scott had seen her looking like a drowned raccoon.

As the thought settled on her, her eyebrows jumped. It was new that she cared what she looked like, as far as he was concerned.

Smiling at her reflection, she filled a glass with water, took several long drafts, and headed out to the restaurant.

Scott was doing a bar inventory, and as she passed behind him, he whistled under his breath.

"Well that's an improvement." Without turning, he spoke to the mirror that multiplied the rows of bottles behind the bar.

Iona slowed her progress. "Say that to my face, if you dare," she whispered. "That smacks of harassment, you know."

Scott spun around and bit his tongue theatrically. "Well, excuse me." He elongated the words.

She laughed, lifting a handful of napkins from the basket. "I'm just saying." She began folding.

Scott walked out from behind the bar and stood opposite her, a pen stuck behind his ear. "Well, I'm just saying…" He paused. "That you look nice."

She saw a wash of color creep up his neck, and the flash of uncertainty in his eyes was disarming. Rather than continue with their customary banter, she smiled warmly.

"Thanks. I appreciate that."

Scott pulled the pen out of his hair, his eyes sparkling. "Right. Enough of that. Get to work, Muir."

~

The lunch shift had been busy with only three servers working. Several of the surrounding restaurants closing on Mondays sent a wave of midday diners into the Bonnie Prince, which Scott never complained about. The place now having emptied out, as the other servers filtered home, Iona cleared down her tables and dropped her tips into the giant coffee jar behind the bar. Her shoulders ached from carrying the heavy trays, and her feet were pulsing inside her still-damp shoes. While the thought of riding home, then sliding into a warm bath, was delicious, she wasn't ready to go quite yet.

Scott was in the back office as she made her way past, heading for the locker room. His long frame was bent over the makeshift desk that ran along the back wall, and as she passed, a tiny pull to her middle made her hesitate at the door. Seeming to sense her presence, he spun around.

"All finished out there?" He gestured toward the restaurant.

"Yep. All done." She nodded. "I'm shattered." She rolled her shoulders back. "Want a coffee?" She watched a smile tug at his mouth.

"Sure. Lead on." He pushed the chair back and stood up, his height blocking much of the sliver of light that was shining weakly in the narrow window behind him.

As she filled two mugs and handed one to him, his unexpected visit, the time they'd spent together, and several of their text conversations ran through her mind like a ticker tape. The experiences she'd had that she'd shared with him, taking him into her confidence, rather than feeling like an exposure, now felt right and nonthreatening. As a sense of calm settled on her, she sat opposite him and began to talk.

Twenty minutes later, Scott sipped his coffee, his eyes never leaving her face. "You went through so much in just one week, and you not only reconnected with your dad but found another father you once belonged to." He pushed his cup away. "I'm amazed you're able to keep it all in perspective."

The word *belonged* detached itself from his sentence and pulled her attention. While an odd way to refer to what she'd discovered, it was nonetheless true. There had been years where she hadn't felt like she fully belonged anywhere—not on her island home, not in the presence of her father, in Edinburgh, in her lectures, or in the musty practice rooms at the Reid School of Music, and not even here at the Bonnie Prince.

As she took in Scott's expression, something undefinable

lifted the last residual weight she'd been carrying. "Yes, I suppose I did belong to him, in some way." She shrugged. "Funny you should say that."

He cocked his head to the side, a trademark gesture she'd noticed many times in the past that now seemed attractively sweet.

"I suppose I haven't felt that I belonged anywhere, for a long time." She bit her lip, fighting the surprising press of tears.

Scott reached across the table and laid his hand over hers. "Well, you belong here." He smiled. "Always have."

EPILOGUE

Iona glanced at the clock as she pulled on her jeans, hopping awkwardly on one leg. She could hear birdsong, and the branches of the giant sycamore tree tapping the bedroom window, and there was a lingering smell of vanilla from the candles they'd been burning the previous night.

Scott's back was turned toward her, and she could see his ribcage gently rising and falling under the bedcovers. His head was buried deep in the downy pillow, and one foot stuck out from the end of the bed, the long toes curling and flexing, indicating that despite appearances, he was awake.

Smiling to herself, she dragged a brush through her hair, then twisted it into a tight bun, and just as she was about to dive onto the bed, he flipped over and grinned at her.

"Had you going, eh?"

"No. I saw your toes moving." She pulled a face. "Got to be better than that." She lay down beside him and draped her arm over his chest. "Are you going to drop me off?"

He nodded against the pillow. "Of course."

She drew a line on his stomach, tracing the downy hair that

ran down from his belly button until her fingers disappeared under the sheet.

Scott clamped a hand over hers. "Ah ah. None of that now. We've got to get going."

She wriggled inside the grip of his arm, but the more she tried to move, the stronger he held her, sending her into a fit of laughter. "Let me go, you perv." She put her index finger inside his ear, something that she knew was guaranteed to make him cringe and release her.

"Get off me, woman." He playfully shoved her away and threw the covers off, sitting on the edge of the bed. "What time do you have to be there?" He spoke to the bright window, where the light of the autumn morning was warming the ivory-colored curtains.

"Eight thirty." She pulled on a sock, dropping back onto the edge of the bed. "On the dot."

She loved being in Scott's flat, on the second floor of a recently renovated Georgian house. The decor was subtle—primarily made up of browns, golds, and natural wood furniture. The long galley kitchen and bright bathroom were always clean and the fridge usually well stocked and, most of all, the entire place was warm in both temperature and atmosphere.

He padded across the floor and disappeared into the hall. "I'll have a quick shower and we can grab a coffee on the way."

"Good idea."

As she heard the water begin thrumming, she went into the living room and opened the curtains, plumped the cushions on the sofa, and picked up the wineglasses that sat abandoned on the coffee table. The room was cozy, and the rug under her feet was spongy as she clenched her toes, feeling the depth of the pile through her socks.

In the far corner her cello was propped on its stand, the black case shining from the polishing she'd given it the previous weekend. Scott had moved an armchair out of the room to make space for it, insisting that it stay in the living room rather than be kept in the tiny guest room down the hall.

On the opposite wall, a huge TV was mounted above the fireplace, and to the left of it, on the narrow bookcase housing Scott's turntable and a collection of his precious vinyl albums, she spotted a white envelope propped up against the sculpture of the ancient Greek Discobolus, twisting in preparation to throw the discus.

She tiptoed over, set the glasses down, and lifted the card. Scott's handwriting was appalling, and as she saw her name scratched in his scrawl, a surge of emotion caught her by surprise. They'd been together for almost six months now, but he never failed to touch her with his thoughtfulness, his kindness, and spontaneous romantic gestures.

She slid her finger under the flap, opened the envelope, and pulled out a card. On the front was an elegant treble clef with a series of quavers and minims trickling from the bottom of the curl, like musical raindrops. Closing her eyes, she traced the image for a second, taking in the feel of the heavy cardstock and the embossed design, like Braille under her fingertips.

As she read what he'd written, her vision blurred.

Iona,

This is the day. You're finally on your way. I'm so happy for you, but mostly, I'm happy for me because I'm allowed to be part of this with you. Best of luck— although you won't need it.

Your personal perv,

Scott x

P.S. I'm cooking tonight.

With her eyes now brimming, she slipped the card back into the envelope just as Scott came into the room, wrapped in a towel.

As she turned to face him, he smiled shyly. "Found it, then."
He nodded at her hand.

"Yes." She flapped the card at him. "You're so soppy." She
walked over and wrapped her arms around his neck. "Thank you.
It's perfect."

He bent down and kissed her, his damp hair tickling her fore-
head. "Glad you like it." He swept the hair away from his face.
"God. Is that the time?" He gaped at the clock on the mantle.
"Give me five minutes, O.K.?"

She shooed him away. "Go. Get dressed."

Scott swung around just as she reached out and grabbed the
end of his towel, sending him scuttling away stark naked.

"Oh, and *I'm* the perv," he shouted over his shoulder.

"Just hurry up."

～

Scott's Volvo was parked in the street, right outside his flat on
Gillsland Road. Finding a space this close was a blessing, especially when the weather was bad, but even more so on days like
today when they were transporting the cello.

Iona hopped from foot to foot as he slid the case into the
boot. "Careful." She slung her bag onto her shoulder as he
wrapped a blanket over the case.

He turned to her, rubbing his palms together. "All set."

They got into the car and put on their seatbelts. Then he
glanced at her before pulling away from the curb. "Not nervous,
are you?"

She nodded. "Actually yes. A bit." She turned to stare out of
the window, the row of double-fronted homes ticking past them
like stone soldiers on parade.

"Well, that's natural, I suppose." He focused on the road.
"Just take it a day at a time, and you'll be kicking Elgar's butt
within a week." He grinned. "Guaranteed."

Iona reached over and squeezed his thigh. "Thanks. You're a star."

Feeling a buzz in her pocket, she pulled out her phone to see two texts—one from Roz, who was with Jim on an aid trip to Uganda, simply saying *Good luck xx,* and then another from her father. *Best of luck. Thinking about you today. So proud. Dad.*

Smiling, she tapped out replies to them both, then slid the phone back into her pocket. The idea that her father and her best friend were both with her in spirit on this auspicious day was supremely calming.

The drive to the Lauriston campus was uneventful and, deciding they had no time for a coffee stop, within fifteen minutes they spotted the distinct red-stone building of the Reid School of Music, with its impressive arched doorway and neo-classical pillars.

Iona stared out the window, feeling a flutter of nerves as Scott indicated, then pulled up outside the building.

"Can't stay here for long." He flicked the seatbelt off and jumped out. "Don't want a ticket." His voice faded as he rounded the Volvo.

Iona slid out of the car and closed the door. Her stomach was tipping dangerously now, and as Scott approached her with the cello cradled in his arms, she took a shaky breath.

His eyes were warm as he handed her the instrument. "Just breathe, Muir. You know this it the right thing. You'll be fine." He leaned in and kissed her. "Your mum would be so proud of you."

"I know. I'm just…" She stopped, catching a movement behind her. Turning, she saw the doors opening and Mr. Halloran stepping out onto the pavement. He wore his trademark tweed jacket, and his feathery hair was even thinner than the last time she'd seen him. His face was aglow, a warm smile lighting the pale eyes behind his glasses.

"Welcome back, Miss Muir." He held a hand out which, shifting the cello across herself, Iona shook awkwardly.

"Good to see you." She bobbed in an absurd curtsy as warmth surged up her neck, tinting her cheeks a rosy red. "It's lovely to be back."

Mr. Halloran looked behind her, and Iona blushed even deeper, embarrassed that she hadn't introduced Scott, who was hovering by the car. "Oh, sorry. This is Scott, my…" She halted.

Scott stepped forward and shook Halloran's hand. "Her boyfriend." He nodded. "Pleasure to meet you."

"And you, Scott." Halloran stepped back, opening his arms wide as in a Shakespearean bow. "Well, Miss Muir. Shall we?"

Iona nodded and kissed Scott's cheek, then hoisted the cello up against her. "Yes, let's."

AFTERWORD

In this book, I touch on two highly sensitive subjects: Motor Neuron Disease (MND), also known as Amyotrophic Lateral Sclerosis (ALS), and assisted dying—death with dignity.

MND/ALS is a cruel neurodegenerative disease, with no racial, ethnic, or socioeconomic boundaries. It affects thousands of people, the world over, every year. My heartfelt sympathy and respect go out to all those who have been affected, or whose lives have been touched by this condition. Research continues around the globe to find a cure, and we live in hope that day will come, soon.

Assisted dying is the most intensely personal choice, and I wish to point out that this storyline and cast of characters are entirely fictional. Any resemblance to real persons is purely coincidental and unintentional. The choices the characters make, and the opinions they express, are not in any way intended to cause offense or to advocate for one end of life choice over another. No disrespect is intended, whatsoever.

Patients who are afflicted by catastrophic and terminal diseases should consult their healthcare professionals, and educate themselves, concerning this subject. Please be aware that the material found within these pages should never be used as a reference guide.

ACKNOWLEDGMENTS

My sincere thanks to everyone who dedicated time, gave sage advice and moral support in the development of this story. First, to my amazing husband and partner in crime, I thank the universe every day for you and everything you do for me.

Heartfelt thanks to Carly Guy, and Lesley Shearer, my staunch allies, brainstorm partners, first readers, and gentlest critics. You are the best sisters anyone could ask for.

Special thanks to Peggy Lampman, my good friend, and talented author, without whose wisdom, humor, and support, writing would not be nearly as much fun.

Thank you to Judith Bond, my friend, and typo-spotter. I so appreciate your eagle eyes.

I am grateful for the friendship and support of my cohorts in Facebook's Blue Sky Book Chat group, a collection of extremely talented authors that I am proud to be a part of.

A huge thank you to all the friends, readers, reviewers, book-bloggers, my wonderful ARC team and members of my High-landers Club, who support me, especially Susan Peterson of Sue's Reading Neighborhood, Linda Levak Zagon of Linda's Book Obsession, Tonni Callan and Kristy Barrett of A Novel

Bee, Denise Birt of Wild Sage Book Blog, Book Gypsy of the Novels and Latte Bookclub, Annie Horsky McDonnell and Serena Soape of The Write Review, Janelle Madison of Green Gables Book Reviews, Wendy Clarke and everyone at the Fiction Cafe Book Club, and Jillian Cunningham and all at The Reading Corner Book Lounge.

Thanks also to Chloe Jordan, Bambi Rathman, Tina Hottinger, Samantha Alvarez, Jackie Shephard, Sue Baker, Linda Keenan, Linda Smith, Amy Connolly, Carla Suto, Tammy Meadal Underhill, Michele Waite, and all the wonderful Instagram bloggers who so generously give their time and support. Every one of you has made this journey more enjoyable for me.

A special thank you to Kate Rock for her spirit, and promotional know-how.

If your name is not here, it's not because I don't appreciate you, so another heart-felt thank you to all those not mentioned individually. Your support means the world to me.

ABOUT THE AUTHOR

Originally from Edinburgh, Alison now lives near Washington D.C. with her husband and dog. Alison was educated in England and holds an MBA from Leicester University.

Dignity and Grace is Alison's seventh book. For more information on upcoming projects go to www.alisonragsdale.com.

Made in the USA
Monee, IL
15 September 2020